Honorable Intentions?

"All men aren't monsters," the Earl of Dudley told Eden Henderson. "You do concede that, do you not?"

Eden couldn't answer. She was lost in the nearness of him, the fierce yearning in his green eyes, the sudden gentling of his touch. He lowered his mouth to hers slowly, giving her time to refuse, but she waited for him. Gently, very gently, his lips settled on hers. Softly they moved, coaxing her own to echo their pressure. Then, long before she was ready, he pulled away. "You see, not all men are monsters, Eden."

She took his lapels in her hands and pulled his head back down to hers for another kiss. This time his mouth was firmer, more demanding, and she wanted to yield all that he demanded as he lifted his head and slid his arms down to wrap around her and press her against his body.

"I'm not a monster, Eden," he said . . . and she felt a monstrous temptation to believe him. . . .

Miss Henderson's Secret

by

June Calvin

A SIGNET BOOK

SIGNET
Published by the Penguin Group
Penguin Books USA Inc., 375 Hudson Street,
New York, New York 10014, U.S.A.
Penguin Books Ltd, 27 Wrights Lane,
London W8 5TZ, England
Penguin Books Australia Ltd, Ringwood,
Victoria, Australia
Penguin Books Canada Ltd, 10 Alcorn Avenue,
Toronto, Ontario, Canada M4V 3B2
Penguin Books (N.Z.) Ltd, 182–190 Wairau Road,
Auckland 10, New Zealand

Penguin Books Ltd, Registered Offices:
Harmondsworth, Middlesex, England

First published by Signet, an imprint of Dutton Signet,
a division of Penguin Books USA Inc.

First Printing, August, 1995
10 9 8 7 6 5 4 3 2 1

This book is dedicated to my two sisters, Donna Compton and Kathryn Ann Compton. They are an indispensable part of my support system and the source of a great deal of the richness of my life.

Chapter One

Early June, 1819

"Where is my daughter, you villain? I demand that you produce my daughter immediately or I shall horsewhip you." Bertram Eardley stood in an aggressive, threatening posture over a young man who was seated cross-legged on the floor in what had once been a drawing room but now seemed more of a storeroom for paint, brushes, carpenter's tools, and wallpaper.

The man on the floor turned slowly and lifted vague green eyes to stare uncomprehendingly at the short, red-faced man who stood over him. The noise of hammering somewhere above them reverberated through the room as he smoothed straight brown hair off his face with long, slender fingers.

"Your daughter? Briggs?" The last word was yelled at the top of a pair of robust lungs, startling Eardley and the two women who stood watching the tableau.

"Here, sir."

"Do I have this man's daughter?"

"Not to my knowledge, sir." Briggs spoke and acted like a butler, but was dressed in rough workmen's clothes, as was the young man on the floor.

"See here, you *are* the Earl of Dudley, aren't you?" You was pointed out to me as such one day in Varnham.

"Occasionally, when I can't avoid it."

"Damn your eyes, stop playing games with me and get up!" Eardley grabbed the young man's collar as if he would lift him bodily.

It was not the safest move he could have made. The heretofore vaguely genial man frowned and pulled himself from Eardley's grasp, then began to rise. He stood up and up and up until the older man found his head forced back onto his shoulders to stay in eye contact. And there was nothing vague about the eyes anymore.

Instead the green eyes flashed what seemed to the three observers to be green fire. "Keep your hands to yourself and a civil tongue in your head or I'll throw you out on your chins."

Eden Henderson fought down the urge to laugh at this reference to Eardley's multiplicity of chins, which were just now quivering in indignation. Mrs. Eardley gasped in alarm and ventured timidly, "Bertram, perhaps—"

"Shut up, Seraphina. When your comments are needed, they'll be asked for."

But Eardley understood at least enough about valor to move discreetly a foot or so away from the tall, powerfully built man who now stood surveying him and the two women.

"Perhaps we had best begin again. My butler was obviously otherwise occupied and didn't announce you—"

"They pushed past me, sir."

"Didn't know he was a butler. Dressed like a workman, what? Anyway, quit pretending you don't know what I'm here for, you licentious seducer, and give me my daughter."

"I never return daughters to men whose names I do not know." The tall man turned his back on his rotund inquisitor to bow to the two women. "I am Roger Brentwood, ladies, at your service."

"Brentwood? But I thought you said you were Dudley?" The older of the two women, a thin, worried matron of perhaps fifty years, voiced her perplexity.

"Dudley is my title but I prefer not to use it, as I told you. Briggs, if one or more of these persons do not identify themselves in the next thirty seconds, throw them all out."

As Eardley sputtered, the harassed-looking woman crossed the room and made a graceful curtsy. "I am Seraphina Eardley, my lord. This is my husband, Bertram Eardley, and our daughter's governess, Miss Henderson."

"Now we are getting somewhere. You are my neighbors to the north, I believe." He took Mrs. Eardley's outstretched hand gently in his own, then turned the now piercing eyes on the tall, attractive young woman next to her. "Miss Henderson."

He gave her a quick, comprehensive, and obviously appreciative masculine survey from the top of her thick braids of dark-brown hair, down her plain, high-necked dress, to the tips of her shabby half boots. He missed nothing, from her smooth golden complexion to her curvaceous figure. Indeed, he lingered just momentarily on her full bosom before returning to meet her large brown eyes, his own alive with interest.

Eden found herself wishing she had taken the time to cover her luxuriant hair with her most spinsterish cap, and to throw a concealing shawl about her shoulders, in spite of the heat.

"My lord." Eden curtsied. How she hated it when that look came in a man's eyes, as it usually did when she was first introduced. It was a lustful look, as she knew all too well. Ordinarily, such a look only irritated her. For some reason this man's appreciative regard both warmed and flustered her.

"I prefer to be Mr. Brentwood," he responded in a deep, richly timbered voice.

"A cursed leveler as well as a vile seducer." Eardley thrust himself between Dudley and the ladies. "Where is she, I say!"

"I take it you have misplaced a daughter, and that she is of a marriageable age, and that somehow you suspect she has come here."

"Not suspect. *Know*. Said so in that note she left to Miss Henderson, after *she*"—he turned to Eden and spat the word at her—"let her read that trash you published in that magazine, all about women's rights and such rubbish."

For the first time Brentwood looked nonplussed. "Women's rights? Magazine?"

"Don't deny it. Read it meself, your name on it. 'A Manifesto on Marriage and the Rights of Women,' by the Earl of Dudley."

Eden spoke quietly. "What he is referring to, my lord, . . . ah, Mr. Brentwood, is an article that you wrote some five or six years ago in *The Legacy*."

Brentwood shook his head ruefully. "Not that! Thought everyone had forgotten about that!"

"Everyone has, fortunately, except for this miserable excuse for a governess here, who for some sinister reason kept it and showed it to my sixteen-year-old daughter. Gel's impressionable. Decided to come to live with you, as you suggested women should do, without marrying and such infidel rubbish."

"She ran away and said she was coming to me?" He addressed the ladies, obviously hoping for more information and less bombast.

Mrs. Eardley nodded her head. "She wrote us a note, my lord. We found it this morning. She must have sneaked away before dawn and—"

"How did she know I'd taken up residence here?"

"The whole countryside has been all atwitter with it since Easter." Disgust laced Eardley's voice. "Though if they'd read that article, all these mothers eagerly preparing their daughters to set their caps for you would hide them instead."

"And rightly so." Brentwood's eyes lit up; Eden thought he winked at her before he turned to Briggs. "Has any sign been seen of such a person this morning?"

"No sir, none whatsoever."

"Well, she's here! Her mare is grazing in your park. Saw her as we came in." Eardley slammed one fist into the other. "Give over, man."

"I swear I haven't seen her, and Briggs would say so if he had, but in the chaos of all this remodeling and repairing, it's possible that she may have entered the house unseen. And she'd likely not pick me out as a belted earl just now." Dudley made a gesture that encompassed his rough clothing, then stooped to pick up the large set of architectural drawings from the floor where he had been studying them.

"Come, let us search for her. Briggs, alert the staff. Could you describe this child, Miss Henderson?"

Some impish impulse made Eden quip, "Why? How many sixteen-year-old girls are you likely to have hidden away?"

Green eyes gleaming appreciatively, Brentwood responded, "I have taken on many new servants here. It would help if I could eliminate any maids I might encounter."

"As if my Bella would be dressed like a servant," Eardley interposed indignantly.

"Yes, well, I'm not sure what the fashionable young lady is wearing to run away this year."

This time Eden was unable to completely contain her bubble of laughter and was forced to cover it with a cough, but Mr. Eardley was not amused.

"You aren't leaving my sight, sir. You'll get no chance to spirit her away."

Eden offered the information before the frustrated earl could explode. "Miss Isabella Eardley is a blonde, sir. She is short, pleasantly plump, and has guinea-gold curls. She is most likely to be wearing a Dresden-blue riding habit."

"Thank *you*, Miss Henderson. Well, Briggs, you heard."

"Indeed, sir." The butler, in spite of his rough clothing, managed to look dignified as he bowed and left the room.

"Come with me into the gold salon." Brentwood motioned his guests to accompany him. "It is not yet torn up. You can be comfortable there while we search."

"We'll do no such thing. Think I'll take your word for it? Or his? In my experience a libertine's butler is a vicious copy of his master. I'll search for her meself."

With that, Eardley bounded from the room. "I'm s-s-s-sorry, Lord Dudley. My husband is somewhat . . ." Mrs. Eardley's voice trailed off, not as if words failed her, but more as if she feared to voice them.

"Quite. Well, shall we join the chase, help run this pretty fox to earth?" He motioned the two women before him. As Eden passed he murmured, *sotto voce*, for her ears only, "She *is* pretty, isn't she?"

"Indeed so, Mr. Brentwood. A diamond." It was Eden's turn to look worried. "Then you really haven't seen her? Where can she have gotten to? She is impulsive and willful, but innocent as a kitten."

"An innocent who wishes to offer herself as mistress to a notorious rake?" His eyebrows were raised skeptically. Mrs. Eardley was far ahead, trying to keep pace with her husband, who was inspecting the interiors of some large cabinets.

"I doubt she has the least idea what is involved, sir. But she is being pressured to marry a man she detests, and that essay—oh, why didn't I burn it years ago? It must have appealed to all of her desperate yearnings to be free."

The amusement died out of Brentwood's eyes. "Forced to marry? At sixteen?"

"Yes, to an older man whose main appeal for her father is that he has a title. You may know him—Lord Nielson? Her father's father made his fortune in trade, you see. Marriage to Mrs. Eardley, who was a Lacey, didn't gain him the entrée into society he craves, so . . ."

"So the daughter is to be sacrificed." Brentwood's mobile mouth turned down in disapproval as he observed Eardley officiously poking in every nook and cranny. For a heavy man he could move with amazing speed, and soon had completed his search of the downstairs rooms. His task was made easier by the modest proportions of Dudley castle, which wasn't a real castle at all, but an eighteenth-century eccentric's modification of castle architecture to Georgian standards of size and comfort.

He was pounding up the central stairway, trailed by Mrs. Eardley, when Briggs reappeared beside Brentwood and Eden. He said nothing, but Eden was sure some communication passed between master and man.

One of Brentwood's high-arched eyebrows rose even higher. He took Eden's elbow and began climbing the stairs with her, looking considerably less jolly. In this mood, in spite of his pleasant, almost boyish features, there was that about him—the firmness of his jaw, the set of his mouth—that suggested a man whom it wouldn't be wise to push too far, a man not to be trifled with.

Eden studied him out of the corner of her eyes as they followed Eardley's peregrinations. He didn't look the part of a rake. She had always pictured him as having black curling hair, dark eyes, and saturnine features.

Instead, his eyes were leaf green, his hair straight and a light reddish brown in color. It fell over a high forehead. He had high-arched, expressive eyebrows, a long straight nose, and a full, mobile mouth.

At five feet eight inches she was generally accounted a Long Meg, yet he towered over her. His pleasant, almost boyish, countenance and playful wit were incongruent with her image of him as a rake. Only his powerful physique seemed suited to the role. All in all, Eden found him unexpectedly, disturbingly attractive.

They watched Mr. Eardley going through the nearest suite of rooms.

"I suppose if he finds her here he'll expect me to marry her?" Brentwood was watching the search a little uneasily.

Testing her suspicion of what the butler had conveyed to him, Eden asserted, "I expect so. Your title and fortune outweigh that of the baron."

"And if I refuse, I suppose he'll call me out, irascible creature that he is."

Eden once again had to swallow her smile, as Eardley just then stormed past her on the way to the next room. Clearly she had been right in thinking that the butler had somehow signaled the earl that Isabella was on the premises. Eden couldn't resist responding in the same vein to his dry humor.

"Oh, indubitably. Unless you would stand still for being horsewhipped?" She widened her eyes and looked up at him hopefully.

Amusement lit his green eyes, though he grimaced theatrically. "An unappealing thought. But mayhap he is a poor marksman. An old man, after all . . ."

"I am sorry to tell you, sir, that he is able to shoot a grouse in the eye at 100 yards."

"No! Is that even possible?"

"Well, he assures everyone it is."

The expressive eyebrows arrowed downward. "I for one would not dare to doubt so formidable an employer."

"Just so. You could choose swords, sir. He is accounted a good man with a small sword, but surely with your reach and youth . . ."

Brentwood looked horrified. "Can't stand the sight of blood, mine or anyone else's! I am doomed." He clasped his heart.

She couldn't stifle the chuckle that escaped her. "Parson's mousetrap for marriage's arch enemy, at last!"

"Langley will be pleased, at least. You say she is pretty. Do tell me she is not a cloth-head."

"Indeed not. A clever and talented child, if a bit overwhelming at times."

"You comfort me." Brentwood motioned her ahead of him out of yet another bedroom suite in Eardley's wake.

Now serious, Eden asked, "But is she like to be found here, sir? You denied all knowledge—"

"And I told true. But unless I misinterpreted him, Briggs has found the child."

"Then why did he not bring her forward?"

"Because Briggs understands—"

But what Briggs understood she wasn't to learn just then, for Eardley approached, shaking his fists. "You make merry at my expense, the pair of you, but you'll pay for it! Especially you, miss. I hold you responsible. And you, Mrs. Eardley."

His face red with anger and exertion on this hot morning, Eardley rounded on his wife menacingly. "Come. It is obvious he has hidden her well. I'll not waste time on a futile search while he makes sport of me. I shall send my seconds to call on you, sir, unless a proposal of marriage is swiftly forthcoming! By sundown at the latest."

They made a ragged procession out to the carriage, Eardley

pounding along furiously, his anxious wife just behind, followed by Eden hurrying to catch up. Brentwood was on her heels, and Briggs rather uncertainly brought up the rear.

At the carriage Eardley practically threw his wife in, but blocked Eden's way.

"Not you, Miss Henderson! You are no longer in my employ. A disgrace to your calling and your sex."

"B-but you can't just leave me here."

"Oh, can't I just." He made to close the door.

Eden thrust herself in the way. "I am a respectable woman, sir, who has done nothing wrong. Just because your daughter took fright at your plans for her, that doesn't give you leave to abandon me on the door of a stranger."

"Aye, and one of England's most notorious libertines. Well, doubtless he'll make you one of his whores and why not? You've been studying for the role for long enough. Treasured his manifesto for the new harlotry for five years, didn't you?"

Brentwood stepped forward. "Hold, Mr. Eardley. You've abused my name sufficiently without distressing Miss Henderson, so take her with you, man. If your daughter turns up—"

"Nay, she's ruined herself and good riddance. Lord Nielson won't have her now. You'll marry her or meet me, and Miss Henderson I toss in for free!"

He thrust his jaw forward and pointed a stubby finger at Eden. "Your trunks will be at my gate at five of the clock this evening. Whether you collect them or they are stolen by the next passerby is of no interest to me."

Eden grabbed his arm as he tried once again to shut the door, a desperate fury in her voice. "You owe me for a quarter's wages, sir, come next Friday."

" 'Tis small enough payment for a lost daughter and a ruined name!" Eardley shook her off and slammed the door, thumping the carriage roof impatiently as he did so. The driver did not hesitate, but immediately obeyed his master's command, starting his cattle with the crack of his whip. Eden jumped back and stared in disbelief as she was abandoned on the Earl of Dudley's doorstep.

Chapter Two

Eden fell back against Brentwood's solid bulk as he moved to pull her out of the path of the carriage's spinning wheels. He was swearing softly but vehemently as he steadied her.

"Much as I agree with your assessment of his character, Mr. Brentwood, I cannot agree that I am 'well out of it.' I am now penniless and without a reference and quite literally in the arms of a famous libertine." She pulled herself away from his supporting arms. Strong arms. She felt an uncharacteristic and most unwise urge to linger in them.

"Am I still famous? I would have thought I'd have been quite forgotten by now. How good to know that fame is not fleeting after all." The green eyes flashed with amusement and masculine admiration as he reluctantly released her.

"It isn't funny," Eden averred, wondering why she felt an insane temptation to laugh. "No one will ever hire me as a governess again, you know." Her voice shook, although her features were composed.

Brentwood took her hands in his. "Don't worry, Miss Henderson. I will take care that you—"

"If you dare to offer me your protection I swear I will call you out myself."

"Such a ferocious look. I do believe you mean it."

"Every word."

He anxiously inquired. "And what kind of shot are *you*?"

Eden huffed a little. "Are you never serious?"

"I am always serious, Miss Henderson. Well, if you won't accept my protection, I suppose I will have to—"

"Eden! Eden! Up here! I'm so glad you stayed!"

Eden and Brentwood looked up to see a very pretty young girl peeping at them over the mock battlements. Leaning over the stonework, she waved excitedly.

"Bella, come down here at once, before you fall."

"Oh, do come up here, Eden. It's beautiful. You can see half of Hertfordshire from here."

"This is the fair Miss Eardley, I take it." Brentwood shaded his eyes with his hand as he peered upward.

"Yes, and I am going to drag her down by her ears. Do order a carriage, Mr. Brentwood. If we take her straight home, perhaps we can recover from this disaster."

"Then you would have her married to Lord Nielson? Fat, old Nielson?"

"Oh!" Conscience made Eden blanch. "I was thinking only of myself, wasn't I? I don't want that for her, of course."

"I am relieved to hear it. Neither do I. We shall have to figure out a way to rescue this fair Rapunzel ourselves. A very short-haired Rapunzel," he ended on a mournful note.

"Happily her hair needn't figure in her rescue."

"Perhaps it shall. I do not care for short hair, you know, in a woman." He let his gaze sweep admiringly up over Eden's heavy braids.

Not entirely sure this was a non sequitur, Eden kept silent, torn between amusement, perplexity, and exasperation.

"Come, let us go in." Brentwood took her elbow, urging her toward the steps. "Briggs will bring some refreshments and our fair Rapunzel to the Gold Salon, won't you, Briggs?"

"Of course, sir." Briggs motioned them before him through the castle doors, held by a roughly attired man.

"Have I told you how much I admire your livery?"

Brentwood chuckled. "It's very economical at least. Actually, all of my male servants are doubling as carpenters just now, as am I, when I am not acting as my own architect. Repairing this old folly is going to be an interesting undertaking."

"You intend to restore it, then?"

"Battlements and all. Though the most dangerous foe this ersatz castle has ever held off has been the tax collector! Here we are."

He opened the drawing-room door for her himself. "Go in and be seated. We must take counsel how to deal with this situation. I must avoid a scandal if possible. I gave Langley my word on that not a week ago and now I have not one but two young women in a compromising situation. And I can hardly marry both!"

Before Eden could ask who Langley was, Isabella appeared at the top of the steps and hurled herself down them. Curls flying, she landed at the bottom, only to throw her arms around her governess in an exuberant hug.

"Father couldn't find me. He never thought to look on the roof! Did he leave you to search for me? You'll help me get away, though, won't you? I haven't been able to find the earl, but the workmen said he was here somewhere. I know he'll help us."

Eden pulled herself free and put her hand gently to Isabella's mouth to stem the flow of words. "Hush, my sweet. This is the earl. Lord Dudley, may I make known to you Miss Isabella Eardley?"

Isabella stared up at Brentwood blankly. Like her father, she had to tilt her head far back to do so. "He doesn't look like an earl. Are you sure he isn't one of the carpenters?"

Brentwood smiled. "I am more a carpenter than an earl these days, Miss Eardley, but I do hold the title. I would prefer, however, that you address me as Mr. Brentwood."

His manner, while friendly, was sufficiently self-assured to quell Isabella's doubts, and she tardily made him a curtsy. The sound of hammering nearby drowned out her murmured apology and greeting.

"Briggs, tell the men to knock off for the morning. I can't hear myself think for that racket, and I do believe I may need to call upon all my mental acuity to solve this problem."

Eden turned to see that Briggs had rejoined them. She wondered how Brentwood had known the man was there. They seemed to have some private form of communication.

"Ladies, please go in so we may discuss our situation." He swept his hand forward, indicating the door now guarded by Briggs.

Isabella bounded inside and began looking around her curiously at the faded room, full of old-fashioned furnishings and objets d'art. "Oh, this is wonderful, like the rest of Dudley castle. I am so glad you are restoring it, but I hope you won't be improving it, because I don't think it can be improved!"

To Eden's surprise, Brentwood put his hand on her arm, keeping her by him near the door as Isabella inspected a knight's armor which was braced against a cabinet. "A very short Rapunzel," he observed in a low, disapproving voice.

"I didn't know there were height requirements for rescue." Eden couldn't resist baiting him a bit.

"There are when rescue may involve marriage."

"I didn't know there were height requirements for matrimony, either."

He stepped closer and looked her up and down meaningfully. "I have always thought it advantageous for partners, whether in marriage or otherwise, to be nearly of a height. I should always be getting a crick in my neck or . . . somewhere . . . with the fair Isabella."

Eden choked back her laughter, trying hard to be angry with him. "Mr. Brentwood, this is beyond—"

"Whereas you, Miss Henderson, are just a fit." He was so close now she could feel the heat of his body.

She stepped quickly away, surprised and alarmed by the warmth surging through her veins. "My height can't possibly have any bearing on the situation."

"Hmmm. Perhaps not. But whether sanctified by marriage or not, the height requirement is about the same."

This highly improper exchange made Eden alarmingly aware of the dangers this man could present to her and to Isabella. She rounded on him. "You mistake me; I should not have jested with you. This is impertinent, in fact insulting. We have a serious situation here. I beg you to give it serious consideration."

"I am fully aware of the seriousness of the situation." Brentwood's grin faded as he took in Eden's angry expression. "Ah, Briggs. Very good. Miss Henderson, will you preside over the tea tray? Come, Miss Eardley, join us. It is a bit early for luncheon, but—"

"Oh, not at all. I am famished. A cold collation, how thoughtful." Isabella applied herself with enthusiasm to the generously heaped tray of delicacies that Briggs placed before them.

Eden poured tea for the three of them and then served herself from the tray. The earl filled his plate with as much enthusiasm as Isabella. Silence reigned for several moments as they battened themselves.

Eden felt strong twinges of conscience as she watched rosy-cheeked Isabella eat as if she hadn't a care in the world. It was in some measure her fault that this innocent little bird had flown her own nest, and landed them both in the paws of Lord Dudley. She still couldn't decide if he was a rapacious tiger or a gentle house cat.

The man's bantering had struck a responsive cord with her own sense of humor, and she had allowed it to lull her to the dangers of the situation. The danger to their reputation was not the half of it.

She began to remember some of the things she had heard of him. His philosophical objections to marriage as it was structured in England did not disgust her, for she had her own strongly-held opinions of that institution. But there had been whispers of multiple mistresses, and of an organization in America where orgies were not only permitted but encouraged. As she thought of what could happen to both her and Isabella if he should act dishonorably, all appetite fled.

Brentwood saw the increasng anxiety in those wide brown eyes and guessed something of her feelings. He rose and went to a sideboard, where he poured some brandy into a small glass. "You look as if you could use a restorative, Miss Henderson." He handed it to her and watched while she took it and sipped at it cautiously. Then he sat down and turned to Isabella, his voice suddenly stern.

"Now, Miss Eardley, you have turned us all upside down today by your actions."

"I am not sorry!" Isabella was instantly on her feet, small fists clenched. "He can't force me to marry Lord Nielson. I won't! He is fat, and old, and odious!"

"So you came here. Did you think your father would simply allow you to take up residence here without a protest? Are you aware that he has turned Miss Henderson off without a penny or a reference, and informs me that either one of us kills the other in a duel, or I must marry you. Forgive me for saying neither one appeals to me greatly."

"No, how could it. I know you despise the institution of marriage. I won't hear of you being forced into it."

"I suppose, then, you came here counting on my killing your father?"

Isabella's eyes grew wide. On a gasp she denied any such intention. "You won't, will you?"

"Despicable man, to so distress such a daughter!" Brentwood stood up abruptly to pace up and down in front of them. "Langley will kill me if I break my promise to him. There is only one way out of this without scandal. I must, I expect, marry you. Sorry, Miss Henderson, much as I would prefer a taller bride, I don't think it would answer. It would solve your problem but not Miss Eardley's."

Eden looked up from where she was comforting Isabella, who had dropped down beside her to cry against her shoulder. "No, of course not. But would you truly consider marriage, sir? Do not trifle with us, I beg you."

Her deep brown eyes were shadowed with worry. He found himself eager to ease her anxiety. "Yes, I will. I suppose it cannot be avoided. I am in some measure responsible for her situation, after all, and have an urgent need to avoid causing a scandal. You, of course, will remain with us as her companion. In fact"—he paused and rubbed his chin thoughtfully—"a governess might be extremely useful—"

"Stop, stop both of you! I don't want to marry you, I don't want to marry anyone. Not ever. I want to be free, the way you wrote that women should be, Lord Dudley. I want to develop my painting talent and earn my own living."

Isabella dashed the tears from her eyes with determination. "And if ever I do marry, I want to marry for love, and you don't love me, you even said you'd rather marry Eden than me. And besides, you're too old for me."

"Isabella!" Eden was torn between horror that her charge was rejecting this solution to their dilemma and amusement over her reaction to the virile young earl, who surely was not above thirty.

"Well, I am afraid your father will expect it, you see, as you have run away to live with me. I really can't kill a man for so reasonable an expectation, even if you weren't prejudiced against my doing so."

The patient tone of his voice as he explained his dilemma once again awakened Eden's risibility, in spite of the seriousness of the situation. She bit her lip to keep from giggling as he plodded determinedly onward.

"And in addition to what I hope is an understandable reluctance to let him kill me, I fail to see how that would solve your problem, for he could then still force you to wed Lord Nielson or someone else very much like him. I would not like to think I must die in vain."

His dry humor was lost on Isabella, who only looked mulish and shook her head.

"Bella, I thought you had more sense than to behave in such a shatterbrained manner." Eden was truly perplexed. Isabella was usually quite intelligent and even precocious in her reasoning.

"Oh, I never meant to live with the earl. But I thought anyone who wrote so eloquently of women's rights to be considered as persons, not chattel, would help me escape my father."

Exasperation written on his face and in his voice, Brentwood demanded, "Then what is it that you want me to do?"

"I want you to take me to my grandmother. She'll take me in, and Eden too."

"I very much fear that won't serve, Miss Eardley. A father has the right to custody of his daughter. Even if your grandmother were willing to fight him in the courts, he'd win in the end."

"I expect what she'd do is shame Father into giving up this scheme to marry me to Lord Nielson. He's terrified of her. Once she makes it clear that she will ruin him forever in the *ton* if he tries to enforce the engagement, he'll give it up. That's what he wants, you know, to be accepted. He thinks if I'm Lady Nielson, it will open doors for him. But if my grandmama speaks against him, he'll find out he's sadly mistaken!"

"Who is your grandmother, Miss Eardley?"

"The dowager Duchess of Carminster." Isabella smiled in triumph.

"Oh, she *will* make him sweat! Old dragon terrifies everyone!" Brentwood dropped back down into his chair, relief obvious in his face.

Eden looked from one to the other. "Do you really think so?" She spoke slowly, dubiously. "I've heard your mother talk about her, of course. But, Bella, I've been with you two years and you've never called on her, nor she on you. That doesn't argue for a close relationship. What makes you think she'll take you in?"

"She despises my father for the way he treats Mama, and for being who he is. She never forgave Grandfather for marrying her daughter to a mere mister, whose father was in trade. After he died, she told my mother if she would leave Papa, we could make our lives with her. I just know she'll be delighted to spike his guns!"

Eden and Brentwood looked admiringly at the precocious sixteen-year-old who had so confidently worked out her own rescue.

"It seems as if we are going to be needing a carriage after

all." Brentwood strode to the bellpull. "Where is the lair of this dragon at this time of year?"

"She is in London. She stays in London almost all year, even in the hottest part of the summer, when everyone else goes to Brighton."

"Excellent." Eden jumped up. "If we leave right away, we can be there before nightfall. Oh! My clothes, my belongings, are all at the Eardleys'. He said he'd toss them out in the lane."

Brentwood nodded. "I'll have someone to collect them for you and send them on to us in London, Miss Henderson."

"Do you go with us, then, Mr. Brentwood?"

"Wouldn't miss it for the world." He winked at her before turning to Briggs, who had answered his summons almost instantly.

Eden watched him as he gave orders to his servants. He was going to behave honorably after all! She let out a long sigh of relief as the fearful tension of the last hour eased. At least Isabella would be safe. All that remained was to convince this formidable grandmother to take her governess as well.

Chapter Three

B rentwood's traveling carriage was not new, nor was it as well sprung as the Eardleys' luxurious vehicle. Nor did its two horses convey it at the spanking speed of her father's fine team of four. All this and much more Isabella observed vociferously to Eden as they bowled along the Hertfordshire countryside, hardly noticing that her governess was making only perfunctory responses.

Indeed, Eden's thoughts were anywhere but on their immediate surroundings. As the carriage bounced and lurched toward London, she mused on the events of this unusual day. She had been carried along on a swift, irresistible current of events since finding her charge gone from her room early in the morning.

How she admired Bella's resourcefulness in discovering a way to thwart Mr. Eardley's machinations. She felt great shame that she, of all people, should have been so slow to take up the girl's cause.

Equally admirable had been Mr. Brentwood's willingness to help. She had been impressed by the swift, efficient way he had organized their expedition to London, complete with sending a note to Isabella's parents by way of the footman who was to collect Eden's trunks.

The note advised them that he was escorting their daughter and her governess to London to stay with her grandmother. Isabella had added a note of her own, and the ferocity which lit her face as she composed it had Eden and Brentwood exchanging bemused glances.

"I've made it very clear to him, for he can be dense when he's in a temper, that if he tries to force this marriage on me, or a duel on you, Grandmother will see that he is never received anywhere again."

"A formidable child," Brentwood murmured in Eden's ear as he handed the two notes to the footman. Eden could only nod, eyeing her heretofore biddable if exuberant charge with respect mingled with surprise.

The earl had chosen to ride ahead of them along with one outrider. "A small guard, but the wilds of Hertfordshire are usually not too threatening, at least in broad daylight," he had quipped. She smiled at the thought of anything wild in Hertfordshire, which was so civilized that even its farms looked like well-manicured gardens, with the holly in the hedgerows trimmed into formal shapes.

No, it was clear that the earl rode outside to protect them all from society's censure, a sensitivity she had not expected from the author of that sternly critical attack on social mores.

When Bella had set up a clamor for him to lead her mare, he had declined, gently but firmly insisting that the mare be stabled until "we learn whether she will be as welcome as you are." Isabella accepted the directive reluctantly, without noticing the phrasing that caused Eden's mouth to quirk upward.

Within the hour they were on their way, and Isabella babbled over her fascination with the countryside and the people they passed. In spite of their proximity to London, she had never been there, and eagerly marked each sign that they drew nearer the metropolis. Eden halfheartedly responded while worrying about their reception at the other end.

There were problems ahead of which neither Isabella nor Brentwood had the least notion. For if the duchess did accept her, she would be living in London, where she might be seen by the wrong person. *Even if I go undetected at first, when Bella comes out next year, I shall surely be expected to accompany her occasionally. And if I do, the chances of discovery are much greater than they were tucked away in a country manor in Hertfordshire.*

Yet what choice did she have? She had nowhere else to go, and was virtually penniless. As Eden mulled over the danger she was so suddenly, unexpectedly facing, she sank into a dismal silence.

By the time they stopped for the last time before reaching London, Isabella had noticed Eden's unusual taciturnity, and failing to draw her out of it, eagerly turned to the earl for conversation as they sat down to a light repast while the horses were changed.

"We heard that you had come home from India a nabob, but I collect it is not true, else you'd have a better carriage."

"Bella!" Eden roused from her doldrums to admonish her pupil. "Your manners!"

Ignoring Eden, Brentwood bent confidentially toward Isabella. "You are on the mark, my dear. My capacity to enrich myself in India was strangely diminished by my qualms about doing so at the expense of the native culture. Indeed, I found the role of my country as the ravisher of that ancient land quite repugnant and soon took myself off to America."

"Then you are still poor! How can you afford to renovate Dudley castle?"

Once again Eden remonstrated, but the earl only chuckled. "My travels took me to the United States and Canada. I have entered into a fur-trading venture with my cousin. It is trade, of course, but does not seem to have the odium associated with the manufacture of cloth, for some odd reason. Not that I care a whit."

"America! How exciting. Did you see any of the wild Indians of which we have heard so much?"

"I saw both wild and civilized men and women of several races." Brentwood's eyes took on a faraway look. "America is a remarkable place. The coastal cities are amazingly like England, but the farther one penetrates into the interior, the more the character of both the land and the people change."

"For the better?" Eden's curiosity led her away from her lowering thoughts.

"The issue is in doubt, I would say. For Lord Dudley, cer-

tainly not for the better, but plain Mr. Brentwood got along
swimmingly, as long as he was willing to pull his weight."

"Whatever can you mean, my lord?" Bella frowned at the
notion of a gentleman "pulling weight."

"No 'my lords,' if you please! What I mean is, if a carriage
is stuck, or firewood to be gathered, or game to be skinned, a
man who is willing to take his turn and work hard is quickly
accepted."

Isabella's blue eyes widened. "You did manual labor? But
you are a gentleman."

"Gentlemen are prized in New York, merely objects of curiosity in Pennsylvania, and positively abhorred in the territories. I found it quite bracing, actually. I learned that I have a
taste for productive activity."

"Is that why you said you were a carpenter today?"

"Just so!" He held up his hands. "Do you think your grandmother will allow me in her drawing room?"

"Calluses," Isabella breathed in astonishment.

"You had better put on gloves, sir," Eden admonished him,
primming her lips to keep from laughing outright at his mischievous pleasure in shocking Isabella.

"Never fear. I still know how a gentleman should behave,
though I may not always choose to act on that knowledge." He
gave her what might have passed for a lascivious leer on a less
pleasant countenance.

"I think you have acted the perfect gentleman, don't you,
Eden? Why, you even offered to marry me, though you don't
want to marry anyone, and though if you had to marry one of
us you'd prefer Eden. I think that is quite gallant!" She
laughed and clapped her hands at his embarrassment.

"It is entirely understandable. Eden is tall, as you said, and
pretty, and much more your age. She is six and twenty, you
know. How old are you? Not that it matters, for Eden doesn't
want to marry, any more than you or I. She's forever turning
down proposals, aren't you, Eden?"

"Isabella, do stop talking and eat, or we shall have to leave and you will go hungry." Eden busied herself with her plate, not wishing to pursue the subject.

"Forever turning down proposals, eh?" Brentwood's eyes caressed the pure oval of her face, the delicious curves beneath her plain brown dress. "I can well believe it, but why? Have no truly eligible gentlemen come forward?"

Before Eden could make some repressive answer that would end this upsetting discussion, Isabella rushed into explanations. "Oh, the vicar was highly eligible. Papa and Mama thought so. Papa was quite amazed that she'd turn him down. He has a fine home and a good living—several in fact, and hopes of future preferment."

"But I expect he was old, fat, and ugly?"

"Not at all." Isabella earnestly cataloged the young, attractive vicar's merits. "And then there was Squire Hamilton. He's older, but also much richer, and extremely handsome. He was struck all of a heap the first time he saw her, and proposed the second, but would she have him? No! So you see, Eden is determined to live her life free of male domination, as you advised. And so will I."

Eden gaped at the young girl. "Isabella, I had no idea you connected my response to those proposals to Lord Dudley's essay. In fact, I thought you only read it yesterday!"

The blond head dipped low. "I have to confess. I went through your trunk ages ago. Papa said there was some mystery about you, when you first came, and I wanted to see if I could find out what it was. I've read and reread that essay, and each time I do it seems truer and wiser." She lifted glowing eyes to Brentwood, who sat back with a look of deep chagrin on his face.

"That cursed article. Would that I'd never penned it. It's done a good deal of harm, and no good that I can tell. Isabella, I've changed my thinking a great deal since then. Not about women deserving fairer treatment before the law, of course, but . . . when we have time, I'd like to discuss this matter further with you. And, Miss Henderson, please don't tell me it is the reason you have refused otherwise acceptable suitors, to bury yourself as a governess."

"No, my l—Mr. Brentwood, you may rest easy on that score. My refusals of those proposals were not the result of that essay, I assure you."

"But, Eden, why did you save it all those years if . . ." Bella tried to voice what was puzzling both herself and Brentwood.

To prevent further discussion, Eden rose. "I believe we should refresh ourselves before continuing our journey, don't you, Bella? We don't want to arrive at your grandmother's looking mussed."

Isabella's grandmother, the dowager Duchess of Carminster, lived in state in an enormous Georgian mansion in Park Lane. The trio of travelers made good time, and arrived before the sun had set. There was some confusion and reluctance to admit them on the butler's part at first, but Brentwood quickly proved that he had not forgotten how to behave like a gentleman by thoroughly intimidating the man into doing his bidding, and they were ushered into an impressive drawing room beautifully furnished in the Regency style, with light furniture and bright colors.

They had only a few moments to admire the centerpiece of the magnificent room, an enormous fireplace with a carved white marble mantel, before the dowager Duchess of Carminster swept into the room. With a sinking heart Eden realized she was every bit the grande dame that Isabella had described.

The dowager's immediate concern was her granddaughter. She received Eden with a chilly nod and Brentwood with an imperiously raised eyebrow, before quickly turning her attention to the young girl.

"Isabella Eardley! Where is your mother? Your father? What are you doing here, and in *such* company?" As she said the last, she shot Brentwood a cold, accusing glance, then thoughtfully surveyed Eden's face.

Isabella stood before her grandmother, wringing her hands.

"Oh, Grandmama. You've got to help me. Papa is going to make me marry Lord Nielson."

"Don't talk rot, girl." The older woman drew herself up indignantly. "The man is twice your age. And far too aware of his own consequence to enter a marriage with an unwilling bride."

"He doesn't know I'm unwilling. I tried being as cold as ever I could be, in fact would hardly speak to him, but it only seemed to encourage Lord Nielson."

"Doubtless he took it as a sign of maidenly reserve. Why not plain speaking? Surely you could have found some way to let him know?" Her eyes strayed to Eden at this point, as if to say, "Why didn't you do something?"

"I didn't dare, and neither did Eden or Mama. Papa said he'd beat us if any of us warned Lord Nielson off. He is quite set on my being a baroness."

A flare of anger came into the cold gray eyes. "Beat you? Does he beat you, Isabella? Has he ever—"

"More than once, and Mama too."

"I knew it! I always despised that man. I told your grandfather how it would be. These little, climbing, pushing men! He expected poor Seraphina to get him into society, as if she could, him such a mushroom, and her so timid. I knew he'd take his disappointment out on her."

"You'll help me, won't you? You won't let him force me to marry Lord Nielson."

The grande dame looked from Isabella to Eden to Brentwood. "Exactly how did you come to be in Dudley's company, missy? Thought you was out of the country, sir."

"As you see, I've returned."

"I ran away to him. I knew he would help me."

"This defies reason. Ran away to Dudley? How could you ever know of him? Oh, do let us all sit down. I'll ring for some tea while we sort this out."

When they had settled in a grouping of chairs in front of the marble fireplace, which was filled with a massive urn of fresh flowers, the duchess continued her interrogation. "Now, tell me all."

Isabella told how she had read Brentwood's essay and decided that a man who could write so eloquently of a woman's rights would be willing to help her escape her father. "And I never want to marry, Grandmama. I want to do just as he says women should—live free of man's domination. I am a very good artist, ask Eden. I mean to study at the Royal Academy and make my living as a portrait painter."

The duchess fell back against her chair in astonishment. "The Royal Academy? Earn your living? Well, Dudley, do you see what comes of your infamous manifesto? Are you proud of yourself?"

"I have changed my views somewhat in the past five years, ma'am, but I still do not believe young girls should be forced into marriage."

"Nor do I. That is not the point. Oh, be quiet, all of you, and let me think." She waved an impatient, imperious hand, and stared into the fireplace.

The clock in the room was all that could be heard as the three obeyed her. The butler entered during the silence, carrying a tea tray which he set on a small table at the dowager's elbow. She waved him off. "My granddaughter shall pour."

Isabella obeyed, her hands shaking slightly, as did Eden's when she took the proffered cup. She stole a glance at Brentwood, wondering how he felt about the old woman's hostility. His face was solemn, but when he caught her eyeing him, he winked. She quickly faced around. The man was irrepressible. Of course, none of this touched him as nearly as it did herself and Isabella. Doubtless to him it was all a day's lark.

"Very well!" The dowager duchess's loud, firm voice startled them all. "You may stay, and I will deal with that worm of a father of yours. Perhaps I can coax Seraphina away from him. He doesn't deserve her, never did."

Isabella, unable to deny her natural affections any longer, darted across the space between their chairs and kneeled, hugging her startled grandmother around the waist. "Oh, thank you, Grandmama! I knew you would. And I shan't be a charge on you forever, you'll see! I'll study ever so hard. I won't even complain when Eden makes me speak in French, for I know—"

"As for Miss Henderson, her services will no longer be required." The duchess disentangled herself from Isabella and put a firm hand across the mouth she opened to protest.

"No, hear me! You are almost a grown woman. The next year will be spent preparing for your come-out. Miss Henderson can be of little help to you there, as she has never had one. And this talk of studying art is to cease."

The dowager stood, as did Eden and Brentwood. "I hold you responsible, Miss Henderson, for my granddaughter's attitude toward marriage. I cannot feel that continued association with you would be in her best interests. My granddaughter won't be forced to marry, but she *will* marry, and marry well."

"But Eden did not—"

"Silence! If you are to stay with me, you must not bedevil me with complaints and arguments." The duchess bent down and urged Isabella off the carpet. "You must begin to behave like a lady. I fear your head has been stuffed with a great deal of useless learning and little knowledge that will be of value to you in taking your place in society."

Isabella moved defiantly beside her governess. "If Eden can't stay, I won't."

Eden turned her around by the shoulders and looked her in the eye. "No, dear, this is the only way. Your grandmother is your best hope of avoiding an odious marriage. And she is correct. I would be of little help in preparing you for your come-out."

"But what will you do? Oh, Grandmama, Father has turned her off without a character, without even her last quarter's salary. We must pay her, must let her stay here until she has found a new position."

"I will pay what is owing to her, but she cannot stay. You do understand, Miss Henderson?"

"I am not sure . . ."

"I live very much in society." The duchess spoke in ponderous, almost menacing, tones. "Should you like to be in the center of society, Miss Henderson?" The cool gray eyes shrewdly awaited Eden's response.

Eden drew back in horror. "Say no more, I beg of you."

"Wait here. Come, Isabella." She held out her hand commandingly, and Isabella reluctantly took it and allowed herself to be led from the room.

Eden lowered her head, avoiding what she knew must be Mr. Brentwood's perplexity. She couldn't, wouldn't explain. In the silence that followed the clock was again heard ticking, but this time its beat was drowned out by the pulsing of her heart. What was she to do? Where was she to go?

Once again, for the second time this day, she was thrown back upon the mercy of Roger Brentwood, Earl of Dudley.

Chapter Four

Brentwood moved closer to Eden, close enough to whisper in her ear, "I begin to perceive that Mr. Eardley was right; you *are* a woman of mystery."

Eden turned away from him in great distress. "Please leave me alone. I can't think what to do!"

"If you would confide your secret to me, I could be surer of offering appropriate assistance." The green eyes weren't twinkling now, but giving her a direct and reassuring signal. For the first time in her life, she found herself wanting to trust a man. She wanted to tell him everything, but fear of the consequences paralyzed her.

When the dowager reentered the room, without Isabella, she found the two thus, staring at one another, a battle of wills underway. "Here is your salary, Miss Henderson. I suggest you go to the Hotel Harndon, a respectable boarding hotel for ladies, and then to an employment agency." She moved in such a way as to force Brentwood to step back. "You cannot wish to go with Dudley, surely?"

"No, but I have no reference. However shall I—"

"As to that, my opinion is that you have been, if not a malevolent influence on Isabella, at least an unfortunate one, as with your background one might well expect. But she is quite fiercely determined you shall have a reference. Perhaps you can find work as a nurse, or companion. I have written you a character that will assist you in obtaining such a position. I could not in good conscience recommend you to help rear another young woman."

The dowager paused as if for once not sure of her next words. "I may even know of a position. I will make inquiries. If you do not find something in a week or so, you may call on me."

"Thank you, Your Grace." Eden humbly, gratefully took the bank draft, small purse, and sealed letter which the duchess held out to her.

The dowager followed them into the entryway. Suddenly Eden remembered her belongings. "My trunks—you had them sent here, didn't you, Mr. Brentwood? Will you store them for a short while for me, Your Grace, until I can get located?"

"That won't be necessary. Send Miss Henderson's trunks to Lord Langley's residence on Curzon Street. She will be residing as Lady Langley's guest for the time being."

Eden had the satisfaction of seeing the duchess's frosty expression warm a fraction. "Of course. You'll see to it, Simpson?"

The butler inclined his head respectfully. "Yes, Your Grace."

When they were on the pavement in front of Brentwood's carriage, Eden thanked the earl for saying she was going to the Langleys'. "Even though it was not true, it took some of the starch out of her. I collect you know them well enough to gain my trunks houseroom for a short while?"

"More than just your trunks, my dear Miss Henderson. I am taking you to Langley straightaway."

"What? Why on earth for? The Langley you refer to is, I think, the Publishing Peer?"

At his nod she laughed. "Why would he have any interest in me?"

"Not only is he an old friend and mentor of mine, he will certainly feel a small measure of responsibility for your plight, and—"

"No, why should he?"

"After all, that infamous essay was published in his magazine."

"But he was out of the country at the time, as I recall, on his honeymoon. Even the government didn't hold him responsible, so why—"

"Where do you think I got the ideas that I espoused in that misbegotten essay?"

"From the writings of Godwin and Wollstonecraft, among others, I should expect."

"Their ultimate source, of course. But the embodiment of all my philosophy when I was a young cub was Stuart Hamilton, Lord Langley. I idolized him, and took every word of his as holy writ. When he, along with two other of my very good friends, suddenly married in one summer, I was a very disillusioned young man.

"He asked me to edit *The Legacy* during his honeymoon, and I took the opportunity to launch an all-out attack on many of what I saw as society's ills, most spectacularly, of course, the institution of marriage."

Brentwood urged her toward the door to his carriage. "Come, get in and I'll tell you the entire tale on the way to the Langleys'."

"Please do not let us be seen entering a closed carriage together." Eden tried to draw back.

"Beg pardon, I forgot. Doubtless the dowager has set her servants to spy upon our manner of departure. Dobson, drive Miss Henderson directly to Lord Langley, if you please. I shall ride ahead."

With economical, firm movements that prevented any hesitation on her part, he assisted her up the carriage steps and closed the door.

Before he could spring away, Eden protested, "I don't want to be an object of charity. Just direct your driver to take me to some respectable hotel for ladies."

"No charity will be involved, Miss Henderson. The Langleys have two children, a girl four years of age, and a boy who is two. Unless I mistake the matter, she is breeding again. They have no governess that I know of, so it is very likely they will be delighted to have you join their family."

After her chilly reception from the dowager Duchess of

Carminster, Eden wondered if anyone would ever again be delighted to hire her. Still more questionable was the wisdom of accepting employment in London. But Brentwood had ordered the carriage into the heavy traffic, so all she could do was agonize over whether she ought to go to the Langleys', and wonder what her reception would be, as the carriage wended its way through the busy streets.

"You've done what? Damn it all, Roger, you promised me you'd stay out of trouble."

"This was not of my seeking, though certainly of my making. She is a very decent young woman who doesn't deserve the treatment she has received. If we don't aid her, she will manage somehow. She's a resourceful, spirited young woman. There will be shame on our heads for failing to help her, but no scandal."

Langley frowned as he looked up at his one-time disciple. Five years of time and travel had changed him, of course. The baron was not exactly sure what sort of man he was dealing with. From the younger man's stiff posture and set mouth, he'd guess a rather determined one, just now.

"Very well, very well, sit down and tell me what has happened and how we may assist you. But we must hurry about it. Gwynneth will be down shortly; we're going to the opera."

Brentwood gave his old friend and mentor a quick sketch of the day's events, leaving Langley shaking his head ruefully. "That old essay, still causing trouble. It got me in enough trouble at the time."

"Not to mention forcing me to flee the country. But something good may come out of it for once."

"What do you mean?"

"Think this woman will make me a fine wife. Marrying her would solve her problem and make me more respectable, all at the same time."

"Hmmmm. Not that I don't appreciate the thought, but when I asked you to be a model of propriety if you joined our political movement, I never meant for you to marry merely for respectability. I would never ask you to go so far. Marriage is too important a commitment to make for such a reason. Surely there must be some other way . . ."

"Some other way than what, dear?" A tall, fair-haired woman in an elegant pale green satin evening gown swept into the room. "Oh, hello, Brent. Have you come to visit? A week in Hertfordshire was enough, I see."

"Gwynneth!" Brentwood kissed her proffered cheek. "Forgive me for appearing in my riding clothes and all the dirt of a fast ride from Varnham."

"Quite all right, but you'll have to change in a hurry. I won't give up my opera for you!" She wagged an admonishing finger at him, smiling to soften the determination in her voice. She did not know Roger Brentwood well, but she was fast becoming very fond of him.

"Can't change just now; my clothes haven't arrived. Have a bit of a favor to ask."

He quickly outlined his request. Even as he finished his sketchy explanation, Eden arrived and was announced. She stood uncertainly in the door of the drawing room, taking in the elegantly dressed pair talking with Brentwood.

"Come in, Miss Henderson." Lady Langley's voice was welcoming. "Our naughty Brent was just explaining your predicament."

"Do you think . . . that is, are you looking for a governess?"

Lady Langley gave her an enigmatic smile. "What I think is that you have had an exhausting, unsettling day, and would profit from a good dinner and an early bed. I am quite selfishly determined not to miss the opera—"

"No, of course I wouldn't think of imposing—"

"It is *The Magic Flute*, one of my favorites, but tomorrow morning over breakfast we can make plans."

"I should go to an hotel. I asked Mr. Brentwood to send me—"

"He did just as he should," Lord Langley's deep intonation interrupted her. "You are another innocent victim of our youthful folly, one of the few we've been able directly to assist, I fear." He crossed the room to the bellpull. "Of course, you'll have to rack up elsewhere under the circumstances, Roger."

"Naturally. Grillon's will do very well for me. Have your man send my clothes over when they arrive. Well, Miss Henderson, it has been quite a day for both of us. At least I am down to only one prospective bride by now."

So saying, the green eyes sparkling with mischief, he bent to plant a swift kiss on her cheek.

"Bride! Don't be absurd."

But she was talking to his back; he had swiftly dashed down the stairs, and only gave her a jaunty wave with his crop as he hurried through the door the footman was scrambling to open.

Eden turned slowly, wide-eyed, to the two elegant strangers who stood beside her. "Sometimes I think he is quite mad."

Gwynneth looked speculatively from her to the disappearing young man. "A bit fey, at times. Well, we can settle all this in the morning. Here is Betty. She will conduct you upstairs and show you your room. As we are not dining in, perhaps a tray—"

"Of course. How I hate the imposition. I—"

"Do not, Miss Henderson. I have an idea it is going to be a distinct pleasure to add you to our circle of friends." Lord Langley took her hand and kissed the air above it.

His unexpected gallantry and warm words alarmed Eden. She had been the unwilling recipient of inappropriate masculine attention more than once in her life. How she hoped she hadn't stumbled into a situation where she would have to fend off the husband's advances and the wife's hatred.

But Lady Langley's golden eyes were just as friendly as her lord's. "I do hate to rush off like this, but—"

"I'd feel even worse if I kept you from your opera."

"Then until tomorrow." She held out her hand. "Get some rest; tomorrow should be a very interesting day."

By the time Eden had washed off the dust of the road and partaken of a generous cold collation, her trunks had arrived.

The kindly maid Betty tut-tutted as she helped her unpack them.

"Just threw all in there together anyhow," she observed indignantly.

"My departure was rather sudden. I only hope they packed everything." Eden didn't offer an explanation to the servant; gossip in that quarter was unavoidable, but she'd give it as little fuel as possible.

With great relief she found her treasured small collection of books had been included, and her locked jewel case, in which resided very few jewels. The offending essay was still in there, as well as a packet of letters. How Isabella had managed to read Brentwood's essay, and more than once, Eden couldn't imagine, but her former pupil was a clever, forceful female. Obviously not even locks intimidated her.

I suppose she read the letters too. Eden sighed. It was a good thing that she and her aunt had always been most circumspect in their correspondence.

Her clothes were few, and quickly inventoried. "All seems to be here," Eden observed with relief.

"Would miss like a bath?" Betty queried.

"Oh, my, how wonderful that sounds. But I would hate to bother the servants at such a late hour."

" 'Tis no bother, miss. Lord Langley has a bath with running water, he does, and the cleverest stove to heat the tank. Two in fact, one on this floor, and one below for the servants, if ye can believe it. 'Tis a condition of our employment that we bathe at least once a week."

"My goodness." Eden was awed. Many in the highest levels of society did not bathe so often. "Then I should love to have a bath."

As she luxuriated in the warm water in the large copper tub, Eden mused on the astonishing day she had just experienced. It had come at the end of an unhappy week, during which Isabella had been vigorously resisting her father's matchmaking attempts, and he had been threatening all three females with bodily harm if he was thwarted.

She had thought she had another year of security before Isabella left for London and her coming-out season. Eden had planned to begin searching for another position as governess within the next six months. Another safe position in the country, for she had known she shouldn't go to London. And now, here she was! Worse, she had probably been recognized, though she doubted the dowager duchess would betray her.

And that mischievous Earl of Dudley, claiming her as a prospective bride. She hoped he was merely teasing, as was his wont, for she hadn't the slightest intention of marrying him, and any attempts on his part to insist must send her speedily out into a world she knew too well was dangerous for a pretty, friendless young woman.

But that pretense of intending to marry her was doubtless all a hum, more of his peculiar humor. His ideas probably had not changed as much as he claimed. He'd been eager enough to avoid matrimony with Isabella, and had exerted himself considerably to that end. He'd surely be no less energetic in avoiding marrying her.

She smiled to herself as she swished the perfumed water to rinse off the soap. He was quite an attractive, amusing, rascal. She rather regretted that she must guard herself so closely against his charm.

Used to country hours, Eden was up before the master and mistress of the house. She found breakfast already in preparation in the kitchen, and would have taken it there, but the servants shooed her into the breakfast room and served her in state. As she was finishing up some kippered herrings and coddled eggs, a stir in the hall presaged a visitor.

She wasn't surprised when Brentwood appeared at the door. "Oh, good. Knew you'd be up betimes. Do you know, I'm an early riser too, can't sleep no matter how late I've been up the night before."

He served himself from the sideboard, waving off the hovering footman. "Go have another cup of coffee, Charles. I wish to be private a moment with Miss Henderson."

Eden eyed him with apprehension, but he looked utterly harmless. He seated himself a very neutral three seats away from her.

In some amusement she watched him spread himself out, utilizing most of the space by his lounging posture and arrangement of china and utensils. He ate heartily, paying her little attention until his appetite was satisfied.

"Better," he mumbled, wiping his mouth on a snowy serviette. "The cook at Grillons must have done his apprenticeship in hell. Everything was done to the texture of leather last night."

"My lord, I—"

"Thought we'd got that 'lord' business cleared up."

"Excuse me. Mr. Brentwood. Last night you said—"

"Want to apologize about that. I realize my offhand manner quite put you off. Mean to do the thing right this morning, though. Shall we go into the drawing room? Much more suitable."

"You surely don't mean to propose to me!"

The high-arched brows reached their maximum height. "I do, actually. Do you object?"

"I won't marry you, sir, so please don't ask."

"You won't?" His astonishment would have been vastly amusing under other circumstances. "Why not?"

"Don't you read your own essay from time to time, Mr. Brentwood? There is a good deal of excellent advice in it, especially for females."

A deep, hearty chuckle from the doorway told her that someone, at least, found the situation comical. "Hoist by your own petard, Roger."

Chapter Five

Lord Langley stood in the doorway to the dining room surveying the two with amusement. "Left England for five years and came back to find that old land mine still packed with enough live powder to explode in your face. Richly deserved, m'boy."

Brentwood shook his head in mock chagrin. "To think I've always run from parson's mousetrap. Apparently I might have saved myself the trouble. In the last twenty-four hours two young women have turned me down in circumstances where you might have thought I'd be nigh irresistible."

The earl's aggrieved tone was belied by his laughing eyes. "The first refusal I was delighted to receive, but yours, Miss Henderson, has cut me to the quick."

"Coming it far too strong, Mr. Brentwood." Eden tossed her head dismissively, but couldn't keep from grinning at his nonsense.

"I say, couldn't we do away with this Mr. and Miss business? It might take a little of the sting out of your refusal." He smiled engagingly. "Call me Brent, that's what my friends call me."

She looked in some perplexity at Lord Langley, who was seating himself opposite Brentwood.

"Not Stu, of course. He calls me Roger—only person in the world who's done so, except for my parents. When I first was introduced to him, I was too much in awe of him to correct him when he began to call me by my first name."

"Now the name sticks, though the awe is long gone." Langley cocked a dark eyebrow in amusement.

"Not entirely, my lord. Yesterday he mentioned you twice in considerable anxiety when he thought he'd landed in the middle of a scandal."

"Good, good. A little awe might help keep him on the straight and narrow. Very important right now, Miss Henderson—I say, I agree with Roger, shall we be less formal? What is your first name?"

"Eden, sir, but—"

"Please call me Stuart. Now, as I was saying, it is very important that all my political supporters avoid scandal, not just now but for the foreseeable future." He shot Brentwood an admonitory scowl.

"Our poor are growing ever more desperate, and the middling sort quite rightly feel left out of the government of the country. We must reform or face the deadly dangers of revolution. The weavers are practicing marching with broomsticks in Manchester. Frame breaking continues in spite of harsh penalties. Riotous mobs are common in the large cities. There have even been rocks thrown and shots fired at the Prince Regent's carriage. Yet the current government's only answer is more repression.

"It is my hope, and that of other progressive thinkers, that we can bring about a bloodless revolution by changing the form of our government."

Fascinated and a little alarmed at the thought of tampering with the British constitution, Eden asked, "Why is so drastic a step necessary? And how can you accomplish it, my lord?"

"Stuart. Because we are continually defeated when we attempt to pass legislation to improve conditions—reform of child labor laws, and reduction of the corn tariff, for example. We must reform the electorate. The rotten boroughs must go. Once England's parliament is more representative of her people, reform will be possible."

"Is there any hope of such a change?"

"Today there is little hope of any change at all. The Prince

Regent has been frightened by hostile crowds once too often. He favors the forces of repression, thinking his safety lies there. Instead, I fear they are going to bring on the bloody revolution they claim to be preventing, by their own actions.

"But we are working behind the scenes, trying to educate the more open-minded of our peers. It will take time and patience, but we have had some success already. We have even made some friends among the royal dukes.

"Whigs and evangelical Christians are our staunchest allies, but many of these would be alienated by any hint of libertinism. We—and all who would work with us—must be most circumspect in our private lives."

"And what could be more proper than for me to take a wife?" Brentwood leaned across the table to take her hand in his. "So you see, Eden, upon your acceptance of my proposal may hang the fate of all England."

"England is in much more danger than I ever imagined, then, Mr. Brentwood." She tugged her hand free.

"Brent. What a heartless wench you are."

Langley chuckled. "Not heartless. Wise, you chucklehead. Marriage is not to be entered into lightly."

"Certainly not before our reform program is enacted. Or is the improvement of women's legal position still on your agenda, Stu?" No longer jovial, Brentwood was leaning forward, his jaw jutting aggressively.

"We will certainly seek at least to even the scales for men and women when it comes to divorce and custody of children. But it won't happen in time for you to take a light view of marriage, certainly."

Brentwood bristled. "Believe me, I do not take a light view of marriage. To be perfectly serious for a moment, I had only planned to suggest to Miss Henderson that we become better acquainted, with a view to matrimony. But there is far more that needs to be done in this area than mere cosmetic changes in our divorce laws—"

"Eden, if you can tear yourself away from our fascinating conversation, my wife is in the nursery, and suggested you join her there when you had finished breaking your fast." Langley obviously did not wish to come to cuffs with Brentwood in her presence.

"I'll go right away." She stood, as did the two men, and hastened to find Lady Langley. Perhaps somehow the subject of her employment as a governess had already been broached. Yet dared she take a position with this socially and politically active family? The scandal which might result if she were recognized while living with the Langleys might harm, not only herself, but the cause of desperately needed reform for her country. *What a quandary. I am terrified of being on my own, yet feel I shouldn't stay here.* Eden mounted the stairs shaking her head in perplexity.

An enchanting sight greeted her when she entered the nursery. Lady Langley, wearing a rather faded morning dress, was seated on the floor pulling a small carved wooden horse in front of her. A chubby little boy of about two years of age, with nearly white hair, clapped his hands gleefully, while a very pretty dark-haired girl of about four leaned against her mother, laughing.

"Good morning, my lady. Lord Langley said you wished me to join you here."

"Yes. Do you mind if I don't get up just now?" Gwynneth gave Eden a winsome smile. "Let me present my children. This is Martin, and this is Madelyn."

Master Martin paid her no mind, having succeeded in getting his chubby hands on the horse, but little Madelyn gave Eden a charming curtsy.

"Set Miss Henderson a chair, will you, Fanny?" A nursery maid who had been hovering in the background hastened to do so.

"Have you breakfasted?" At Eden's affirmative, Lady Langley sent Fanny away with the tray. "It has become my custom to breakfast with the children, and then we spend an hour or two on their studies. Madelyn is making excellent progress at reading and writing, and Martin is beginning to learn his letters."

She spoke with great pride, the unusual golden-hazel eyes glowing. "Brent indicated that you had been a governess, and would like another position caring for children?"

"Yes, my lady."

"Please call me Gwynneth, if you don't mind my using your first name."

What an informal household, Eden thought, ducking her head a little in embarrassment. *One could so easily forget one's place among such people.*

"Do you think that's wise? I mean, if I am to work . . ."

"I think it is wise to be comfortable among ourselves, don't you? Of course, we'll behave ourselves when outsiders are about."

Eden couldn't resist the conspiratorial grin the other woman threw her. She nodded her acceptance. "Please call me Eden, then."

"A lovely name." Gwynneth paused as if pondering what to say. "I had not thought of engaging a governess just now, as I don't feel children need intensive instruction at such an early age, do you?"

Eden shook her head, her hopes plummeting.

"But Stuart and I talked it over last night. Madelyn is almost ready for a governess, and with another baby on the way, I shall surely need help with them soon. Right now teaching the children is one of my chief pleasures, so I hope you won't take it amiss if I participate in your lessons for a while yet."

"Oh, no, that would be quite acceptable. Actually, my l— ah, Gwynneth, I have not taught such young children before. My first position was at the school where I was a pupil. I taught the older girls music and art. Then, when our head-mistress died . . ." Eden felt her composure slipping and looked away. She still couldn't think of Kitty Robinson without deep emotion. "When the school was closed, I went with the Eardleys at Isabella's insistence. She was one of my most talented art students."

"Well, then, for now you can work with them along with me, and perhaps act as my secretary, too, for in addition to my social obligations, I help Stuart with *The Legacy* now he is so busy with politics. If you decide you don't like working with small children, you can take your time seeking another position. How does that sound?"

"Perfect! I don't doubt I'll like the children, you understand. It's just that I'm not sure about appropriate teaching methods . . ." An unhappy memory surfaced of her own governess, chosen by her father over her mother's protests, strapping her into a harness to keep her spine rigid, and then making her stand for hours reciting French verbs. If that was Lady Langley's notion of how young children should be treated, she could never manage it.

"I find that making lessons seem like play works best." Gwynneth proceeded to demonstrate her theory with a lively guessing game that had both children looking for objects around the room that illustrated the letters of the alphabet. As the morning progressed, Eden began to feel increasingly confident both of her welcome and her ability to be a good governess to the Langley children. When Martin fell asleep on her lap, she rocked him back and forth, and felt tears coming to her eyes, tears for the children she would never have.

"They are both so beautiful. You are very fortunate."

"I know. There are times I can still hardly believe my good fortune. Two healthy children and a husband who truly loves me. Speaking of which, you seem in a fair way to attaching Brent." Gwynneth's golden eyes twinkled.

Eden shook her head vehemently. "He is teasing. I do believe he would joke at his own funeral. No, this mention of marriage is all a hum, but even if he were serious, I am not interested in marriage."

"Well, of course you wouldn't want to rush into it the way he was suggesting, but—"

"Not ever. I am resolved never to marry. Please, my lady— Gwynneth. If I am to stay, you must not try any matchmaking. In fact, it is my wish to stay very much in the background."

Gwynneth stood, brushing her clothes down carefully. "Is it that wretched essay that has given you such a disgust of marriage? Will you not let me refute it, if so, with some arguments of my own, not to mention the examples I can point to of happily married couples?"

Eden smiled and stood, carrying the sleeping child to the indicated bed. "No, it is not just the essay. I have much more direct and personal reasons for abhorring matrimony. Thank you for your concern, though."

Gwynneth studied the young woman curiously. *I always thought it was men who avoided marriage*, she mused. What an ironic reversal it would be if Brent were serious, and Eden the one determined to remain single.

Eden spent the rest of the day with Gwynneth, learning what was expected of her in her secretarial capacity. Gradually, rather shyly, Lady Langley revealed that she did a great deal of the editing for Lord Langley's various publications now, especially *The Legacy*, his magazine devoted to women's writing. "He is just too busy now, with politics and estate matters. Of course, I don't let anyone know."

"Why? I would think Lord Langley would wish it known. Wouldn't it validate his views of women's abilities to have it known that his wife so capably manages his publications?"

Gwynneth frowned and bit her lip. "Yes, he does wish it. It is the one area in which I let him down, I fear. I do not like to attract notice to myself, you see. If for no other reason, for fear of alienating those men who might assist him in his reforms."

Eden didn't entirely understand. "Isn't improving the status of women one of his hoped-for reforms?"

"Yes, but until we can expand the electorate, all is doomed to failure. Look at how impossible it is even to get a law against using children as chimney sweeps. Until we can break the Tories' stranglehold on the Parliament, all other reforms will fail."

Eden leaned back in her chair. Now it was her turn to worry at her bottom lip. That such a little thing as knowing his wife edited his magazine might cost him votes! Only think if she, as a member of his household, were exposed. It might discredit his whole movement.

Eden declined the Langleys' invitation to dine with them. They expected several guests, so she urgently begged to have a tray in her room.

"It appears Roger's pretty friend is even shyer than you, my dear." Langley watched his wife in the mirror as he arranged his cravat while dressing for dinner. "Did you learn sufficient of her background to satisfy yourself that she would be acceptable as our governess?"

Gwynneth wrinkled her nose. "I didn't learn much, actually. Her parents are dead. She described them as very obscure country gentry. Her only previous position was at the school she attended. She stayed on there to teach after she reached the age of eighteen."

"Well, that's something, though. We can write the headmistress . . ."

"I'm afraid not. She is dead. According to Eden, a virulent influenza killed her and several of the school's pupils, and it was closed. Isabella Eardley was one of her pupils, so she was hired to teach the girl at home."

"Hmmm. Touchy business. We can hardly go to the Eardleys for a reference. I'm not too pleased with Roger for putting us in this position." Langley gave the cravat a final tug and turned to face Gwynneth, his long face furrowed with worry. "See here, our children come first. If you think it isn't safe—"

"I like her. She is very gentle and loving with the children, and obviously very intelligent. Her French is impeccable, and she says she is quite advanced in music and art, areas where I am most deficient." Gwynneth spoke with conviction.

"And I shall work beside her until I am quite satisfied that she is suitable, before leaving her alone with the children."

"Then she shall stay. I like her too, did so on sight! And I've an idea that Roger is quite honestly attracted to her, in spite of his tendency to treat all subjects with levity."

"Poor Brent. I hope not."

"Why ever not?"

"Because she is as adamantly against marriage as any disciple of William Godwin and Lord Langley ever thought about being."

Langley swore softly. "I wish to God there were some way to call back the written word."

Gwynneth lifted a laughing face to him. "The written word has proved a poor bulwark against love in *some* cases!"

"Minx!" Her husband laughed at her reference to their courtship, which had almost gone awry because of what Langley himself had written against marriage. He sat down beside her and gave her the kiss she craved. "Then there might be hope for Roger."

"If he comes to love her, and can win her love. Marriage is too sacred, and she's far too fine a person for him to marry her on a whim, or to please you."

"You needn't sound so fierce, lady wife. I agree with you entirely, and said as much to Roger today. To my surprise he did not argue the point. We had a frank discussion, and though he ended with some joke about having secret reasons for wishing to marry soon, he left me feeling much satisfied with his intentions."

"You mean toward Eden?"

"Not specifically. Toward the whole subject of marriage, which he now seems to value as he ought. Though he did say that he and Eden were very much alike, both full of secrets and surprises."

Gwynneth said nothing, but privately shuddered. Secrets had very nearly destroyed her chance for happiness with Stuart. And the disastrous results of one of Roger Brentwood's surprises, in the form of that essay in *The Legacy*, were still being played out in all their lives.

Chapter Six

Dinner was going to be interminable. Brentwood looked around the drawing room with consternation. Langley's guests tonight were from the groups he had sternly warned Brent not to alienate, the reforming Whigs and Evangelicals. While Brentwood had an ever-increasing respect for their willingness to act on their principles, he did not expect to find any of them to be lively, conversable companions.

The one exception so far was a young man about his age, Lord Pelham. He and his pretty wife, Davida, were not as starched up as the others. Scion of an old-line Whig family, Pelham was, Langley had informed him, very eager to see reform in the British constitution.

"But in his morals he is as strict as a dissenting minister, and that attractive young wife is a model of propriety, so watch yourself," Langley had warned him just prior to introducing the pair.

Brentwood had exchanged a few pleasantries with the Pelhams. Now he once more stood beside Stuart, a little apart from the other guests, who seemed uneasy in his presence.

"What the deuce? Why is that old libertine here?" Brentwood turned in perplexity to his host as a familiar couple were announced at the drawing-room door. Gwynneth moved forward to graciously greet Sir Alfred Morley and his lady wife, Alana.

"Surprisingly enough, he has found a political patron. He sits in the House of Commons at the pleasure of Lord Derwent. He pretends to be ardently interested in reforming our government."

"An arch-tory sponsoring a reformer. Not likely."

Langley grinned. "No, he and Alana have been sent to inform on us, of course."

Comprehension dawned. "And you allow them rather than risk a cleverer, better disguised government agent."

"Just so." Langley looked extremely pleased at his pupil's perspicacity.

Brentwood had been vexed to learn the delectable Miss Henderson had refused to join them for dinner. It was to further his acquaintance with Eden that he had remained in London, when his remodeling project really required his attendance in Varnham.

"Well, at least Alana is conversable, and will not look at me as if I had two heads," Brentwood observed, before joining his hostess to greet the new arrivals.

As Sir Alfred abandoned his wife to join a group around the sherry decanter, Brentwood turned to Alana Morley with relief. He had fond memories of their brief association at Nicholas Verleigh's country house party five years before. She had been most generous with her favors and expert in her tutelage. What a clodpole he had been at lovemaking, before she took him in hand!

"I do not need to ask how you have been keeping, Alana, for you are quite as lovely as ever," he murmured as she willingly allowed herself to be drawn into a tête-à-tête.

It was not precisely true, he thought even as he spoke the compliment. The golden hue of her hair now looked as if it owed more to her hairdresser's art than to nature, and she had added a bit more avoirdupois.

Still, for a matron in her mid-forties, she was very well-looking indeed, and the welcoming warmth in her still-vivid blue eyes was pleasant after the chilly reception he had received from most of the other women in the room.

"I thank you, my lord. You may take the compliment as returned, for you have grown into a most attractive man." Her eyes caressed his tall, muscular frame.

He winked at her. "Not quite the beanpole I was, at least. By the by, please call me Brentwood, or Brent. I eschew the title among my friends."

"Though I cannot but regret such democratical notions, I am proud to be included in such company." She batted her eyes at him. "Speaking of company, have you not brought back anyone from America?"

"No, why should I?" He was suddenly wary.

"I have a cousin who makes her home now in America, in New York. She wrote me a most astonishing account of your harem there. It sounded fascinating."

Seeing no judgment in Alana's eyes, Brentwood relaxed. "I regret to disappoint you, but it was nothing so interesting as a harem."

"But there was some foundation to the rumors?"

Brentwood nodded reluctantly. "My cousin started a colony that was to be along the lines of Coleridge and Southey's Pantisocracy—have you ever heard of it?"

Alana shook her head.

"Ah, well, not surprising. They abandoned it before it could begin, but the idea always intrigued me." He looked around to be sure they weren't being overheard. "Ours was to include an experimental kind of marriage. A half-dozen couples pledged themselves to one another, to form an economic and social unit—"

"You held the women in common, then?" Her look was avid.

"That is the wrong way to describe it. The intention was just the opposite—to give the women freedom, rather than be acquired like a piece of property. We were all, male and female, to be free to pick our partners, and to change partners at will."

"I should turn from you in horror, you know," Alana said, her bright eyes showing no sign of that emotion.

"Yet the concept is not so very different from the behavior of the typical English aristocrat." He grinned at her.

"Tell me, Brent, why ever did you return to stuffy old England, then?"

His smile faded. "I learned quickly that social experimentation can lead to very unexpected—and unwanted—results."

Deciding that the conversation was heading into dangerous territory, Brentwood challenged Alana, "I am as surprised as I can be to find you and Sir Alfred here in Langley's political circle."

"Oh, pooh!" Alana tried for a girlish pout, though the expression no longer flattered her features as it once had. " 'Tis Arthur's latest start. You know I care nothing for politics. But now you are here, the association won't be so dull." She shifted her body toward him, so that her full bosom brushed against his arm. Her eyes moved over him in an assessing way that Brentwood found unpleasant, as if he were a stallion being considered for stud, not a person.

"I am afraid you will find me the dullest of the lot. Langley's politics are of supreme importance to me, in fact the reason I came back from America, *en fin*."

"I did not say I opposed his politics, my lord . . ."

"Brentwood," he said curtly. "Ah, dinner is being announced. May I take you in?"

His dinner companion on one side was an elderly and rather deaf matron who looked as if she smelled something bad every time he drew her attention to himself. "Brentwood?" She queried. "You mean Dudley, don't you?" When he admitted to the title, she harrumphed, "Can't say as I blame you for not wanting to use that name, after the infamy you brought upon it." She then focused her attention with single-minded zeal on her dinner.

It was a relief, then, to turn to the person on his left, Davida, Lady Pelham. The pretty young brunette was wary of him at first, but he was soon able to win her over by his mischievous comments upon the social and political scene. Mindful of Langley's cautions, he was careful not to stretch the bounds of propriety.

But as he talked to Lady Pelham about everything and nothing, he found himself wondering if he had changed or Alana had. Six years before, an unlicked cub, he had been thrilled when she had turned her attentions from his mentor, Langley, to begin a flirtation with him. At that time she had seemed warm-hearted and kind. Had he missed the hard, calculating look in her eye? And what had seemed delightfully inviting in her attention to him then, seemed unpleasantly bold, almost aggressive now.

When at last dinner was over, Brentwood found more to hold his interest in the political discussion the men entered into over their port, but his mind kept straying in spite of himself. He knew exactly where Eden was staying, and he kept picturing her there in the gold bedroom. Gold would become that golden complexion, that sienna hair, and those warm brown eyes.

When the men rose to join the ladies, Brentwood managed to be left behind, and as soon as he saw the drawing-room door close on the last of Langley's guests, he took the stairs two at a time. He was almost on the third-floor landing when it dawned on him that he could hear faint but unmistakable evidence that someone was in the Langley's music room on the second floor, playing some intricate piece of music with vigor.

He reversed course and opened the music-room door quietly, closing it behind him to keep from attracting other listeners. Bent over the keyboard of Gwynneth's new pianoforte was Eden, her eyes closed, lost in the music. She played with a sure touch and interpretive fire.

Brentwood drew in his breath in admiration, both of her playing, and at the picture she made, her dark brown hair caught up loosely in a ribbon and flowing down her back. It swayed as her body moved. Her involvement in the music was seductive in its intensity.

When she came to the end of the piece she drew in a deep breath and then wiped beneath her eyes. Brentwood realized she was crying, and crossed the room to comfort her, quite forgetting that she was unaware of his presence. She gasped and spun around, her elbow playing a frightened glissando on the keyboard.

Brentwood reached for her, and she jumped up, knocking the piano stool into his knees. As he grabbed his legs in a reflex of pain, she shoved past him and scurried out of the room. He stood rooted to the spot, staring. Her face had been full of terror. Gradually his surprise, and his chagrin at losing the opportunity to be alone with her, was replaced by a cold, intense fury. What man had made Eden Henderson so afraid?

She never should have gone down to the music room alone. She never should have played that particular piece of music. And she certainly shouldn't have reacted so wildly when Brent happened upon her. What must he think of her—that he'd introduced a madwoman into the Langley household?

How could she explain to him, without explaining how that piece always evoked for her the spirit of its composer, her dearly loved mother, and the savage fury of her father on one memorable evening when she had played it against his orders? How could she explain, that is, without explaining so much more that couldn't be said?

Eden lay awake long into the night, remembering things she'd tried so hard to forget. By the time she joined Gwynneth and her children the next morning, her eyes were ringed with dark circles. She fully expected to be greeted with a suggestion that she seek other employment, but apparently Brentwood had said nothing to her employer, for Gwynneth greeted her cheerily, then inquired if she was feeling poorly.

She admitted to a poor night's sleep just as the nursery door opened and Brentwood entered briskly. Her heart began to race, half in fear, half in admiration. He was dressed as befit the most discriminating Bond Street Beau today, and looked exceedingly handsome.

Madelyn abandoned the geography puzzle she was working on to make him a pretty curtsy. Eden studied him anxiously as he lifted the child to his shoulder. Had he come upstairs to warn Gwynneth off?

Setting the giggling child down, Brentwood folded his length onto one of the small nursery chairs beside Eden. He helped Martin clamber onto his knee, as he observed in a low tone, "You must have run into some very severe music critics in your life."

She looked at him blankly.

"To flee from me in such terror last night."

"Had I known I'd had an audience—"

"Yes, you would have doubtless exerted yourself more. But if you had remained for my review, you'd have found it highly favorable."

Her tension dissolved at his bantering tone. "And are you a qualified judge?"

"Speaking as one with not one ounce of musical ability, but a great deal of appreciation, I'd say you were a very talented and accomplished musician. Now, aren't you sorry you ran away?"

"Eden ran away from you?" Gwynneth looked from one to the other with curiosity.

"I crept upstairs to listen to her playing the piano. When she caught sight of me she fled as if I were going to send her back to practicing her scales six hours a day."

"It was a very improper situation—"

"Oh, *that* was why you ran." The gentle tone of mockery told her he knew better.

"Improper? What have you been up to, Brent, you scamp?"

"Only because we were alone, very briefly, in the music room. Not even long enough to steal a kiss, not that I'd do such a thing, of course." He winked.

"Perish the thought!" Gwynneth was grinning openly; Eden kept her eyes carefully lowered, wanting to respond to his flirtation and knowing she mustn't.

"I'm hoping you'll let me show Eden some of the sights of London, Gwynneth. Stu has loaned me his curricle. I have to go back to Varnham this afternoon, so I'm hoping you can spare her for a couple of hours this morning."

"Oh, no, I couldn't!" Eden shook her head.

"Of course. It is an excellent idea." Gwynneth beamed at them both.

"Come, Eden. A governess should know all about the Towneley sculptures, the Elgin Marbles, and the Rosetta stone." At her shaking head, he persisted. "Or perhaps you'd prefer a visit to the Tower of London? No? Madame Tussaud's more your style? Or how about Week's Mechanical Museum?"

Fighting the urge to laugh as he moved rapidly down the intellectual scale, Eden kept on shaking her head. She wanted to go with him, and feared her eyes were giving her away. She primmed her lips and tried to look fierce. "I am newly employed. I can hardly take half a day, on my second day of work, sir."

"Not even if your employer encourages you?" He saw that she meant to refuse him. "Well, by the time I come back you will have earned your half-day. Promise you will spend it with me?"

It seemed to be the price of making him leave, so Eden agreed. He was on his way to the door when it opened to reveal the Langley butler, looking very perturbed.

"Madam, there is a young lady who insists on seeing Miss Henderson."

"Who is it, Parker?"

"A Miss Eardley. She is in a highly emotional state, my lady."

"Isabella!" Eden rose and hastened down the stairs. In the entryway, pacing back and forth, was her former pupil. Rather than the tears which Eden had been expecting, it was clear that the young girl was in a tearing rage. When she saw Eden she burst out, "The injustice of it. The unfairness. They can't do it, can they? They can't keep me from attending the Royal Academy just because I'm female, can they?"

"Bella, never tell me your grandmother took you there?"

"No, of course not. You heard her yesterday. I must give up painting. Well, of course I didn't say no, but I can't, can I? It is my life. But how am I to improve without more schooling? You said yourself you'd taught me all you could."

Eden led Isabella into the front drawing room. Brentwood followed them in and took a seat nearby as she drew the girl down to sit by her on a sofa. "Ah, Bella, I never told you that you could be admitted to the Royal Academy."

"No, but you told me two of the founding members were women—Angelica Kauffmann and Mary Moser. So if women were founding members, why can't a woman study there?"

Gwynneth let herself quietly into the drawing room and crossed to sit by Brentwood as they talked.

"It is very unfair, Miss Eardley." Brentwood leaned forward earnestly. "Your best hope will be to convince one of the instructors who teaches there to take you as a private pupil. Some of the most famous artists have been known to take on gifted pupils."

"But I want to attend the classes." Isabella's face took on a determined look. "Do you have any influence with the trustees? Or does Lord Langley?"

"No, I fear not, though if either of us had, you may be sure we'd support you."

"Did you go to the Academy on your own, Isabella? I saw no sign of a maid or footman with you." Eden's mind was still occupied with the terrifying notion of Isabella wandering London's streets unaccompanied.

"Certainly. You didn't think Grandmother would take me? Nor any of her servants. She is a poky old thing, Eden. Don't do this, don't do that! I shan't like living with her above half."

Eden looked at Brentwood in some alarm. "She's been going about London all alone!"

He shook his head and stood up. "We'd best restore her to the grandmother's hearth, don't you think?"

"I don't want to go there. I want to stay here with you, Eden."

Eden glanced quickly at Gwynneth's wide-eyed response to that suggestion. "That is impossible, Bella. I am here as a servant. I can't take in another person. Not that your father would permit it."

"Oh, Father, that is another thing. When he arrived last night he was vitriolic. He virtually threatened to disinherit me. He was all for insisting you marry me, Mr. Brentwood, but my grandmother said you wouldn't do at all."

"Your grandmother has my eternal gratitude."

"Well, mine too! As if I'd want to marry a man half again my age, and twice my height! Besides, I don't want to marry at all, but no one listens to me. Eden, couldn't we live together somewhere? You could teach music, and I could teach art, and—"

Eden shook her head until her braids threatened to fall from beneath her lace cap. "Absolutely not, and if you run off from your grandmother like this again, I seriously suspect she'll see you married to some very elderly and repressive husband just to get you off her hands."

"Mayhap even one older than me, Miss Eardley." Brentwood lowered his eyebrows and pinned the girl with a narrow-eyed stare.

Isabella looked from one to the other, hoping for some sign of weakness or pity. Seeing none, she sighed and rose. "Well, if that is how it must be, I shall look for an old, doting husband who will let me do just as I please. Perhaps I should marry you, after all, Mr. Brentwood." Mischief suddenly brought out enchanting dimples beside Isabella's full lips.

"No, I thank you for the compliment, but I must decline. I have decided I can never marry without affection."

She tilted her pert face up to his. "I can be very affectionate."

"Oof! She is beginning to be dangerous, and only sixteen! Let's go, minx. Eden, you'll accompany us, of course."

"I, uh . . ." Eden looked to Gwynneth for guidance.

"I expect you had better, Eden. Else Isabella's grandmother is like to draw some drastic conclusions when Brentwood returns her from running away a second time."

* * *

The dowager Duchess of Carminster was not pleased to have her missing granddaughter show up once again in the company of Brentwood and Miss Henderson. First she sent Isabella up the stairs with the threat ringing in her ears, "If you leave this house unaccompanied again, I shall send you to a convent in France where they know just how to keep wild young English misses under control until they are old enough to marry."

Once Isabella was out of the way, she furiously turned on the pair in the hall. "If you are angling to marry that gel, you can think again. Dudley. I've heard about all your wives, and you shan't add my Isabella to the list."

"All my wives?"

"Rumor has it that in America you belonged to some sort of heathen sect, and had four wives."

Eden couldn't tell if it was fury or embarrassment that made Brentwood turn a dull shade of red. For a rare moment he seemed speechless. At last he replied, "I am vastly disappointed, ma'am. If rumor was going to supply me with a multiplicity of wives, it could have at least been more generous than a mere four. Surely twelve would be more proportional to my merits."

"Get out. I never want you to cross my door again. And you, Miss Henderson. I make some small allowances for your background, but beware! Any more leading Isabella astray and I will throw you to the wolves. Or to one wolf in particular."

Eden flinched and the color drained from her face. "I beg your pardon, Your Grace, but—"

Brentwood did not give her a chance to finish. "Neither of us had anything to do with Isabella's actions this morning. We only brought her back to you safe and sound. When you have had time to calm down, I am sure you will recognize that fact. Let us go, Miss Henderson." He placed her hand on his arm and marched her out of the room. Eden was glad for Brentwood's supporting arm, for the duchess's threat had left her knees feeling rather watery.

"The old baggage has a funny way of showing her gratitude for bringing her lost lamb home safe and sound." Brentwood tooled his borrowed curricle through the traffic as he muttered.

"She can certainly ring an impressive peal over one's head." Eden struggled to control the trembling that had overtaken her body.

A large masculine hand came down to cradle hers where she was wringing them in her lap. The gesture was touchingly comforting, and Eden gave her escort a tremulous smile in response.

"I think ices at Gunthers might help our battle scars heal," his deep voice urged. "What do you say?"

Eden shook her head. "Thank you, no, What I do say is, you've been very kind and patient in allowing yourself to get embroiled in other people's affairs, and with scant appreciation for it! I haven't had a chance yet to thank you for the position with the Langleys."

"Do you think you would be willing to show your gratitude in some tangible way?"

Eden studied his suddenly mischievous expression warily. "What way did you have in mind?"

"Spend the rest of the morning with me. First, ices. Then, the British Museum. Or Week's Mechanical Museum. Your choice."

She let her eyes meet his, and the hopeful, eager expression there was her undoing. "Very well, Week's. I have always wanted to see the mechanical tarantula."

"Week's it is. But you have managed to surprise me, Miss Henderson."

"I often surprise myself, Mr. Brentwood."

"Brent." He took her left hand in his and, turning it to expose her wrist, lifted it very briefly to his lips, rendering her by far the most surprised of the two as a jolt of pleasurable sensation shot through her at the touch of his warm lips on her skin.

Chapter Seven

Eden knew a few uneasy moments at Gunthers, where those of the *haute ton* who were still in town were likely to gather on such a hot day. But Brentwood sent a young boy for their treats, and they ate delicious strawberry ices in the carriage. Though there were other carriages around, with other passengers similarly occupied, she attracted no notice.

She had chosen Week's Mechanical Museum as their destination because it was the place least likely to be attended by someone of the *ton*, someone who might be as observant as the duchess. True to her wishes, it was not very crowded, and those who were in attendance were the middling sort, or governesses with their noisy charges.

She and Brentwood spent some enchanting moments there. The musical clocks and mechanical animals were fascinating, and even though she was prepared for the tarantula, it was sufficiently lifelike to cause her to jump back in alarm, giving a most agreeable excuse for Brentwood's arms to steady her.

She felt a rush of pleasure at this impromptu embrace. To cover her embarrassment, she burst into hurried conversation. "Martin would love this place. And Madelyn, too. I must bring them here soon."

Brentwood chuckled. "You'd best have young master Martin on a leash. He'll want to get his hands on those delightful creatures."

Eden nodded. "Perhaps he *is* just a little young. But how his eyes would light up." Her own eyes were glowing.

"You like the children, then?"

"Oh, yes, they are adorable. I've never had the opportunity to be around very young children before. I had no idea they could be so engaging."

Brentwood looked inordinately pleased. "Do you think you could come to love children even if they weren't your own?" His voice dropped in disgust. "Some people can't, you know."

"Oh, yes, I am halfway there, already. I shall be quite heartbroken if the Langleys decide I don't suit."

"Perhaps it would be wisest not to become too attached to the Langley children. I was thinking of—" He stopped suddenly, like someone who has thought better of what he had been about to say.

"Ah, I mean . . . perhaps soon you'll have an opportunity for children of your own."

She looked up at him in alarm. "Oh, no, that will never— can never be. Do look at the time. We must be getting back. It's past nuncheon, Gwynneth will be needing me to start on her correspondence." Eden trotted hurriedly through the museum, Brentwood following behind.

Just as she reached the door, his hand on her elbow stopped her. He looked around. They had no audience at the moment. He dipped his head and pressed a quick, firm kiss on her lips. "People change their minds about matrimony, Miss Eden Henderson. I have, and I plan to see that you do."

Before she could reply, he hustled her through the door and onto busy Haymarket Street. Her mind in a turmoil, she didn't speak to him on the way back to the Langleys. When they arrived he helped her down, then regretfully bade her good-bye.

"I must leave for Varnham, if I am to arrive before dark. I can't leave my remodeling at this point, or I would stay to further our acquaintance. In a week or so I shall return. Do try not to lure Isabella on any more outings in the meantime, Eden."

"You mean to deny me all pleasure, I see."

He flicked her nose, the laughter in his eyes belying his solemn tone. "Only because if you continue corrupting the child the duchess may reveal the terrible secret she keeps threatening you with."

"What . . . what do you mean?" She blanched.

"I wish I knew. Her dark insinuations seem to have meaning only to you." His expression sobered. "You wouldn't care to tell me, I suppose?"

"Don't be silly." Eden attempted a lighthearted laugh. "She only refers to the fact that I've failed, in her eyes, as a governess." In spite of her attempt at sang froid, Eden was trembling.

He cupped her face briefly in his large hand. "As you say. But someday, my dear, we will trust one another with all our secrets."

Eden went straight to her room, though she was very hungry. She had to get command of herself. She had feared exposure, always. But she had never feared that she might fall in love. Yet she knew she was in a fair way of doing so with the tall, green-eyed earl. And it was impossible, just impossible.

As if I hadn't a sufficiently dangerous enemy, I have become my own worst enemy, Eden thought, remembering the flush of warmth when Brentwood had kissed her wrist, the way she had yearned to turn into his embrace when he had steadied her after the tarantula jumped. And that kiss. Oh, how she had wanted it to last. She lifted trembling fingers to her lips as she looked at her flushed face in the mirror. What was she to do?

Alana Morley tugged sharply on her husband's arm. "Look, there, on Langley's steps. Who is that?"

Sir Alfred sat up in the carriage, lifted his quizzing glass, and stared. "Why, that's young Dudley, of course. You remember him, I'm sure."

"Of course I remember him, I'm speaking of her. Who is he with?"

Morley turned his head as their carriage carried them on down the street. "Can't say as I recognize her. Damn fine piece, though."

Alana dropped back against the cushions in irritation. "I wonder why she looks familiar to me?" A surge of possessive fury swept through her. When she had learned of Dudley's return from his wandering, she had not been terribly interested. Their brief affair had been, for her, a diversion and a sop to her ego because of Langley's rejection. The earl had been too young, too thin, too callow a youth to make much of an impression on her.

But the Dudley who had returned, insisting on being called Brentwood, was a very different person. He was a man now, filled out physically, and with the strong sense of self-confidence that she found so irresistible in a lover. His peculiar sense of humor still perplexed her, but all in all his presence had bidden well to compensate her for the dull task of spending time with that former shopkeeper, Gwynneth Langley, pretending to a friendly interest in their husbands' politics, when in truth she hated the woman and still yearned for revenge upon her husband for spurning her.

Before dinner last night, Brentwood had seemed quite interested in her. She had expected him to come to her side directly when the men joined the ladies, as he had been wont to do in Guilford five years ago. But he had never joined them. He had, as her husband teased her later, "done a flit," and her hope of reviving their affair had been dimmed.

Now he was standing in intense tête-à-tête on Langley's doorstep with a very handsome brunette. Alana clenched her fists in determination. She hadn't taken all that trouble to teach him how to please a woman, only to have some other woman reap the benefits now he'd become a man.

"Let's call on the Langleys, Alfred."

"Oh, no, my pet. Prosy bores, the lot of them. Bad enough I have to spend so many evenings with them."

"Then get out and let me call on Lady Langley."

"Lady Langley, ha! You've your eye on Brentwood. Ah, well, just remember Aunt Agatha, dearest. Be very discreet." So saying, her loving husband signaled their driver to stop, and exited the carriage. He tipped his hat to his wife, and she blew him a kiss before instructing John Coachman to circle around and pull up in front of the Langleys' again.

How very fortunate she had been in her choice of a husband. Though his pockets were often to let, he was the most complacent of husbands. If only his dour, straightlaced, but very rich aunt had not recently threatened to disinherit him if he and his wife failed to live up to her ideas of morality. It required a much greater degree of discretion and self-control than either had been accustomed to exercising. But as they had been living on their expectations from her, they were united in their determination to keep her blissfully unaware of their extramarital affairs.

Lady Langley was from home. Alana chewed the inside of her lip for a moment upon hearing this from the stately Langley butler. "Ah, Parker, perhaps you could assist me, then. Just a few moments ago I saw Mr. Brentwood outside escorting a young lady here. At least, I think they were coming here. I recognize her, but can't recall her name. So embarrassing."

Parker looked at her stonily.

"She is tall, and has dark brown hair, a very attractive young woman. She was dressed very modestly."

"You possibly are referring to Miss Henderson, the new governess."

Alana tilted her head. "Henderson? No, I don't recognize the name, either. Perhaps she merely resembles someone I know. Ah, well, no matter. You'll tell Lady Langley I called?"

"Of course, madam."

A governess. Of course. He was attempting to set up a flirt. She must act quickly. "Ah, Parker, Mr. Brentwood isn't staying here, I take it?"

"No, madam."

Impatiently Alana reached into her reticule. Perhaps a guinea would loosen the man's tongue. "Where is he staying, then, Parker?"

Palming the coin without losing a shred of dignity, Parker informed her that Mr. Brentwood had returned to his country estate near Varnham. He allowed himself a slight smile as the inquisitive Lady Morley took herself off. *That* reply had clearly not been to her ladyship's liking.

* * *

Eden's days with the Langleys were busy but pleasant. Mornings she spent with the children. After three days Gwynneth apparently felt comfortable enough with her to leave her alone with them for an hour or so each morning, but for the most part the two women worked together, either teaching the children or discussing plans for their education.

In the afternoons she turned her hand to a variety of tasks from answering correspondence to making fair copies of poems and essays that had been submitted to *The Legacy*. They were about to go to press with a quarterly edition, and there was much to do. Once assured that her spelling was excellent, and that she could punctuate intelligently, Gwynneth entrusted her with some proofreading chores, and observed that she would doubtless be able to do some editing for them when Gwynneth was confined.

The warm praise she received from both Langleys was very rewarding to Eden, whose efforts for Isabella had been appreciated by her pupil, but often denigrated by Mr. Eardley, who had no understanding of how difficult it was to teach the ladylike accomplishments to so lively a charge as Isabella.

Eden and Gwynneth got along so well that they were more like friends than employer and employee. In fact, she often had to remind herself and Gwynneth of their relative positions, to prevent herself from being included in the Langleys' activities.

Eden kept to her determination not to be drawn into the Langleys' social life, though they both urged her to join them for dinner when they were at home, and invited her to go to the theater and various musical events with them. Instead, she played the piano or sewed during her free time in the evenings, after the children were tucked in and surrendered to the care of the nursery maid.

She tried not to count the days until Brent would come again. She almost convinced herself he wouldn't come, that it had all been an idle flirtation. Doubtless he was immersed in his architectural drawings and his carpentry, all thought of her banished. Doubtless one of the local beauties had attracted his interest by now. This thought was in almost equal parts a relief and a sorrow.

On the week's anniversary of her employment with the Langleys, the mail arrived while both Stuart and Gwynneth were out. Parker brought it to her. "I expect you'll end up dealing with most of this anyway," he observed, giving her a surprisingly friendly smile. The servants had decided to like Miss Henderson, who didn't give herself airs and made few demands—indeed, so politely asked for what she needed from them that it was plain to all that she was a real lady fallen on hard times.

Eden took the sizable stack of mail and began separating it into his, hers, and *The Legacy's*. At the bottom of the stack was a large, oilskin-wrapped packet addressed to Mr. Roger Brentwood, in care of Lord Langley. Eden weighed it in her hand—it would be a month's wages for her to pay the postage for so voluminous a correspondent. It had come all the way from New York, in America!

Ignoring the little dance her heart did at the sight of Brent's name, she tried to concentrate on her previous task, copying out a rather tedious poem for the typesetter. But the realization that the packet for Brentwood was from America recalled the dowager duchess's ugly accusation that he had had four wives there. From the size of that letter, all four of them must have written him.

Eden had read Tory scandalmongering accounts of his activities that hinted at libertinism under the guise of new forms of marriage. The thought was disgusting to Eden, but she wondered if there was any foundation to the talk. Or was it as ridiculous as most of the scurrilous nonsense published in the popular press?

When Lord Langley saw the packet on his return, his response was not calculated to negate the duchess's insinuations. "Hmmmm." He hoisted the packet, studying the writing carefully. "A feminine hand, wouldn't you say, Eden?" Brentwood had warned his friend not to discuss this expected correspondence with Eden, but Langley couldn't resist the temptation to pique her interest and possibly make her a little jealous.

"Yes, it appears so to me."

"He's been expecting this communication. Ah, me. Roger, I hope you don't land us all in the soup over this!" With that enigmatic comment Langley retreated to his desk to write a hasty note. As he summoned a footman, he winked at Eden.

"Roger will be glad of the excuse to come to London, I don't doubt."

Eden was perplexed. Why did Lord Langley not simply send the packet on to Brentwood in Hertfordshire?

"I've invited him to stay here. I hope you don't mind." Langley gave her a rather sheepish look.

"No, I—"

"He usually does stay with us when he comes to town, and as you are, after all, an employee . . ."

"Yes, sir, of course . . ."

"And now moved to the nursery floor, next the children . . ."

Eden laughed at his worried expression. After a moment he joined in. "Do I protest too much?"

She sobered. "Gwynneth promised me she wouldn't try any matchmaking. I hope you will do me the same kindness."

Langley dropped down into a chair near her desk. "A pity you couldn't take to the boy. He seems quite smitten, and . . ."

Eden frowned. "I like him very well, but that is all there can be to it, my lord. Please accept that, and help him to do the same."

"And you? Do you need help accepting that, too, Eden?" The look the dark-haired lord sent her was far too penetrating for Eden's comfort.

Barely above a whisper she nodded her agreement. "And me."

It was Langley's turn to frown. Roger was right. There was some mystery about the girl, some secret she kept from them all. He hoped it wasn't one that could hurt the children, or cause a scandal. Still, he could not believe that, whatever her secret was, it arose from any evil in this young woman, for like Gwynneth he felt strongly that she was a decent, upright person.

Three days later a reply came from Brentwood. Eden was helping Gwynneth with her correspondence when it came. Langley was seated at his desk, making voluminous notes for a speech to the House of Lords when the post came. He took out his own mail, and opened one letter as he carried the rest over to Gwynneth and Eden.

"Roger is going to be here early Saturday, and stay over a few days," Langley informed his wife after a quick perusal of the letter.

"Good," was all her reply, leaving Eden to wonder what was going on. One of those secrets Brentwood had hinted at?

She found not looking forward to Brent's return was much harder when a definite date was fixed for it. She had a sudden impulse to complete the stylish new ecru walking dress she was making. Surely it was merely that her clothes had become very dowdy, far too dowdy for a creditable appearance in a household where the lowliest servant was clean, well-fed, and respectably clothed. It couldn't have anything to do with Brentwood's imminent return, could it?

Alarmed at her lack of control over her own emotions, Eden took herself firmly in hand, and put the new dress in the bottom of her clothes press, out of temptation's way.

Chapter Eight

The morning papers were strewn about the breakfast table. Gwynneth as usual was breaking her fast with her children above stairs. Eden was immersed in the *Morning Chronicle*, and Langley was muttering over the latest report of unrest in Nottingham, when Brentwood strode into the breakfast room.

Radiating vigor, he dropped his length into the chair next to Eden and leaned forward eagerly, almost before she could fully take in his appearance. "Pining away for me, I see," he teased, his eyes scanning her well-filled and partially demolished plate of food. "No need to starve yourself in your grief. I told you I'd be back."

He took a roll from her plate, neatly dodging as she swatted at his hand. "Ready to go to the solicitor, Stu?"

"Almost." Langley folded his paper haphazardly. "Are you quite sure about this, Roger? You are taking on quite a responsibility, you know."

"Quite." Brentwood's jawline firmed, the teasing light left his green eyes. "I mean to have them."

Eden studied him curiously.

"You don't dare ask, do you, except with those expressive brown eyes. For if I told you my secrets, you might feel obliged to answer some questions of mine in return." Brentwood snagged a generous bite of ham from her plate and stood. "We've much to do. Shall we be off?"

Langley rose and tossed down his napkin. "If you're determined, let's be about it. Eden, tell Gwynneth we don't expect to be home much before dinner. Oh, and you may dine with us tonight. We are going to be strictly *en famille.*"

Brent had already reached the door. He stopped in midstride and turned, a look of disdain on his face. "*May* dine with us tonight?"

"Perhaps I should say, 'must.' Miss Henderson is the one keeping up the social barriers, lad, not us, so come down out of the boughs." Langley clapped him on the shoulder and gave Eden a wink. "Bring the children down for a visit before dinner. 'Twill be a salutary lesson for this young buck."

Leaving her to ponder that remark, and wonder at Brentwood's mysterious mission, the two men disappeared into the day.

Eden dressed for dinner reluctantly, yet with a sense of excitement, almost of joy, that she tried hard to repress. She had been unable to think of any reason why she should not join the other three for the evening meal, particularly when Gwynneth had requested that she play for them afterward.

They dined in the room where they usually breakfasted, and in this intimate setting conversation was general, free-ranging, and fascinating. Naturally, politics formed a considerable part of their topics, but music, poetry, and art all received their share of attention. She found that not only Langley, but Brentwood, eagerly sought Gwynneth's opinions and obviously respected her answers.

She found herself drawn into their discussion as naturally as if she were entirely their equal. She could hold her own in politics and music, but could only listen with wonder as the men's interests ranged into the new inventions of the day and how they would change the world.

She was astonished to learn that Lord Langley believed steam, which already was gaining ground as a source of power for ships, would one day replace horses as the nation's chief motive power. "We'll ride about in carriages powered by it, mark my words." Brentwood disagreed, calling it a "nightmare vision."

"Speaking of nightmare visions, what of Mary Shelley's vision of science run amuck in *Frankenstein*?" Gwynneth asked.

"Precisely what I mean. We will create monsters with some of these new technologies." Brentwood shook his head gloomily.

"Whether we are hurt or helped by our inventions lies in our own hands." Langley stroked his chin thoughtfully. "I think on balance we will benefit. Consider the indoor plumbing which you were ready enough to adopt—"

"Hardly new. The Romans had as good or better before Christ was born."

"And the gaslights," Eden interjected. "And the improved roadways."

Brentwood rejoined, "And the spinning jenny that puts workers out of work!"

Evidently feeling the conversation was getting rather heated, Gwynneth changed the subject. "Speaking of Mary Shelley, have you dropped in on Godwin since you've returned, Brent?"

"Oh, yes. The old man is actually pleased with his daughter's marriage." The disgust in his voice startled Eden. Her puzzled look drew an explanation.

"You surely know of the scandal of Shelley eloping with Godwin's daughter and stepdaughter."

"Yes, of course. Everyone has heard."

"But I don't see why Godwin shouldn't be pleased at the marriage, for he was horrified at her living with Shelley as his mistress." Gwynneth looked from one to the other in perplexity.

Brentwood nodded, but his expression had suddenly become mischievous. "Shelley eloped with both Mary and Claire, but he couldn't marry them both, you see. I was in much the same situation recently vis à vis two young ladies, so I know just what a quandary it is."

Eden's face flushed. "Nonsense, you never were."

"Poor Godwin. His teaching did a great deal of harm to his children." Gwynneth looked solemn.

"They've done harm to a great many people's children," Langley growled. "Here are Miss Henderson and her young charge Isabella as the most recent victims of Godwinian radicalism."

Brentwood looked troubled. "From the way everyone still reacts, my essay in *The Legacy* must have caused quite a stir."

"It was incredible. Gwynneth and I returned from our honeymoon to find government censors, irate husbands and fathers, and infuriated parents all demanding your blood."

At Brentwood's muttered imprecation, Langley grinned. "I do not exaggerate, either. Remember Colville, Gwynneth?"

"Remember? I'll never forget. I thought I'd be a widow by nightfall."

Eden gasped as she looked from one to the other.

"You speak of that old roué, Lord Colville?" Brentwood leaned forward eagerly. "I've heard of him. Now, there's an unlikely champion of marriage."

"Since he was newly wed, and his sixteen-year-old bride had left a copy of your editorial on his pillow on their wedding night in her stead before disappearing . . ."

"No!" Brentwood chuckled. "I can't say I'm sorry to hear it. That diseased old sinner didn't deserve a young wife."

"When he couldn't find you to get satisfaction, he sued me. He's good at that. Always going to law with someone about something."

"Did he win?"

"We settled out of court at my solicitor's suggestion."

Brentwood sighed. "Another debt I owe you."

Langley made a dismissive motion with his hand. "The money doesn't matter, but I always worried about his young wife."

"Why, was he cruel to her?"

"Doubtless he would have been if he could have laid his hands on her."

"You mean he never found her?"

"No. Disappeared from the face of the earth. Her relatives believe her dead."

Brentwood dropped his head into his hands. "Poor child. I never dreamt the harm my ill-considered words might do."

Eden spoke then, her voice low but taut with controlled emotion. "Better off dead than married to such as he."

The three looked at her in surprise. "You knew him?" Gwynneth asked.

"I . . . knew his like. You did the young woman a favor, inspiring her to reject her marriage, so do not feel any need to retract your words."

Langley frowned thoughtfully at her over his wineglass. "In the final analysis it is deeds, not words that count. Look at Godwin. He dismissed marriage as a cruel system of human property, yet married Mary Wollstonecraft. He wrote contemptuously of the family, yet has been a loving husband and father."

Gwynneth reached across the table and touched her husband's clenched hand. "And look at you."

Their eyes met and Eden felt tears come to her own at the tenderness, the love that passed between them.

"You see, Eden, all our past ravings should be ignored. You should throw that old essay in the fire and read from the book of life now." Brentwood's green eyes held her. She felt her resistance weakening, but it was not a weakness she could allow herself.

"The book of life, unfortunately, has much more written in it of the sorrows of marriage and family than the joys, Mr. Brentwood." Eden strove to lighten the mood. "I think you both should realize that your writings have brought, if not justice as yet, then at least hope, to some women."

"Shall we leave the men to their port, Eden?" Gwynneth stood hastily, for she sensed the tears threatening to break through Eden's composure. "Do not be overlong, though. Eden has promised to play for us tonight, and if the sounds I have heard through the music-room door are any indication, we have a rare treat in store for us."

When Langley and Brentwood joined them not long after, there were no more moments of controversy. Eden played sev-

eral difficult pieces to their acclaim, then Gwynneth accompanied them while the other three sang popular songs. Langley
had a deep, thrilling baritone. Brentwood, too, was a baritone,
though he was off-key more than on. He made up for this lack
by an enthusiasm that Eden found endearing.

The next morning she was surprised to find Brentwood,
handsomely attired in a blue morning coat and buff trousers,
preparing to escort herself and Gwynneth to church. "What,
are you not a deist like Lord Langley?" she asked curiously.
Gwynneth's husband felt that church attendance on his part
would be hypocritical.

"No, I am not. The Church of England has its flaws, like
any human institution, but I find that my spiritual life needs
the sustenance which only the church adequately provides
me."

There was neither banter nor flirtation in his manner. As
they worshipped together, it increased her regard for him to
discover that there was no hint of superficiality in his participation. Apparently he was sincere in his religious convictions.

The next day they were greeted by a fine June morning after
several cool, rainy days. Gwynneth proposed a drive to Rich-
mond. "I'll have Cook pack a picnic. The children will adore
it."

Brent was enthusiastic, and thus Eden found herself spending more hours in the company of the young man who seemed
determined to woo her in spite of all her resistance, the only
man she'd ever met who could make her wish she could encourage him.

He was obviously fond of the children. It was an education
to Eden to see the two men romping and playing with them.
Her eyes followed them from where she and Gwynneth lay
stretched out, replete, under the elm tree where they had pic-
nicked.

"An endearing sight, isn't it?"

Eden nodded. "I have never seen men take pleasure in the
company of children before."

Gwynneth said nothing. By now she was fairly sure that

Eden's father had been one of those domestic tyrants of whom Brentwood had written. Her mother's marriage doubtless had been so miserable that Eden feared trusting herself to a man. It would do no good to try to argue her out of it, and so she had told Brent last night, after Eden had climbed the stairs to the nursery floor. Let her observe the Langley household, she had advised him. She would soon realize that not all men were monsters, nor all marriages miserable.

"Don't crowd her," she had counseled. "If you want her for your wife, give her time to know you."

As she stretched out under the tree, pleasantly tired, Gwynneth felt satisfied that her advice had not gone unheeded. Brent had made none of his pointed remarks this morning, had not flirted with Eden at all, but had merely been friendly. Eden's relaxed acceptance of his presence seemed to indicate that Gwynneth's suggestion had been a good one.

Brentwood had no doubt that the advice Gwynneth had given him last night was well meant, and probably wise. But as he watched the two women out of the corner of his eye while acting as Madelyn's "horsie," he wondered if he would go quite mad trying to court Eden at this pace. She looked so desirable, stretched out there at her leisure in the shade of the gigantic elm.

He yearned to stretch out beside her. He could not remember desiring a woman so much before. Still, he knew Gwynneth was right. Eden would not respond to hasty wooing.

When the children became fussy, he suggested they join their mother, now fast asleep, for a nap. Their father seconded the suggestion, and even agreed to nap with them.

Eden sat up to make room for the children and found herself being pulled to her feet by Brent. "What—?"

"It would not be at all the thing for you to nap on the same tablecloth as Lord Langley, you know, Miss Henderson. Who knows what vile rumor would begin circulating if some busybody spotted you." He led her away as Langley, smiling, settled the children between himself and his wife, curving his body protectively around them.

"We'll stroll a bit—unless of course you'd like to get a blanket from the carriage and curl up with *me* for a nap?" He looked at her hopefully out of widened green eyes.

"Don't bother trying for the innocent look, Mr. Brentwood. It doesn't work for you. Something about the eyebrows." She tossed her head and strode away from him, setting a brisk pace. "Actually, a walk is just what I need."

He's going to try to kiss me. Eden knew she should refuse this walk, with the opportunity for intimacy that it afforded, but she couldn't. She was torn between panic and desire.

Brentwood surprised her, however, by launching into a chronology of his travels which was amusing and informative. He told her of his lightning-fast tour of Europe, then his decision to go to India.

"I was in such bad odor at home, and my pockets were to let. As marrying for advantage was anathema to me, I determined to go to India and seek my fortune."

"I believe you mentioned that to Isabella. You didn't care for what was going on there, as I recall."

He looked pleased that she remembered his words. "No, I have no quarrel with earning profit through trade, not even the usual aristocratic prejudice against certain kinds of mercantile ventures, but driving out native rulers in order to earn profit at the end of a gun was not to my taste."

"But you were not in the military."

"No, but it is upon our military conquests, still going forward, by the by, that our trading opportunities rest." He paused a moment before adding in a low growl, "I doubt I would have found India compatible at any rate."

He was silent for so long that she stole a glance at him and found a haunted expression upon his face. He met her eyes ruefully. "I shouldn't speak of what will distress you."

"Please, I am very interested."

"One of my chief objections to English society was its treatment of women, but what I saw in India . . ." He passed his hand over his brow as if to rub away the sight. "Girl children are very unwelcome there, at least until a man is comparatively wealthy and in possession of several sons. A woman who gives her husband only daughters is in disgrace. Firstborn girls are often killed."

"Killed!"

"Yes. Usually starved. Compassionate parents soothe their hunger pangs with opium until they die."

Eden bowed her head. "Poor things."

"And then . . . I suppose you've heard of suttee."

"No, I haven't. What is that?"

"When a woman is widowed, she is expected to throw herself onto her husband's funeral pyre in grief. If she declines the honor, there are usually loving relatives to see that she does so."

"Why would they want—"

"Money, m'dear. Desire for any inheritance she might have, or retention of her dowry."

" 'Tis horrible! Surely we do not allow it?"

"In the areas falling under English control, we are beginning to put a stop to these practices"—his scowl puzzled her, until he continued—"but what the ultimate effect on India will be, I do not know. If Malthus's calculations are correct—"

"Ah, but we can not allow such means to control population, surely."

"In India the climate and culture lead to early and fecund marriages. And they show even less interest than most Englishmen in other means of limiting their families. I fear their future must be vast increases of population and poverty."

Fascinated yet deeply embarrassed by the direction their conversation had taken, Eden turned the topic to his observations of native practices in the former colonies.

"What is not generally appreciated here is that the American natives are not of one culture, but many, and it is difficult to generalize about them. Some are nomadic and warlike; some are agricultural and peaceful. I found our relationships with them to be generally congenial, however. I speak of my cousin Dominique's trading company in Canada, in which I have invested. There is a vast country full of every sort of fur-bearing animal, and those who trade with the Indians can make a very fine profit."

"Without the odium of conquest." Eden smiled approvingly.

"Well, there has been conquest, too. And cheating. But Dominique and I are determined to make our money through honest and fair trading, or not at all."

"In that you are to be commended."

He smiled down at her. "I had hoped to earn your approbation! I did not return from my exile a nabob, but at least I can offer a wife and family a comfortable existence."

This was a subject Eden wished to avoid. She looked around her and found that while he had held her attention so completely, they had covered a considerable distance and now stood on a hill with a fine prospect. Past the Star and Garter Inn they could see the Thames winding its way through a tree-filled valley. A small craft, a pleasure boat, was the only traffic on the river. "What a fine view," she observed.

"Magnificent." He smiled down at her in shared pleasure.

"We must be going back now," she murmured.

He stopped. "Why did I guess you'd say that? Well, then?" He turned and offered her his other arm.

She took it, disappointment warring with relief. He wasn't going to try to kiss her after all. Apparently he had given up on wooing her. It was for the best, so why did her heart feel so heavy as they retraced their steps toward the blanket on which the Langley family was arrayed?

Chapter Nine

For three days and nights Roger Brentwood conducted himself like a disinterested friend. When Eden refused to accompany the Langleys and himself to the opera, he acquiesced gracefully. When she scurried from the library to avoid being alone with him, he offered to leave himself rather than upset her routine. When she came downstairs on the third night to dine, thinking the Langleys would be there, and found it was to be only the two of them, he charmed her into staying.

After a delightful dinner spent for the most part discussing history and Shakespeare's liberties with it in his plays, she agreed to play the piano for him. The Langleys returned from their dinner party to find the two of them bent over a chess set.

So comfortable had she become with Brentwood that Eden didn't even demur when, on the fourth day of his visit, he suggested taking the children and herself on an outing. The Tower of London was selected, with the zoo expected to be the highlight of the trip.

As the two adults and their excited charges were being seated in Langley's brougham, Alana Morley saw them and ordered her driver to stop their carriage. "When they move, I want you to follow them, and set me down where they get out."

Alana had seen Brentwood briefly at the opera two nights before. She had been disappointed to find him merely cordial, without showing the least partiality toward her.

"What are you about, my pet?" Sir Alfred cocked a wary eye at his mate.

"I want to get a close look at her."

" 'Twill only make you feel worse, m'dear. That chit is not a day over twenty, mark my word."

"That is not to the purpose. She looks familiar to me; I want to see her up close."

"Well, I confess to some curiosity myself." Her complaisant husband settled back to enjoy the drive through London's busy streets.

"Oh, tiresome bother. They are going to the tower." Alana stepped from the carriage and opened her parasol against the blazing July sun. "Do let us catch up with them right away and then we can leave."

Sir Alfred huffed to keep up with his wife's rapid though short strides, which changed abruptly to leisurely ones when close enough to her quarry to call out to them.

"Oh, do look, Alfred dearest. It is the darling Langley children." The older pair closed the distance between themselves and Brentwood's party.

"Lady Morley, Sir Alfred!" Brentwood could hardly hide his surprise; a more unlikely pair to find about to enter the Tower of London could hardly be imagined. He politely introduced Eden to them.

"We're taking the children to view the tower. Not exactly in *your* line, I would have thought," he couldn't resist observing to Alana, who was studying Eden with narrowed eyes.

"No, of course not, Brent. We saw you get out and decided to hail you." Alana hoped her honesty was disarming. "I thought I recognized Miss Henderson, but I see I was mistaken. You remind me so much of someone, but I can't quite recall who."

Eden felt subtly menaced by this woman. She did not wish to encourage any line of questioning that might prompt the lady's memory, so she rushed into speech. "I have that sort of face, I believe. I am forever being told that I look like someone. Will you join us for a walk through the zoo? Madelyn and Martin are eager to see the lions."

Sir Alfred, who had gallantly taken Eden's hand and kissed

it, laughed. "Gad, no. Smelly things, lions. Lovely creature like yourself—shouldn't like it above half, I'd say. Why not let Alana and Dudley take the children? I'll show you the more interesting sights in the tower. Do you like jewels, m'dear?"

Eden snatched her hand back and scooped up Martin, who had been clinging uneasily to her skirt as he eyed these new-comers. "Thank you, sir, but I am most eager to see the lion and the other animals in the menagerie. Come, Madelyn, give me your hand." She wasn't about to let that old roué lead her off.

"Well, ta ra, then, enjoy yourself." Alana flashed Eden her most pleasant smile, then favored Brentwood with a more suggestive one. "Brent, you said you'd call on me for a tête-à-tête before you left town again. Don't forget!"

Brent turned from staring indignantly at Sir Alfred to briefly nod at Alana. "If I can," he said vaguely. As he hurried to catch up with Eden and the children, he puzzled over the look that had flashed across Sir Alfred's face just as Eden had pulled her hand from his. The older man's eyes had widened in astonishment, as if he had suddenly realized something. What was that all about?

"Eden, do you know those people?" He studied her frowning countenance as they walked. She looked very uneasy.

"I never saw either of them before, how should I? I have heard of them, though. One reads of them occasionally in the gossip columns. They seem to spend a great deal of time visiting other people."

Brentwood chuckled. "As Sir Alfred's pockets are usually to let, that is an economical way to manage."

Eden smiled, but her heart was pounding in alarm. That old man had stared at her like he had seen a ghost. Like the dowager duchess, he and Lady Alana probably had known her mother. Had he made the connection?

Back in the Morleys' carriage, Alana settled herself pettishly. "Well, that was a waste. Except to confirm that his new flirt is young and looks elegant even in a shabby governess's dress, I gained nothing. I still don't know who she is."

"Never mind, m'dear. I know."

"You do? Who? Do we know her? I can't think how."

"Now, we must tread carefully here, m'dear. You know my Aunt Agatha has some odd ideas. Thinks rather more of Langley and his bunch of Godwinian radicals than a God-fearing woman ought."

"Tell me, tell me!" Alana gave her husband's arm an eager tug.

Sir Alfred grinned at his wife's eagerness. "She is the image of her dear departed mother. I wonder if her husband knows where she is?"

The zoo had been a great success, but the tower itself held little of interest to such young children, so Eden and Brentwood left off their attempts to tour it, settling for an expedition to Green Park instead.

"They're so busy. Quite exhausting, really." Brentwood stood, hands on hips, watching closely as Madelyn and Martin attempted to make friends with some ducks.

"Small children are a very large responsibility," Eden said, chuckling. "They are my responsibility, after all. If you wish to do something else—"

"Don't be ridiculous. I am enjoying myself enormously. And I have to get into practice, don't I?"

"You do?" Eden turned startled eyes on him.

"Of course. Going to be a father soon."

Eden turned her head away. "I didn't know." She tried without success to keep disapproval from her tone.

"Of course, to some extent it depends on persuading my intended to marry me."

Relieved and alarmed at the same time, Eden huffed indignantly.

He laughed. "I am hoping that—" Suddenly his expression changed to one of dark fury. "Watch the children, Eden. That wretched chit! If the duchess doesn't send her to that convent in France, I am going to take her there myself!"

Catching up Martin and Madelyn's hands in her own, Eden turned, perplexed, to watch Brentwood storm across the greensward and catch up with a much smaller man. He reached out and grabbed the young man firmly by the elbow, turning him abruptly around. They began to exchange angry words. Eden hurried over as fast as she could coax the children to move.

As she drew near the young man struggled out of Brentwood's grasp and started to dash away. He almost crashed into Eden. "Oh, Eden, it's you, I'm sorry!"

The high-pitched feminine voice had Eden taking another look. "Isabella?"

The irrepressible girl giggled. "Yes, it's me. I fooled you, did I? Fooled everyone but Mr. Brentwood." The sight of his scowl made her thrust her lower lip out. "But why he's in such a pet I do not know."

"What are you doing dressed like that, for heaven's sake!"

"Well, hello." Ignoring her former governess, Isabella bent down to speak to the two children. "Who are you?"

"Are you a wady?" Madelyn's eyes were wide.

"Oh, no, you too." Isabella stood up, laughing. "Don't look at me so, Eden. I want to be able to attend classes at the Royal Academy, and the only way I could think of to do it was as a man. My maid bought me these clothes secondhand. Don't you think they are an excellent fit?"

Eden studied her former pupil. The breeches and boots were a good fit, but the well-endowed young girl was stuffed into the coat in seam-bursting volume. "In truth, you look a little like a pouter pigeon, Bella."

Brentwood exploded in laughter. "And walk like one too! That's what made me notice you first."

"Well, the boots are too heavy. I feel like I'm trying to walk with anvils tied to my ankles."

"May I suggest we continue this discussion in the brougham?" Brentwood hoisted Martin up on his shoulder and shepherded the rest of them to the waiting carriage. "Miss Eardley can explain her latest start to us there."

Brentwood purchased stick candy from a vendor to occupy the children. Isabella eyed it so enviously that he turned back around and bought a stick for her, too, winking at Eden as he did so. Laughing and something more tender bubbled up in Eden at the conspiratorial grin that spread over his face.

In the carriage Isabella explained her woes. "Grandmama won't let me go anywhere but to call on old ladies. Says I'm not ready to be out yet. We spend endless hours on deportment and fittings and oh—turn your head, Mr. Brentwood—Eden, she makes me wear a corset." This last remark was uttered in a loud, hoarse whisper.

Choking back embarrassed laughter, Eden lowered her voice to reply, "You've worn a corset since—"

"Yes, I know, but you and Mother never made me lace it tight! I declare I can't breathe!"

She sat back against the carriage seat. "You can listen again, Mr. Brentwood." Then she continued her litany of complaints. "Of course, I can't paint or even draw, as I have no supplies. My maid wouldn't buy me any because Grandmother specifically told her I wasn't to have any, but she didn't think to tell her not to buy me some men's clothes."

Brentwood turned his head back, a look half-sympathetic, half-amused twisting his mouth into a strange smile. "Poor child!"

"Poor duchess. Isabella, don't you know you could disgrace her by such behavior? And I must say you do not make a convincing young man. Do you have any idea of the dangers you are risking?" Concern for her former pupil made Eden's voice uncharacteristically severe.

Isabella began to cry. "But, Eden, I'm so unhappy. I can't live like this, I just can't!"

Martin began to cry in sympathy with Isabella, and Eden felt tears coming into her own eyes. Brentwood scowled and clenched his fists. "I'm going to have a talk with that old dragon. I'll have the coachman drop Bella and me there first and then he can take you and the children on home."

Eden nodded, then pulled Bella into her arms. "Sweetheart, a woman's lot in life is never easy, but you are going to make it very much harder if you don't begin to conduct yourself as your grandmother expects."

Bella returned the comforting hug. "I know." She wiped her eyes. "I'll try."

As Brentwood helped Isabella down out of the carriage, she called back to Eden, "If only you could come back to be my governess again. I'm going to ask Grandmother one more time."

"I doubt that is possible, dear. Even if she would permit it, I have accepted another position now. But perhaps she would hire a companion for you." Eden turned to Brentwood. "A young woman who knows how to go on, but who is near enough Bella's age to give her some enjoyable company."

Brentwood nodded. "I'll suggest it."

The scratch at her door startled Eden out of a reverie. She was drying her hair in front of the fireplace in her room, wrapped in a faded turquoise brocade robe.

Thinking it was the nursery maid, she called, "Enter."

She started to scramble to her feet when Brent stuck his head in the door. Since standing up would expose a long length of leg, she hastily resumed her previous position, sitting on the hearth in front of the fireplace.

"Mr. Brentwood! I thought you had gone with the Langleys!"

"I did, but it became an incredible bore." Brentwood eased himself into the door frame. "I find I am not quite as much a democrat in actuality as I am in theory." His high-arched eyebrows invited her to laugh with him.

Curiosity distracted Eden from chasing this highly improper visitor away from her door. She knew he had accompanied his hosts to a dinner with several leading manufacturers who were eager to see parliamentary representation increased in the populous manufacturing centers. "Are they so very different, then?"

"No, that is the odd thing. They are so very much alike! In spite of my protests, they *would* use my title, and the instant we rejoined the ladies, they began parading their eligible daughters before me, precisely as any self-respecting mama of the *ton* would do. 'Elizabeth plays the harp; play something for Lord Dudley, dear.' Elizabeth had studied the charming posture of a harpist to perfection, but could not find the strings. Then it was, 'My Mary sings like an angel.' Whereupon Mary proceeded to howl like a dog!"

Eden began to laugh in spite of her determination to urge him to state his business and leave. "You are a severe critic, sir!"

"No, just an honest one. Speaking of which, you are honestly the loveliest sight I have ever seen, with your long hair spread out around you. It gives off fiery red highlights in the glow of the fireplace." As he rhapsodized, Brentwood began a lazy advance from the door frame, into the room, and toward the fireplace.

"Brent, you must leave." Alarmed at his expression, which was at one and the same time mischievous and hungry, her voice grew shrill with insistence. "You can't come into my room with me alone, and late at night at that!"

"But I can. I have." He smiled at her in a way that set her heart to racing in her breast. Deprived of speech by conflicting emotions, she could only glare at him.

Ignoring her scowl and her words of warning, Brentwood settled beside her and lifted a long, curling tendril of hair to enjoy the fragrance. "Mmmm. Lemon and verbena. Like you, Eden. A little tart, yet very sweet, and full of hidden fire."

She drew back. "There is going to be nothing hidden about my fire if you don't leave!"

"I thought you might want to hear about my interview with the dowager Duchess of Carminster today."

"I do, but some other time." She caught and held the green eyes, her own expression stern.

Brentwood sighed and stood up. "You are a hard woman, Eden Henderson. Well, as I have much to do tomorrow, I will tell you and then leave." He began a leisurely retreat to the door. "After some home truths from me, the duchess allowed that she had been too strict with Isabella. She thought your idea of a companion was a good one, and even better, she promised to arrange art lessons for the girl in exchange for good conduct. Isabella was so ecstatic that I believe she will keep her end of the bargain."

"I am very glad to hear it!" Eden smiled joyfully. "She is really very talented."

"Well, then . . ." When Brentwood reached the door, he stood hesitant, reluctant to leave. "Soon I will have to go back to the country again, to finish my remodeling project."

Seeing that he was going to leave, Eden relaxed a little. "I envy you, in a way. I still haven't gotten used to all the noise of the city, and the rank odors." Her nose wrinkled in distaste.

"You dislike the city?"

"Not dislike, exactly. The country suits me better, though."

"You think you could be happy spending your life in the wilds of Hertfordshire, raising children?"

"Hertfordshire?" She deliberately misunderstood him, though her heart was pounding. "I wasn't aware the Langleys have property there."

Abruptly he walked back across the room, bent down and grasped Eden's upper arms firmly, pulling her up in front of him. "Eden," he growled, "you are driving me mad. You know what I mean."

"Don't. I don't want to know what you mean." She tried to free herself.

"Just because your father was a monster doesn't mean all men are."

Panic-stricken, she stared up at him. "My father . . . what do you know of my father?"

"Someone made you despise the marriage bond, and you've sworn it wasn't that foolish essay I wrote."

She ducked her head; he tilted it up with one imperious forefinger. "I'm right, aren't I?"

She couldn't answer. She was lost in the nearness of him, the fierce yearning in his green eyes, the sudden gentling of his touch. He lowered his mouth to hers slowly, giving her time to refuse, but she waited for him. She wanted this, though she knew she shouldn't allow it.

Gently, very gently his lips settled on hers. Softly they moved, coaxing her own to echo their pressure. Then, long before she was ready, he pulled away. "You see, not all men are monsters, Eden."

She took his lapels in her hands and pulled his head back down to hers for another kiss. This time his mouth was firmer, more demanding, and she wanted to yield all that he demanded. Breathing as if he'd just run a mile, he lifted his head and slid his arms down to wrap around her and press her against his body.

"I'm not a monster, Eden."

She burrowed her face into his chest. "I know. I know."

At the utter despair in her voice he put her just far enough away from him to look at her face. Tears drenched her eyes. "Please," she begged. "Please let me go . . . *make* me go!"

"Go, then." He loosened his grip on her, stung by her reaction. She stumbled backward several paces, clutching her robe tightly around herself.

"I apologize for distressing you." Turning abruptly, he walked from the room without a backward glance.

Chapter Ten

"You said you planned to stay several days."

"It seems pointless now."

Langley and Brentwood were pondering the finer points of French brandy and West Indian cigars. Gwynneth had bid her husband good night at the bottom of the stairs when she saw the look on Brentwood's face.

"Rushed your fences."

"Yes, and after your good wife warned me, too. Well, I'll try again, of course, and try it Gwynneth's way, but I don't think it will make any difference. I'd made up my mind to marry Eden before I was in her company half a day, but it appears she'd made up her mind never to marry anyone long before that."

"Patience . . ."

"Were you able to be patient with Gwynneth once you were sure she was the one woman for you?"

Langley tossed his head back and laughed. "Touché, my lad. No, I all but abducted her."

At the kindling expression on his young friend's face, Langley held up his hand. "Hold, Roger! Please remember your pledge to me. No scandals."

"Damn you and your politics to hell." The words were fierce, but Brentwood pronounced them equably. "If I thought she'd eventually come around, I'd do it. But there's something here I don't understand, and if I've learned anything in my travels, it's to go carefully when you don't understand the ground."

"That's right. Patience. Time is your friend in this situation."

"Not really. Have you forgotten what's coming from America?"

Langley looked at his young friend in consternation. To be sure, he was in a difficult situation. If Eden was shy of him now, how would she react when his surprise arrived from America?

At breakfast the next morning Eden learned that Brentwood had departed at sunup. Lord Langley had given her a rather censorious look as he informed her of this fact; clearly he knew something of what had passed between herself and his friend the night before.

She had spent many sleepless hours during the night pondering what she should do. She knew little about the male sex, and most of what she did know had made her loathe them. Never had she expected to meet a man who could make her doubt her opinions. Brent's humor, kindness, tenderness, had challenged her impression of the sex. The strange feelings he was able to arouse in her with a touch, sometimes even with a look, she supposed were the dawnings of attraction, of lust, perhaps even of love.

Unfortunately, she could not afford to allow those feelings to develop. Brent wanted to marry her, which was impossible, and she would not allow herself to become any man's mistress.

Adding to her sleeplessness was the danger she was exposed to here in London. Not only the duchess, but now Lady Alana and her husband had responded to her resemblance to her mother. Sir Alfred might even have realized exactly who she was. If so, she must leave, and immediately. But where would she go? And how would she explain matters to the Langleys, whose treatment of her went beyond mere kindly treatment of a servant? They had become friends, a concept as dear as it was rare in Eden's life.

If she told them the truth, she might be endangering them,

for she realized that the Langleys as well as Brentwood would insist on trying to help her. Bitter experience had taught her that those who helped her could be made to suffer.

Eden was toying with her breakfast, her dilemma still unresolved, when Parker entered the breakfast room. "Miss Henderson, you have a caller."

Panic gripped Eden. "Who . . . who is it, Parker?"

"The dowager Duchess of Carminster, miss. I put Her Grace in the blue drawing room." Parker looked benignly at her. That was the most formal and elegant room in the Langleys' home. Apparently Parker thought her consequence had gone up with a duchess for a caller.

"Excuse me, Stuart?"

"Of course." Langley watched her leave, full of curiosity. Eden was looking decidedly down-pin, which he felt was all to the good as far as Roger's suit was concerned. Probably it meant that she was regretting having rejected him. Langley hoped the duchess wouldn't do anything to muddy the waters.

"I truly do not blame you anymore, my dear. It is now clear to me that Isabella will be a rare handful, no matter who has charge of her, and that you doubtless would be a moderating influence upon her. But when she begged me to let you return as her governess, I decided I'd best speak to you privately first. As I hinted when first we met, your resemblance to your mother is pronounced, and cannot help but be remarked in my circle of friends."

Eden was surprised at the frank, friendly manner in which the dowager was addressing her. "I thank you for keeping my secret, Your Grace."

"Bah! I have excellent reasons of my own for despising Colville. Nor did I disagree with everything that young Lord Dudley wrote in his infamous essay, you know."

Eden studied the older woman in some astonishment. The duchess seemed an unlikely convert. "I agree I cannot return to being Isabella's governess. The fact is, ma'am, I fear I am already in danger of discovery. Do you know Sir Alfred Morley and his wife?"

The dowager made a rather rude noise. "Paltry pair."

"Mr. Brentwood introduced us yesterday. I believe they made the same connection you have done."

"Then you must leave London, and at once, for I know that woman. She is spiteful to the core. She would notify Colville without a moment's hesitation."

Eden jumped up, agitated. "I knew it! I felt it. But where shall I go? If I leave the Langleys on such short notice, I can't very well ask them for a recommendation, and besides, my funds are very limited."

"Would they be so unhelpful, once they understood the situation?"

"No, in fact, they might be too helpful, which is why I don't want them to know. Colville is capable of anything. He might do them an injury. At the very least, it might open them up to another scandalous lawsuit. You know how Colville likes to go to law. He's already sued them once over Brentwood's essay, pretending it had something to do with my flight. They are trying so hard to bring about peaceful, constructive change in this country. I would feel very guilty if public outcry diminished their hopes of success."

"Quite. And if young Dudley finds out, he'll doubtless try to do something rash—"

Eden whirled around. "Oh, Your Grace, that is my greatest fear. And he mustn't! I could never bear it if he came to harm because of me."

"Sit down and calm yourself, miss. You didn't successfully hide from a canny monster like Colville for all these years by being hen-witted."

The duchess's stern tone braced Eden. She sat down and forced herself into a semblance of calmness.

"That's better. Now, I have an idea. Been thinking about your situation for a while. I have a friend. She's an invalid, living on her own in Wales. Too stubborn to live with her children. She'll take you on if I ask her."

"But will she want me?"

"No, she won't. She don't want anybody, hasn't for years. But she needs you. Won't be a sinecure, my girl. She's blind and often in pain. Hadn't the most equable of temperaments even when young. You'll earn your salary, and then some."

"I'm not afraid of hard work, Your Grace."

"No, I don't think you are. And one could not ask for a more isolated situation, if only we can get you there without being tracked."

The duchess then proceeded to lay out a plan that Eden thought showed considerable capability for intrigue. The crux of it was that Eden was to leave while the Langleys were out for the evening, in a hired hackney. It would drop her at a designated corner, where she would rendezvous with the duchess's own traveling carriage. It would carry her in complete privacy to Wales.

Though deeply regretting the need for such secrecy, Eden agreed to the plan. "They will doubtless worry about me, though. I will have to say *something* to them."

The older woman nodded. "You must say something that will give them a disgust of you, else they will make inquiries that will attract Colville's attention."

"A disgust of me? But I don't want to hurt people who have been so kind . . ."

"It will be kinder in the long run, though. You certainly are intelligent enough to know you can't communicate with them from now on. Isn't that why your own relatives think you dead?"

Eden stared at the duchess. She wanted to argue, but the old woman's reasoning was as strong as her implacable countenance. Except for her mother's sister, all of her other relatives had given her up for dead long ago, because she had never communicated with any of them, save for a very minimal and carefully coded correspondence with her aunt.

"You have the right of it, Your Grace. It has to be so. And Isabella, too, will have to think I have just abandoned her." She shrank from the thought.

The duchess reached forward and patted her clenched hands, surprising her. "I will contrive to see that Isabella is more contented than she has been. Your suggestion of a young companion for her was a good one."

"Brent said you might consider it." At his name Eden felt a stab of pain. Her disappearance—what would it mean to him? Was she never to see him again? The thought gave her almost unbearable pain. She bowed her head and fought down tears.

"So the Langleys dine out tonight?"

Eden mastered herself. "Yes, and I believe they go to the theater after."

"Good. The children are not left solely in your care?"

"No, ma'am. The nursery maid sleeps in the room with them. I usually tuck them in around 7 P.M. After that, my evenings are my own."

"Then best do it tonight. No point in delay." Isabella's grandmother stood. "You're a brave girl. Colville can't live forever, you know."

"He's only sixty, ma'am, and it is said only the good die young."

"Bosh, I'm going strong at seventy, ain't I?" It was the first time Eden had seen the dowager smile, and suddenly she realized why the woman had once borne the reputation of a great beauty. She stood and held out her hands to her benefactress.

The two pairs of hands, one young and smooth, the other old and wrinkled, joined for a long moment before the dowager moved off, leaving Eden with an address and a time. "I will arrange for the hackney and for my traveling carriage. The less attention you attract to yourself the better."

The rest of that day was like a waking nightmare to Eden. She had to fend off Stuart and Gwynneth's touching concern at her pallor and obvious distress. She had to play with the children and put them to bed without telling them good-bye or explaining why she must leave them. She had to pack her trunk and carpetbag and ask them to be carried down just as the hackney was due to arrive, without offering a word of explanation to the surprised servants, who had been nothing but kind to her and deserved more civil treatment.

The vales she left with Parker to distribute would hardly reconcile them to her behavior. But there was no point in brooding about the consequences of her abrupt departure, since failure to flee might well be fatal.

Alana Morley had pondered all day what to do with the knowledge she now possessed about the elegantly attractive governess known as Eden Henderson. She cared not at all about the consequences which her decision might have on the pretty brunette. No, her concern was all for how the information might affect her relationship with Brentwood.

If she simply notified Colville of the location of his long-vanished wife, he would doubtless claim the girl immediately, thus removing her from competition. But when Brentwood found out, he might decide to act the hero and rescue her. Knowing Colville's ruthlessness, she realized this could result in the younger man's death. Even if he prevailed, he would doubtless feel he had to marry the chit. No, that path could well drive Brentwood straight into the so-called Miss Henderson's arms.

Alfred had been no help at all. "Keep mum," he'd advised. "Meddling in their affairs might make us enemies of the Langleys. We don't need enemies now, pet. Especially enemies Aunt Agatha admires."

It was not until she was dressing for the theater that the solution came to Alana. It was so simple, really. She knew Stuart Hamilton, Lord Langley, well enough to know he wouldn't be shocked to learn that he had been sheltering another man's wife. He might have behaved like a choirboy since his marriage, but he was far from an angel. For all she knew, he too was enjoying the missing viscountess's favors in exchange for hiding her from her husband.

However, he would be well aware of how shocked many other people would be to find Joanna, Viscountess Colville a member of his household. And Alana was perceptive enough to know that Langley did not court scandal. The temper of the times was changing. A new moral conservatism was in the wind. To further his own political aims, he would avoid unnecessary public challenges to the established order.

"I have it!" She whirled and dashed into her husband's bedroom. "Say nothing. Let me handle it." She quickly explained her plan to her admiring husband.

When the theater lights went up for intermission, Lord and Lady Langley were surprised to find Lady Alana Morley already entering their box. "I have something very important to tell you. It is for your ears alone," she informed Langley.

Masterfully controlling her curiosity, Gwynneth moved toward the box opening, giving them some privacy as she greeted other guests.

Seeing nothing to be gained by playing cat and mouse, Alana went straight to the point. "Stuart, do you know who your governess is?"

"I thought she was Eden Henderson. Obviously you plan to tell me otherwise."

"Alfred recognized her because she is the very image of her mother. You have heard of her mother, I am sure—Anthea Fortman?"

Perplexed, Langley searched his memory. "I don't recall . . ."

"Perhaps you never had occasion to meet her. She made her come-out when I did. An accredited beauty and an heiress, she made an unfortunate match. Her marriage to Sir Edgar Trent was a disaster. She ran away from her husband and was forced to go back by the courts, even though he beat her."

"Poor creature. No wonder Eden has such a poor opinion of men."

"I expect it has as much to do with poor Eden's own husband, Viscount Colville."

"My God! Eden married? To Colville? Are you sure?"

"Unfortunately, yes. She is the very picture of her mother.

Alfred and I both recognized her when we came across her with Brentwood and your children yesterday afternoon. Colville doubtless would be quite interested to know that his long-missing wife is a member of your household."

"That diseased old rake." Langley clenched his fists in impotent fury. Alana was watching him carefully. He couldn't tell if it was malice or concern that narrowed her eyes, but she wasn't in any doubt that her news had hit him like a Congreve rocket.

Alana leaned forward. "That 'diseased old rake' is capable of making a great scandal, you know."

"Well do I know it." Langley's brows almost met as he scowled. Alana clearly wanted something.

"Better you help 'Miss Henderson' to quietly disappear, n'est-ce pas?"

"How kind of you to concern yourself."

"I wouldn't wish Brent to be hurt by his association with her."

After a moment's consideration, Langley nodded his head. "Now I understand. If 'Miss Henderson' disappears, you think Roger will renew his affair with you."

"As long as he doesn't see me as a villainess."

"Silence in return for silence."

"Do you not think it a fair exchange?"

Langley bowed his head. What could he do? Scandal as terrible as any he had ever imagined faced him. That particular runaway wife, in his own household? What might the Tories make of it? Moreover, there was the strong possibility that that young hothead Roger would challenge the old roué. And Eden—if somehow Colville got his hands on her—the results would be unthinkable. Langley's mind was abuzz with conjecture, but one thing seemed clear. He had to agree to Alana's terms. This secret must be kept, at least for a time.

"*D'accord.*" He gave his agreement ruefully.

"If you need any help in finding her a situation . . ."

And put the poor child completely in your power, Langley thought grimly. "No, I thank you, I will think of something."

"Then good evening, Stuart." Alana gave him a smug smile and sauntered from the box.

Chapter Eleven

As the duchess's luxurious traveling coach carried her across England and into Wales, Eden was enchanted by the beauty of the countryside, a small but welcome compensation for what she had given up to go into this exile. The wooded hills, the lovely rolling valleys and ancient, narrow-streeted villages charmed her.

At Llangollen she purchased sketching supplies, spending no small amount of her available funds to provide herself with a pleasurable distraction from her unhappy thoughts. Anytime the carriage halted, even if it was only for a change of horses, she made pencil sketches of old buildings or particularly fine views.

Concentrating on drawing helped keep her from thinking of what she had left behind. That way lay a broken heart.

On the fifth day the duchess's dour maid, who had accompanied her, broke her usual silence to inform Eden that a half-day's journey over bad roads would bring them to Colin Molyneux and her new mistress.

Though the maid, Maigret, had not shown any interest in being her confidante, Eden couldn't help but worry aloud, "I wonder if Lady Humphrey will take me on? After all, she isn't even expecting me."

"She'll do it," Maigret responded with conviction. "She 'n my lady were thick as inkle weavers when they were young 'uns. But it's wondering I am if you'll be stayin' with her? She's not a kind-hearted lady like Her Grace."

Eden found herself imagining Brentwood's grin at this de-

scription of the dowager duchess. But she smothered any inclination to smile. "Indeed, the duchess has been incredibly kind
to me, providing me with a fine carriage, a maid, a coachman,
and two footmen. I quite feel like royalty."

"Aye. Lady Humphrey will know you are of importance to
Her Grace. But it won't make her any more gracious. An old
tartar, she is."

It was the most Maigret had ever said. Eden felt a little ap-
prehensive about trusting her destiny to a woman who struck
the dowager Duchess of Carminster's maid as a tartar. Still,
it was far better than facing her fate if returned to her husband.

Toward evening the coach rumbled up a long, unkempt
drive, toward an Elizabethan manor house of impressive proportions. Humphrey Manor was structurally sound but had a
general air of neglect. The impression of recent neglect was
strengthened as she entered the main hall. The solid overarch-
ing wooden beams were smoke-grimed, the walls in dire need
of whitewash. The floor was worn and, like the furniture, none
too clean.

An ancient butler greeted them with a resentful air. He ac-
knowledged Maigret, and eyed Eden speculatively when told
the duchess had sent her. Still, he informed them firmly that
her ladyship had retired for the evening and was not to be dis-
turbed. Maigret loftily waved him aside. " 'Tis as well. Miss
Henderson is very tired after her journey. I'll show her to her
room myself. See you get her hot water for a bath, and send up
a tray for dinner."

Not giving him a chance to reply, she steered Eden upstairs
like one well acquainted with the house. Once she had selected
a bedroom she began, muttering between her teeth, to strip the
bedclothes. "Damp! It's a disgrace!"

Eden moved to the other side of the massive bed and helped
her. "I hope there are fresh linens."

"Aye, but as to whether they'll be any dryer, I don't know. I
doubt there's been a fire lit in here this age."

Maigret left Eden to unpack her valise, and returned shortly after with clean bedclothes. "It'll be unpleasant duty working here, Miss Henderson. The servants know she's blind and are takin' advantage. I'm sure you're used to much better management."

"Perhaps she will let me help her with managing the house." Eden knew she would find it difficult to live in such a place and not intervene to bring it up to snuff.

Maigret looked doubtful, but merely sniffed, "Perhaps."

The interview the next morning with Lady Humphrey was anticlimactic. Though of an age with the duchess, the baroness seemed at least ten years older. Her thinning gray hair hung in wisps beneath an elaborate old-fashioned cap. Her clothes hung on a gaunt frame, and her pale blue eyes were clouded by cataracts. She was propped up in her massive bed like an old rag doll.

"How like Helen to simply send me a companion without a by-your-leave. I don't need a companion, I say! Told my daughters and my sons so, a hundred times." The woman's voice was shaky with age and anger.

Eden swallowed her fear; now was the time to be bold. "But you do need a housekeeper, ma'am. And a groundskeeper too, I vow. All is going to rack and ruin."

Lady Humphrey puffed up angrily. "Explain yourself, miss!"

Eden proceeded to describe the rutted drive, the weed-infested park, the dirt and grime and air of neglect of the entire house. Her prospective employer listened in seeming indignation, occasionally interrupting with loud exclamations. Eden fully expected to be ordered off the premises when she finished. But instead the old woman sighed and sank back against her bed pillows.

"I don't doubt it's true. 'Tis what servants will do when there's none to make them behave. And then, they are old, like me. Doubtless the house is become too much for them."

"Then pension them off, my lady, and let me hire some new ones. At least a pair of maids to dust and polish, and a strong young man to set the park to rights."

Lady Humphrey sat quiet for so long Eden thought her mind might have wandered. "You are musical?" she finally asked.

"Yes, ma'am. I play the piano, the harp, the flute, and the violin."

"Not the harpsichord?" A querulous note of disappointment crept into the old woman's voice.

"That, too. It's what I learned to play on."

Lady Humphrey mused, as if not hearing Eden, "Of course, I could buy a pianoforte. I've been wanting one, but my daughters never learned to play well enough to make it worth the expense, and I can't see the music anymore, so there seemed no point."

Her voice seemed to become almost enthusiastic as Lady Humphrey continued to muse on Eden's potential usefulness. "And you can read to me. I like to keep up with all the gossip. I'll subscribe to the papers again."

After a brief silence which Eden hesitated to interrupt, she continued, "If you're really from Helen, and not a spy for my interfering daughters. They want to take charge of me, you know, and thus of my money." Lady Humphrey looked challengingly at Eden, as if she expected to be doubted. But Eden knew too much of the corroding influence of money unequally distributed in a family, and of treachery by one's nearest kin, to question the charge.

"Truly, my lady, I do not even know their names, and shall have no claims upon you beyond the salary you will pay me."

"See you don't make the mistake of expecting more and we'll deal well together."

Thus began Eden's new life. It was a very busy life. Running a household such as Humphrey Manor was not child's play, though once the servants learned that Lady Humphrey intended to dismiss them if Eden recommended it, her task became much easier.

She read the papers to her employer each morning while they breakfasted, and afterward took dictation as Lady Humphrey gleefully resumed her once-extensive correspondence. At night Eden read to her from books of sermons or played the harpsichord. The only time she really had to herself was in the afternoon when Lady Humphrey took a long nap.

Eden soon had the house set to rights, and without any hesitation took the afternoons for her own pursuits. She walked, marveling constantly at the beauty of the Welsh countryside. She sketched and did watercolors of her favorite views. Sometimes she visited the tenants, though lacking transportation, she couldn't go far enough to call on all of them. She had an opportunity to observe firsthand the distress the agricultural classes were experiencing, distress which was bringing the country to the brink of revolution. With her employer's permission, she did what she could to assist the impoverished farm workers.

Lady Humphrey had no riding horses, nothing at all but an ancient carriage that was only taken out on Sundays, when Eden assisted her in attending church services in the nearby village chapel. The horses that pulled it were just as ancient, so Eden had to make do with shank's mare when she wanted to go into the village for any reason.

But in truth, once she had posted a letter, carefully coded as usual, to her aunt, Eden had little need to go into the village. The cook had been in the habit of purchasing most of what was needed for the household. Eden let her continue, feeling she was safer by keeping to Lady Humphrey's boundaries as much as possible.

The isolated life she led was peaceful, but somehow not restful. She found that her thoughts often strayed to London, to the friends she had left there. Alas, friends no longer, after the way she had left them. She bitterly regretted the necessity of writing the callous, misleading notes she had left behind.

She couldn't keep herself from wondering how Langley's political plans were progressing, whether Gwynneth had gotten the latest issue of *The Legacy* out on time, and how the children had taken her abrupt departure.

Was Isabella contented, or still creating crisis after crisis, headlong on the road to ruin?

Even more often her thoughts strayed to a tall, green-eyed man with a fey sense of humor. She found herself wondering how he would react to various situations she encountered. She yearned to discuss with him the news of the day, and the latest novel. Had the Langleys shown her notes to Brentwood? Of course they had. He probably despised her now.

She pondered the immediate attraction that had sprung up between them. Likely it had been merely infatuation for both of them. Surely she could not have formed a serious attachment in so short a time? But if not, why did he continue to invade her thoughts so often?

As for the earl's eager courtship of her, she convinced herself that he had reached the age that a man, especially a nobleman with a title to pass on, looks about him for a wife. She had been thrown in his way at the crucial time. If she had not come along, he would have courted another woman. Doubtless by now he had begun to do so. His delightful old folly of a castle was surely remodeled by now, freeing Brentwood to survey the marriageable misses for a likely countess to begin filling its nurseries.

Each day as she read to Lady Humphrey the gossip columns she delighted in hearing, Eden was glad of the opportunity to look for gossip about her London friends. A little nervous flutter accompanied her reading of each engagement announcement, sure that the next one would be for Brentwood's coming nuptials. When she was brave enough to be completely honest with herself, she could admit how relieved she was not to find it.

Lord Langley had quite a struggle with his conscience as he sat next to his wife in the carriage on their return from the theater. He had never deceived Gwynneth in anything yet, but he had given Alana his word that he would keep quiet about Eden's identity. He could not quite see how he was going to find the young woman another situation and send her away without either breaking his promise or lying to Gwynneth about the reason.

As for Gwynneth, she sat with her hand engulfed in his, perfectly trusting that whatever Lady Morley had found to whisper in her husband's ear, it had nothing to do with their personal life. Doubtless it was some political matter. He would tell her about it if he could, but she would not press him. Instead, she analyzed the play, and commented on the audience, aware that her husband was participating in the conversation while only half listening.

Langley did not know whether the situation had been made better or worse when, on arriving home, they discovered that their governess had left.

Parker informed them of the matter as soon as they entered the foyer. "Asked for footmen to carry down her trunk, bold as brass, and there was a hackney waiting for her at the door. Planned in advance, m'lord. And someone helping her, for none of us here summoned the cab, and she spent the evening in her room."

Gwynneth's exclamation of astonishment was quickly followed by a question. "Did she offer any explanation, or leave any notes?"

"Yes, ma'am, there was one for each of you on the table in her room. As for explaining herself to us, she did nothing but issue commands." Resentment at such Turkish treatment from a woman he'd respected reverberated in Parker's deep voice.

"Let's read her notes." Langley turned on his heel. When they reached Eden's room, Gwynneth took up the folded, sealed note eagerly. As she perused it, Langley broke the seal and read his own. An oath escaped his lips.

Gwynneth looked up from hers with tears in her eyes. "I simply don't understand this. She says nothing about where she is going, only that she found working with the children irksome and felt it was necessary to make other plans. This is the coldest, rudest thing—"

"If yours is rude, mine is impertinent. She informs me that

she has decided that she wishes to travel and know some of the luxuries of life, and has found a man who will provide her with them without requiring that she marry him. She says she knows I will wish to keep the matter quiet to avoid scandalizing my political allies."

"That hussy!" Gwynneth threw her note down and stomped from the room. "I regret the day Brent brought her here. What will I tell the children?"

Langley followed her. "And what will I tell Roger?"

There was more to that query than Gwynneth could know. For Langley now found himself faced with a double dilemma. The secret information Alana had given him, which he had wondered how to keep from Roger and Gwynneth, raised vexing questions about Eden's sudden departure. Had she really left as some man's mistress, or had she left under duress? If the latter, who had forced her? Or had she been carried off?

The note she had left him gave him the perfect out if he wished to keep Roger in ignorance and guarantee that he would turn from her in disgust. Yet a lingering doubt that Eden would have really taken up such a disgraceful life made him unsure of what to tell the others. Perhaps she needed help; shouldn't they somehow seek her out and rescue her?

In the end he decided to make his own inquiries before involving Brentwood. The next day his questioning of the servants revealed a groom who had heard the direction given to the hackney driver.

"Ethan, are you sure she said Curzon Street? 'Tis but a few blocks from here."

"Yes, m'lord. Ee didn't look surprised, either. I quizzed him on getting such a short fare. Ee told me ee'd already been paid, an' well."

"I'd give a pretty penny to know who paid him!" Langley rested one hand on a fine bay carriage horse's flank and stared gloomily at the rafters of the stable.

"I kin ask 'im if you like, m'lord."

Langley turned eagerly. "Do you know the man?"

"Aye, I see 'im from time to time taking passengers 'ere and there. I know where 'is usual stand is."

So they went together in search of the driver of the hackney coach. They learned little, but what they did learn convinced Langley that Eden had indeed joined a wealthy lover, rather than being carried off against her will. The hackney cab driver told of being hired by a footman in expensive livery to pick up a fare at the Langleys' address and deliver her to the address on Curzon Street. He had done so. A luxurious traveling coach awaited her there. A footman had loaded her trunk, while a maid had assisted her into the carriage. She had shown no reluctance, indeed had seemed eager to be on her way.

"Was there a coat of arms or any other means of identifying the coach?"

"No, my lord. That is, there was a coat of arms, I expect, but it was draped with black cloth, so's no one could see it. 'Twas a fine coach, but much like any other."

"Describe the livery to me."

"They was all in black. In mourning, like."

Langley groaned. Footmen and coachmen dressed in mourning clothes? That meant there was no way to trace them to any member of the nobility through their livery. He thanked the hackney cab driver and returned to his home.

Only a few minutes of thought were required to make his decision. Eden had obviously left willingly, so she had not gone with her husband. She had left in circumstances of luxury which Alana Morley could certainly not afford to provide. She had, he concluded, done just as her notes said. She had taken a wealthy lover, doubtless a married one of high station, who had both the will and the means to hide her from her dangerous husband.

He would not tell Roger or Gwynneth what Alana Morley had told him. He was well rid of the baggage, and could only be glad that her need for secrecy had driven her to elope so discreetly; otherwise she might have embroiled him in a double scandal.

He thought, *good riddance to Eden Henderson*. He could only hope that Roger Brentwood would feel the same.

Chapter Twelve

Langley returned from his investigations satisfied in his own mind that Eden had left voluntarily. It wasn't difficult for him to convince his wife that Roger should not be notified of Eden's elopement. "He might decide to go after them, get himself in a duel or something. Let's let her get well away before we tell him. She mentions travel. Doubtless that means on the Continent, where she won't be so easily recognized."

"She? You mean her lover, don't you?" Gwynneth wrinkled her nose in perplexity. She was still reeling from the abrupt, cold departure of the young woman she had so quickly learned to regard almost as a sister.

"Yes, of course." Langley let out a long breath. He wasn't accustomed to deceiving his wife. He would need to guard his tongue carefully. "At any rate, don't you agree we should give them time to get away, for everyone's sake?"

Gwynneth nodded her head. "Poor Brent. I believe he was truly attached to her."

"I hope not. I had wondered if he was just in a hurry to marry. Perhaps it won't be such a blow to him as you think."

Gwynneth looked dubious. "We can only hope not. The children certainly were upset by her disappearance. They'd grown very attached to her." She began drifting toward the door. "I'm going to look in on them."

"I'll go with you."

The two climbed the stairs to the nursery and crept quietly into their children's room. Holding hands, they basked in the beauty of the little sleepers. "Irksome," Gwynneth whispered, shaking her head. "How could she!"

Langley put his arm around his wife in comfort, while cold fury against Eden Henderson grew in his heart, replacing all pity at her plight. Had she to hurt his wife and children just because fate had dealt her a bad hand? She'd better not come back and expect anything but contempt from him!

Brentwood stood in the middle of the park in front of Dudley castle and admired the effect his remodeling had wrought. No more sagging *faux* battlements. No more leaking roof, or stained stone. The windows were all clean and newly leaded. Those which had been boarded up in response to the window tax had been uncovered, restoring symmetry to the outside as well as light to the inside.

Within, he knew that all rooms but one had received fresh paint or wallpaper, and suitable furnishings had been installed. The nursery had been expanded and equipped with the newest toys and books. It had taken longer to accomplish the remodeling than he had expected, but the two weeks had been well spent.

The one room he had left undone was to be Eden's bedroom. Her dressing room, really, for he intended that she would sleep with him. He had left this room for her to decorate to her own tastes.

He frowned as he thought of the dearth of letters from London. Caught up in the frenzy of activity caused by his remodeling project, he had still found time to dash off two breezy notes to Stuart, fully intending that he would share them with Gwynneth and Eden. It would have been too much to expect Eden to write him. If for no other reason, propriety would keep her from it.

Still, it seemed as if Stuart or Gwynneth might have written him. A little niggle of uneasiness worried at him. As soon as the workmen had finished installing the plumbing for his indoor water closet and bathing room, he was going to nip down to London for a visit. *See if absence does make the heart grow fonder,* he mused. Another week and all would be in readiness for his American visitors, and for his bride if he could but persuade her to join him.

"You'll have to tell him something. I can't bear to think of him rushing in here expecting to see her, and . . ."

Langley nodded his agreement. In his hand was the letter from Brentwood that had arrived with the morning's post. It informed them that he would be in London in a few days. "I've dreaded this. Hard to know what to say to the boy."

"Why not the truth?"

Langley turned sharply, studying his wife with narrowed eyes. "What do you mean?"

"I'm not sure." Her golden-hazel eyes met his, full of the same look of hurt and perplexity he had surprised there more than once since Eden had left. He was uncomfortably aware that he had deceived his wife, if only by omission, and he suspected that somehow she sensed the fact. If so, he was paying a price for keeping his vow of silence to Alana, and he wondered if it wasn't too high. But he wasn't one to break his vows easily, so he looked away, avoiding eye contact as he growled, "That's right, we don't know the whole truth, just enough of it to know we're better off now she's gone."

Gwynneth rose and brushed down her skirts. "I'm going to be in the nursery."

Langley unhappily watched her leave, worried by her stiff posture. "Devil take that Eden Henderson, and Roger Brentwood for bringing her into our lives," he muttered, taking up his pen to write his reply.

"I don't believe this! It is a lie!" Brentwood had just finished reading the notes Eden had written to the Langleys. Stuart's letter had caused him to drop everything and hasten to London.

"This is not like her. She might have had difficulty with the idea of marriage, but she would never accept *carte blanche* from a man. If she'd been so inclined, I have every reason to believe she would have given me the opportunity, for I know she was as attracted to me as I was to her. Yet she took care I knew better than to suggest such a thing.

"And this one about finding the children irksome—ridiculous! I saw the look on her face as she spoke of them. She adored them."

"Why would she lie?" Langley was surprised by his young friend's vehement defense of Eden. He had expected outrage at her betrayal.

"Likely for the same reason she ran away. I don't know what it is, but she was afraid of something."

"Why didn't she turn to us for help? Surely she knew we would stand her friend?" Gwynneth leaned forward, hoping Brentwood could come up with an explanation.

"Some dangerous secret haunted Eden. The duchess alluded to it more than once."

Gwynneth suddenly sat up straight. "The dowager Duchess of Carminster?"

"Yes. Each time we visited her, she seemed almost to threaten Eden with exposure if she did not stay away from Isabella."

"That might be the answer."

Both men looked to Gwynneth for an explanation. She turned to Brentwood, subtly shutting out her husband. "The last morning she was here, Parker told me they had been closeted together for over an hour.

"Eden looked so miserable that day, like she had learned of a loved one's death. But she wouldn't tell me what was wrong. I thought she was worrying over her relationship with you, Brent. At the time I thought that was a good sign. It wasn't until after she left that I realized something had frightened her. I had no clue as to what, but I felt that the duchess was somehow involved."

"Why didn't you tell me this?" Langley took his wife's elbow to turn her to face him. What he saw in her eyes told him he'd made a bargain with the devil, and had paid with his wife's trust.

"That's it, then! The old harridan said something to frighten her and she fled." Brentwood snapped his fingers decisively.

"It didn't happen that way." Langley turned his head to contradict Brentwood. "A hackney called for her, and she was delivered to a rendezvous with a very expensive carriage, with the crest covered. She went to it quite willingly. There were several servants, in expensive but unidentifiable black livery."

Brentwood stared at him. "You are sure?"

"I talked to the driver of the hackney. He had no reason to lie."

"Then that proves it has something to do with the duchess. She would have the means to take Eden away in such a style. I want to know where, and why, and what she did to her to make her write these brutal letters to you." Brentwood was halfway to the drawing-room door when Langley stopped him.

"Wait up a moment, Roger. I need a word with Gwynneth and then I'll go with you. Possibly I might have more luck getting information from the duchess than you will."

Brentwood halted reluctantly. "I suppose you might. She certainly made her disdain for me known on many occasions. But don't be long."

"She's been gone almost a month. You can give me five minutes. There's something important I need to discuss with my lady wife."

The ominous tone to his voice unsettled Brentwood, who paced the foyer impatiently. He hadn't missed the subtle signs of conflict between husband and wife, and wondered how they related to Eden's disappearance. Had Gwynneth helped her leave? Did the two women suspect Brentwood of somehow planning to force her . . .? No, that was too Gothic. Was Langley responsible? Had he become Eden's lover? Jealousy rippled through him at the thought.

As Brentwood paced and fumed, Langley shut the door and stalked his wife, who had retreated to the window that looked over the garden. "Why didn't you tell me about your suspicions before now?"

"I think you know." She toyed with the golden tassel on the

drape cords. "Was I wrong to link her disappearance with what Lady Morley had to say to you that night in our box at the theater? You didn't seem very surprised by Eden's disappearance, or at all inclined to find out why she would behave in a manner so contrary to what we believed was her character."

"Ah, Gwynneth, forgive me! I should have told you what Alana said, but I didn't think it had any bearing on Eden's flight. Those letters seemed genuine to me. I was so furious at the girl that I was glad to be rid of her."

"But Alana did tell you something about Eden?"

"Yes, but she swore me to secrecy. She meant to expose the girl and cause a scandal unless I sent her away in such a manner that Roger wouldn't suspect Alana had a hand in it."

Gwynneth gasped. "*You* spirited her away? And let me think—"

"No! Absolutely not. I would have helped her find another place, and you would have had plenty of warning. But when I saw she was gone, I was relieved, for it solved the problem of what to tell Roger."

"I don't understand."

"Eden Henderson is married."

Gwynneth stood perfectly still for a long time, her golden eyes searching his brown ones for confirmation of the truth. At last she sighed, "I wondered if she might be."

"Sometimes I think you are a witch. Why?"

"Her insistence that on no account could she marry Brent just didn't jibe with her obvious attraction to him. So she is a runaway wife?"

"Her husband is one of the older generation's most infamous rogues. We've had dealings with him, as I'm sure you'll recall. She is married to Viscount Colville."

"The one who sued you?"

"The same."

"No wonder you didn't want her found here. What a fuss he would have made. Is that why she crept away? To save us embarrassment? But surely she could have explained herself, instead of writing those distressing notes. We could have helped her."

Langley paced away from his wife. In many ways she was still an innocent, and he hoped to shelter her from knowledge that could only distress her. "I expect she was terrified that he might somehow find her through us if she took us in her confidence. He is known for his cruelty. Perhaps she learned of it firsthand on her wedding night. That is when she ran away, you remember."

"Oh!" Gwynneth dropped into a nearby chair. "Poor Eden."

"Yes, and poor Roger."

Tears threatened at the thought of her friends' plight. "Hopeless!"

"Until Colville dies." Langley's expression lightened marginally. "Which shouldn't be too long, actually. He was obviously diseased and decaying from within the last time I met with him over that settlement."

"What are you going to tell Brent?"

"The truth?" Langley looked as if hoping for guidance.

Gwynneth's brow wrinkled. "What will he do then?"

"God only knows. Not just drop it, I suspect."

"Oh, no! He'll pursue the matter."

"That could prove dangerous for him."

"But if he learns the truth from someone else—"

"He may not be as forgiving as my wife." Langley pulled Gwynneth from the chair into his arms. "You do forgive me?"

"Ye-es." The slight hesitation was accompanied by a quiver of her lips.

"You'll never trust me quite as much again." Langley bowed his head against hers, nuzzling the flaxen hair sorrowfully.

"Actually, I think I'll just be a little more persistent in asking for the truth." Smiling tenderly, she offered him her lips in a reassuring kiss, then drew away. "The truth, I think."

"Yes," Langley sighed. "I'll tell him before we pay our visit to the duchess. But you must realize, as must he, that Eden still may be just as bad as I thought her. The fact that she's married to a villain doesn't make her an innocent, incapable of being corrupted. Still, I know he won't accept that until we've eliminated all other possibilities."

Gwynneth nodded agreement. "I think you'll find his instincts are right in this."

Brentwood sat dumbfounded before his mentor. "Married! How do you know?"

Langley hesitated. "I am not at liberty to say who, but an acquaintance recognized her, or rather, her remarkable resemblance to her mother, and deduced her identity."

"Married." Brentwood staggered to a chair. "The one thing I never guessed at! Of all the possibilities, why didn't I think of that?"

"She had an untouched air about her."

"Yet if she ran away on her wedding night, I suppose she must have had the worst sort of initiation into womanhood." Brentwood looked up at his friend as if hoping for a contradiction.

"Knowing her husband, that's not hard to believe." Langley's expression was grim.

"You know her husband? Who is he?"

"Do you remember our discussion of the viscount who sued me because his bride ran away?"

"Colville, wasn't it?" Brent's eyebrows arched in shock. "But that couldn't be. Wasn't his bride sixteen? That would mean she can't be above twenty-two now. Isabella said Eden is twenty-six."

"Either the bride's youth was exaggerated, or Eden is younger than she has pretended to be."

"Which wouldn't be too surprising in a young woman hoping to be employed as a governess." Brentwood jumped up and paced the length of the library, shaking his head. "I can scarce take it in. She sat there quietly and listened while we discussed the situation. Though I do remember her saying something about the runaway being better dead than married to such as he."

Brentwood turned to Langley, fists clenched. "Tell me about Colville. I've heard of him, of course, but never met him."

"He had a reputation for every kind of dissipation and particularly for cruel treatment of young women. My father was no saint himself, but he stopped inviting Colville to house parties because female servants were not safe around him. I am not speaking merely of backstairs fondling, either, but rough treatment. Also, he had survived two wealthy young brides already, by the time he married Eden."

"What could have led her father to marry her to such a man?"

Langley shook his head. "I know very little of her family, but I do know the father was helping to search for the girl, until he died."

Brentwood headed for the door. "Well, I must have some answers, and I know someone who has them."

"Roger!" Brentwood turned at the peremptory tone.

"Remember, nothing that I have told you precludes Eden's having left with a lover, just as she said."

Brentwood shook his head angrily. "I would have to see that with my own eyes. I held her in my arms. I kissed her—I *know* what kind of woman she is. Are you coming with me, or not?"

"Young man, I don't know what you are talking about. Abducting Eden Henderson! It is an absurd insult." The duchess stood with her back to the carved marble fireplace, ramrod stiff and as haughty as she had ever been.

"Actually, Your Grace, we did not think you abducted her. Just that you might be able to shed some light on her sudden disappearance." Lord Langley attempted to calm the duchess's ire.

"Eden Henderson is a wanton. I spotted her as such the day the three of them first arrived here. I didn't want her around my granddaughter. A very bad influence. I am not at all surprised that she ran off with some man."

"Who said she ran off with a man? All I said was that she had left suddenly."

Momentarily discomposed, the duchess stuttered, "S-stands to reason, don't it? Didn't she leave any notes for you, Lord Langley?"

Langley eyed the duchess with dawning comprehension. "By Jove, you were right, Roger. She knows all about it, probably planned it."

"I know nothing about anything. I want you two to leave."

"Not without knowing where Eden Henderson is," Brentwood advanced on the duchess.

She stood her ground, her eyes like flint. "Doesn't it occur to you, Lord Dudley, that if she wanted you to know where she is, she would have told you?"

"It occurs to me that somehow you forced her to leave. I need to know that she is safe. I must tell her that there are those who will help her. You see, we know about her past."

"Her past wantonness, you mean!"

"We know that she is married."

The duchess absorbed this information before abandoning her pretense. "You know about her marriage?"

"Yes, and to whom."

"Then you should know that there is no help you can give her, that won't expose her to danger or sink her deeper in disgrace. If she had remained here, someone else would have remarked her incredible resemblance to her mother, and that would have brought Colville running. What would you have done then, my lords?" The old woman challenged the men.

"You both are well versed in the law as regards women and marriage. She is his property. That loathsome old man could claim her, and there would be nothing you could do for her, short of eloping with her."

"Then I would have eloped with her."

"A selfish approach, as Eden realized herself. That would expose your political friends to scandal and ridicule, not to mention being an immoral act. She is her mother's daughter.

Doing what is right is a concern that weighs with such as her, whether it does with you or not."

Brentwood stood before her, hands clenched in impotent fury. "How do you know he won't find her? Hasn't, already?"

"He hasn't, and won't, if you don't make a fuss and lead him to her."

Langley touched Brentwood gently on his shoulder. "Come, Roger. We've found out what we wanted to know. The duchess is right. Eden wanted us to keep our distance or she never would have written such letters."

"I'm not satisfied with that explanation. You threatened her more than once, Duchess, in my hearing, because you thought Isabella was harmfully influenced by her. I believe after that last escapade you frightened Eden into leaving, intimidated her into writing letters that would burn her bridges with her only friends. Under those circumstances, I can't trust that you have found her a safe haven somewhere."

Brentwood took one step forward. "I must, I *will* know from her own lips that she is safe, and reasonably content."

The old woman threw back her head in arrogant defiance. "Find her if you can!" She moved to ring the bell for her servant. "Simpson will show you out."

"I think not. I haven't mixed much in society since I got back, Your Grace." Brentwood crossed the distance to the fireplace, and leaned one long arm with affected nonchalance along the mantel.

The non sequitur caused the duchess to stay her hand at the bell-pull, a betraying gleam of uneasiness in her eyes.

"I think I will visit all my clubs and old, rakehellish friends. I should be able to dine out for, oh, a week, maybe two, on the exploits of your granddaughter, Miss Isabella Eardley. Amusing little harridan. Ought to titillate the *ton* no end, to learn of some of her escapades—for example, throwing herself on my protection? And her excursion in men's clothing should make fascinating scandal broth, don't you think?"

Chapter Thirteen

The duchess faltered for but a second, then rang the bell vehemently. "You base creature! Claiming to respect women, to seek to better their condition in life, then threatening to use the lowest form of blackmail against an utter and complete innocent to force me to expose another young woman to your unwanted attentions. Get out!"

His conscience quickly informed Brentwood that this savage attack was not entirely unjustified. He would have to convince the duchess of his sincere concern for Eden. "I beg your pardon, Your Grace. You have called my bluff magnificently. Of course I would do no such thing, but I am so worried over the fate of Miss Henderson, it is driving me to distraction."

Langley shot Brentwood a repressive frown before turning to soothe the duchess. "Perhaps you could have Eden write to us, to reassure us that she is well-treated and safe. That would content you, wouldn't it, Roger?"

"No, it damn well wouldn't. Such a letter could be written under duress, just as the ones she wrote to you were." Brentwood's casual posture had been abandoned. His voice betrayed his agony.

The duchess's expression softened ever so slightly. "Those letters were my idea, but she wrote them willingly, Lord Dudley. She hoped to prevent this kind of pursuit when she wrote them. I offer you my personal assurance that Miss Henderson is well-housed and congenially employed. You recall I suggested to her, on our first meeting, that she take a position as a companion?"

Brentwood nodded. "More of an order, actually."

"Well, I had a particular person in mind. I was able to arrange the position, and Eden was most grateful, for it seemed that you had become importunate, Lord Dudley."

Flinching at this reference to the kiss he had stolen the last night he saw her, Brentwood asked, "Did she run away because of me, then?"

"Not entirely. She was beginning to worry about how to deal with you, but more significantly, she thought someone else had recognized her, someone who might well inform her husband."

"Morley! I thought he looked at her strangely."

The duchess nodded her head. "If you knew her husband as well as I do, you would not blame the girl for getting away, and making sure she couldn't be followed. Leave her be, gentlemen."

"I will never be entirely comfortable about her until I can speak to her myself. But I can see that you won't be moved, so I bid you adieu." Brentwood opened the door for himself, and discovered the reason for the butler's tardiness: he was downstairs ushering in Miss Isabella Eardley and another woman, an attractive red-haired woman of about thirty.

"Oh, Mr. Brentwood, have you come to see me? And Lord Langley too! Let me introduce you to Mary Fenton, my dear companion. Grandmama took your advice, you see, and now we are all quite·content."

Before Brentwood could properly acknowledge the introduction, Isabella was tugging on his arm, trying to lead him back into the drawing room. "Don't go now. You've come from the Langleys, I see, so you know. Isn't it shocking how Eden just simply disappeared. So unlike her."

"Very!" Brentwood's pinched features as he glared at her grandmother, and the old woman's steely demeanor did not go unnoticed by her granddaughter.

"Isabella! Lord Langley and Lord Dudley were just leaving, and you must needs go straight up and change clothes, for you are promised for a drive in the park."

Surprisingly docile, Isabella responded, "Yes, Grand-mama." She gave the two men a pretty curtsy, and as she arose, her large blue eyes met Brentwood's green ones. "Perhaps another time, Mr. Brentwood?"

"Of course." In tribute to her very grown-up attire and behavior, Brentwood took her hand and bowed over it before following Langley out the door.

"She is certainly a formidable old dragon. Quite makes you alarmed to think what might happen if women were able to wield power directly." Langley sank back into the squabs of his town carriage as his friend folded his long legs in beside him.

"Yes. She stood her ground and won the day, didn't she. Puts me in mind of Boadicea."

Langley's lips curved. "I must say an encounter with the dowager Duchess of Carminster gives one a certain insight into that legendary queen's character."

"Yes, and also the Amazons. Until today I've never met a woman I could imagine would actually cut off a breast to accommodate her shield." Brentwood's tone was admiring, almost jocular.

Langley stared at his young friend. "You're surprisingly cheerful for a man who was just bested in combat."

Brentwood nodded. "That's true. We know very little more about Eden's fate than we did before we called on the duchess. But I expect to know a great deal more, very soon."

Langley stirred uneasily. "What are you up to, Roger? Nothing to do with that villainous threat you made, I hope. For I must tell you I couldn't countenance—"

"Of course not. Nor would I have done such a thing, as she well knew. It was a desperate but empty threat."

"Then what are you going to do?"

"Absolutely nothing. All I have to do is wait."

"Wait?"

"Yes, await the visit of a certain precocious bundle of mischievous energy known as Isabella Eardley."

"Ah, that's the way of it. You think she knows something?"

"If she doesn't, she'll find out. A very resourceful female, is Isabella Eardley."

"You have a high regard for her! Perhaps you'll end up marrying that chit yet."

"Not a chance. I admire Isabella, but I don't desire her. Nor does she feel the least inclination of a *tendre* toward me. No, I will marry Eden Henderson."

"There is no such person, unfortunately."

Brentwood glared at him. "What do you mean?"

"There is only Joanna, Lady Colville, runaway wife."

"Whose husband has one foot in the grave. And I may just see about giving the old rogue a push."

Langley eyed the younger man with alarm. He knew too well that Roger's capacity for rash action should not be underestimated.

Brentwood thought he might have to cool his heels for several days before Isabella managed to get away to talk with him. But he had reckoned without the young woman's resourcefulness and determination. She presented herself, very properly chaperoned by her attractive companion, at 11:00 the next morning.

To outward appearances she was calling on Lady Langley. After greeting her politely, Isabella turned sparkling eyes on Brentwood, who was sitting with Gwynneth in the drawing room. "Oh, and here is Mr. Brentwood, Lord Dudley, whom you met yesterday, Mary. Have you come to call on Lady Langley, or are you staying here, Mr. Brentwood?" She batted innocent blue eyes at him.

"I'm staying here for a few days." Brentwood wondered if the minx would discuss Eden in front of her chaperone, who appeared surprised to see him. Very likely she had been warned by the duchess to keep her charge away from him.

"I am so glad you are here. Would you look at my leader's right foreleg?" He was favoring it, I am sure. My coachman says he was not, but I think he's been in the gin already this morning." Isabella fairly danced to the door. "Oh, don't get up, Mary. You were going to show Lady Langley that poem you hoped her husband might print in *The Legacy.*"

Torn between duty and literary aspirations, the attractive young companion chose ambition, and turned eagerly to Gwynneth, fumbling in her reticule for a sheet of paper.

Brentwood willingly followed Isabella out of the drawing room. "Where can we talk?" she asked, her eyes darting along the foyer.

Brentwood suggested they go into the library, knowing that Langley was there, reading his mail.

She went willingly. "Good morning, Lord Langley. I was sorry not to be able to talk with you yesterday. I have been wondering if either of you had heard from Eden?"

Isabella seated herself and turned her big blue eyes expectantly up to Brentwood. "Did you come to visit to tell us where she has gotten to?"

Disappointed, Brentwood sat beside her. "No, I came to try to convince your grandmother to tell me where she is."

"Grandmother!"

"Yes, I have reason to think she arranged for Eden to leave." Brentwood was not going to confide the entire tale to Isabella if she did not know it. It was pointless to distress her unnecessarily, and also he could not trust so young a child not to reveal such a juicy bit of gossip.

Isabella looked thoughtful. "Why would she do such a thing?"

Carefully excising any mention that Eden was anyone other than she purported to be, Brentwood explained about her grandmother's visit, followed by Eden's sudden, unannounced departure. He told her about the hackney being met by a fine coach, which carried Eden off, escorted by well-dressed footmen and a maid. Her eyes grew ever wider as his narration progressed.

"I wonder what the maid looked like?"

Langley entered the conversation. "All the hackney driver

could tell us was that the servants were dressed in black, as if for mourning."

"My grandmother sent her maid Maigret to Wales to visit her sick sister the day before I knew that Eden had left." Isabella looked from one man to the other. "I was surprised to see her send 'round the heavy traveling coach escorted by footmen and all, just for her maid. My grandmother is not given to excessive coddling of servants. And they were dressed as for mourning, which I thought most peculiar at the time. Now it makes sense."

"Wales! Where in Wales?" Brentwood leaned forward eagerly.

"I don't know. Didn't ask. Maigret won't tell me, of course, she's Grandmama's oldest and most trusted servant, and besides, she'd fear being turned off. But my maid might have heard something below stairs. I shall look into it."

She stood abruptly. "I shall find out the truth," she said with a determined glint in her vivid blue eyes. "My grandmother means well, but she can be quite unfair and tyrannical. She shan't get away with exiling poor Eden!"

"My companion and I will be going driving with Wilfred Marshall tomorrow. Perhaps you could accidentally meet us in the park tomorrow afternoon at the fashionable hour, Mr. Brentwood?"

Brentwood had stood when she did. He bent over her hand with a smile. "My pleasure, Miss Eardley." He walked her to the door, and watched as she rejoined the ladies. Then he turned, grinning at his observer. "Well, Stu, like to make a wager on the young Boadicea against the old one?"

Langley laughed. "I won't give you long odds. There is definitely a similarity of character between Isabella and her grandmother."

Isabella had very little luck with her maid, Jane, who was by now quite wary of involving herself in her mistress's concerns. The dowager duchess had very nearly discharged her after the incident with the men's clothing. Another mistake and she was out. "I don't know, miss, I'm sure, and that Maigret is as close as a clam. She don't talk about that trip at all."

"And the others?"

Jane sniffed. "Don't associate with grooms 'n such, miss,"

Isabella put her hand on her hip, vexed. "You are more snobbish than a titled lady, Jane."

Her strategy would have to be revised. There was no point in talking to the coachman, for the simple reason that he, like Maigret, was a loyal old servant who would not discuss the matter with her. But Isabella knew that one of the two men who had accompanied them, an ex-soldier by the name of Joshua, was a loquacious man. He was usually employed outside, as a groom, but when the duchess was entertaining he was occasionally pressed into service inside, as he had been a captain's batman and knew some of the domestic arts, too.

She had once spent a very enlightening afternoon with him while he cleaned the silver for a dinner party. He had told her all kinds of things about the war which she would never have heard anywhere else. Her grandmother would have been scandalized by the gruesome details conveyed to her delicately raised granddaughter, and horrified at the eagerness with which the girl absorbed them.

Isabella approached Joshua the next day by deciding to go riding at the exact time when the head groom had his afternoon tea, liberally laced with gin. This was after she had solemnly informed her companion that she had the headache and could not go on the planned drive in the park with Wilfred Marshall.

In the head groom's absence she requested that Joshua accompany her. As she expected, he was delighted with this assignment.

As they clattered through the busy London streets she called out to him, "Was it pretty in Wales?"

"Eh, miss?"

"Wales. When you went to Wales earlier this month, with Maigret. What is it like?"

"Oh, Miss Eardley, if it's pretty pitchures yer after, that is a place for them. Lovely for the eyes, hard on the horses, all them hills."

"Did you get to see Cardiff? I've heard there's a marvelous castle there."

"No, miss, we went more to the north, like. We saw Llangollen, though. That's an old town, it is. Narrow streets, like."

"What were the roads like? Was it terribly rough?"

"The roads was good as long as we was on the mail road. We made good time through St. Albans, Coventry, Wolverhampton. It begun to git a mite rough after that. Jiggled us a good bit till Oswestry, then they really got bad. Them Welsh roads are little mor'n cart tracks. The worst was the last few miles, getting from Colin Molyneux to Humphrey Manor. Had to hitch six of them Welsh ponies to the carriage, 'n still I never thought we'd make it."

This detailed account of the roads between London and Wales at any other time would have bored Isabella to tears. But she listened intently, aware that she was getting a virtual itinerary of their trip.

"Is that where Maigret's sister lives, Humphrey Manor?"

Joshua looked puzzled. "Maigret's sister?"

"That's what the trip was for, wasn't it, to take her to visit her sick sister?"

"Oh! Oh, yes, miss, that be right. Her sister. Right sick, she was." Joshua's sheepish look told of suddenly remembered instructions to be silent about the journey.

Hiding her smile, Isabella changed the subject. Now she knew exactly what route Eden had taken and her destination.

Brentwood returned to the Langleys' feeling extremely frustrated. He had arrived at Hyde Park at the fashionable hour hoping to meet Isabella Eardley. But she was nowhere in sight, and he found himself accosted by Lady Morley. She was with her husband in their curricle. Distracted by his search for Isabella, he gave her disjointed answers to her questions, only realizing after the words were out of his mouth that he had agreed to dine with them on the morrow.

He had managed to extract himself from that conversation, and greet his many acquaintances without becoming embroiled in lengthy conversations, but by the time the fashionable hour had ended, he had still not been able to locate Isabella.

"Not there?" One look at Brentwood's face and Langley reached for the brandy decanter.

Taking the proferred libation, Brentwood scowled. "No. The entire remainder of the beau monde was, but no Isabella. I wonder if that old dragon caught her trying to get information?"

As the two men discussed what their next move might be, Parker interrupted them. "Your pardon, my lord, but this arrived for Mr. Brentwood." He held out a small, sealed paper wafer.

"How did this come?"

"A street urchin, sir."

Brentwood broke the seal. The note was succinct. "Humphrey Manor, near Colin Molyneux, Wales," It was signed with an elaborate, ornate capital "I."

"She's done it!"

Langley took the paper that Brentwood triumphantly waved in front of him. "Or thinks she has. Surely you're not going to tear off to Wales on no more information than this."

Brentwood lifted expressive eyebrows. "No, you're absolutely right. Perhaps I'll look up old Colville first."

Chapter Fourteen

"Exactly what do you have in mind, Roger?" Langley was almost literally holding his breath.

"I want to have a look at this sixty-year-old man who married a child and frightened her so badly that she has hidden herself from him for five years."

"Have you considered the consequences?"

"That I might be unable to restrain the impulse to choke the life out of him?" Brentwood's lips curved upward but his eyes glittered dangerously. "It will be a great temptation, but I will resist. I mean to be Eden's husband, which implies that I must avoid becoming gallows bait. However, if he should prove to be fit to meet me . . ."

Langley shook his head. "You won't murder him, you know, no matter how tempted you may be, and I doubt he has ever had the courage to meet a man in a duel. No, the consequence I fear is that you will somehow lead him to her. Your interest in her will draw his attention to us. He wouldn't have to investigate very long to learn that she has been here."

"Then I'd best just go to Eden."

Langley looked worried. "What if Miss Eardley decides to discuss this situation with others? The child has no reason to understand the vital need for secrecy. It may seem merely interesting scandal broth to her. The old rogue might get wind of Eden that way."

Brentwood scowled darkly and fell silent for several long minutes. At last he rose and stretched. "I had better let the grooms know that I will be leaving early tomorrow."

Langley watched him from the room, frustrated and alarmed by the younger man's lack of communicativeness.

As for Brentwood, he spent a nearly sleepless night, as he had each night since learning of Eden's marriage. He found that each time he closed his eyes, visions of what she might have suffered at the hands of her beast of a husband tortured him. This night an added anxiety kept Morpheus at bay. He had, in fact, put Eden in danger.

He had introduced her to Sir Alfred Morley, who probably knew who she was. He had encouraged Isabella Eardley to find out her whereabouts. Unlikely though it was, he feared that a careless word by either of them, heard by a person who could put the two incidents together, might indeed lead Colville to Eden.

He broke out in a cold sweat at the very thought. Before the dawn had quite lightened the sky he left his room and made his way to the dowager Duchess of Carminster's spacious mansion. He was waiting for her when the dowager descended for breakfast. One look at his face and she motioned him into her drawing room.

"I have made a mistake; now you must help me, or rather Eden, once more."

The duchess listened without speaking while he told of his enlisting Isabella. "She knows nothing of the marriage or the scandal. Now I am worried that a careless word might—"

"Quite!" The old woman's mouth was bracketed by lines of fury. "Well, I shall have to reveal the facts to her, much as I dislike doing so. She will keep the secret, for she would never knowingly hurt Eden. And I suppose you are still intent on going to see her?"

"Yes. I am sorry, Your Grace, but I must. For all the reasons I've already stated, plus, she must be warned."

"I think it is you who must needs be warned. Her husband is no mere rake or rogue. He is a devil incarnate. A cold-blooded murderer, a torturer of the helpless. He is clever, knows the law, uses it, and works his own will within it, but he is not restrained by legality. He will hire the worst dregs of humanity to achieve his aim." The duchess's voice quivered with deep, profound emotion.

Brentwood stared at her. "You know something more of him than mere society gossip."

"His first wife was my young cousin Melissa. He was nearly thirty, she was sixteen and had a plump fortune. He charmed her, married her, drained her fortune to the dregs, and then killed her."

This explains the duchess's willingness to aid Eden, Brentwood realized. "Killed her! Yet he wasn't brought to justice."

"I wasn't positive until the second wife died in much the same way. I believe that they were both poisoned. He, of course, was miles away from them both at the time of their deaths. My late husband made many and careful inquiries, hoping to find something, some way to bring him to justice.

"Though what we learned only convinced us of his guilt, we never could prove anything. He is ruthless, and he is clever. Do not underestimate him because he is old and sick, young man."

"You say he is sick. What is his illness?"

The dowager made a dismissive gesture. "Any one of a dozen illnesses that can be acquired by debauchery and over-indulgence. I don't know. But understand that until the man is dead and in his grave he is still dangerous."

"I believe you. I won't take him lightly. As it happens, I have some property in Wales, so I have a legitimate reason to travel there. I will be careful."

The duchess only shook her head. Suddenly she looked very old and tired. "Determined as ever. Well, then, God go with you."

Alana Morley was in a fine rage. She had thought Brentwood seemed vague when she spoke to him in the park, inviting him for dinner. So she sent a handwritten invitation, to remind him. And still he hadn't come.

As she remembered his manner, she decided that what she had first interpreted as distraction was actually coldness. And why should he be cold to her? Why should he be so lacking in *politesse* as to neither reply to her invitation nor attend the dinner? It could only be because Langley had not kept his word to her! Langley had told Brentwood of her threat to expose his flirt's whereabouts to her husband.

"Now, pet, I'm sure he didn't. Lord Langley is a man of honor. He'll keep his word."

"Most men don't consider it dishonorable to lie to or cheat a woman," Alana spit out bitterly. "Especially men who prate about women's rights."

"Well, don't do anything hasty, my dear."

"You must help me."

"Anything, my angel." Sir Alfred was genuinely interested in pacifying his wife. If she stopped cooperating with him and scandalized his Aunt Agatha, the fortune he hoped to inherit would be whistled down the wind.

"Call on the Langleys tomorrow. Try to find out why he didn't come to our dinner. I am so angry I am afraid I would scratch Langley's eyes out, and besides, calling on Lady Langley is a very shabby pretense, as she knows quite well that I despise her."

The next day Sir Alfred gloomily reported that Mr. Brentwood had left for his home in Hertfordshire. "Langley didn't know about the dinner invitation. Apologized for him, said the lad had been distracted lately. So I took a chance and asked after his governess. He very frostily told me she had taken a position elsewhere."

"I knew it! He's told Brentwood, who's taken her under his protection." Alana strode back and forth in her dressing room, eyes narrowed in fury.

"Pet, I really do not wish you to pursue this matter. If we cause Langley trouble, Aunt Agatha—"

"No, of course not." Alana stopped her peregrinations abruptly. "But there is nothing to prevent an anonymous letter from alerting the forlorn husband to the probable whereabouts of his bride, is there?"

Sir Alfred chewed on his thumbnail, worried about the outcome of his wife's revenge, but knowing she wouldn't be denied.

Eden stood on her favorite bluff, overlooking the picturesque village of Colin Molyneux, with Mount Snowden soaring in the distance. Her spirits were oppressed, and the magnificent view was not sufficient to lift them. Lady Humphrey's daughters had arrived a week ago, full of alarm at the new companion who was threatening to steal their inheritance by making herself indispensable to their mother. They had accused her of plotting behind their backs, and had exerted pressure on their mother to dismiss her.

Their efforts had failed, and they were planning to leave, but they had uttered dark threats of investigating her background to see just what kind of adventuress their mother had engaged. Eden knew the duchess would not fail her, but still, the thought of those two asking questions around the *ton* was sufficient to alarm her.

The worst of it was that their bickering, their insinuations, their pressure, had had terrible consequences for Lady Humphrey. She had visibly deteriorated during their visit, and just yesterday had suffered an attack which for a while looked as if it would carry her off. Her physician had insisted that they leave and give their mother peace and quiet.

Eden sighed deeply. She had become fond of the crusty old lady during her time with her. She had been kept very busy, had worked very hard for her salary, but had been rewarded for it by the satisfaction of seeing not only the house and grounds, but their mistress, improve. Lady Humphrey had begun to exercise leaning on Eden's arm, and to eat better while listening to Eden read the gossip from the newspapers. She had gained weight and color, and her temperament had improved. Now Eden greatly feared the setback would be permanent.

"It is little less than murder," she complained loudly to the wind.

"That's true. I almost pined away and died when you disappeared."

Eden whirled at the unexpected, but dearly familiar, deep voice. "Brent! What?" She stepped backward and he abruptly caught her by both elbows.

"Come away from there. The duchess already pretends to believe you ran away to free yourself from my unwanted attentions. Topple over that cliff and she'll have me up on murder charges."

"The duchess told you where I am?" Eden pulled herself free of his hands, suppressing firmly the desire to step forward into his arms instead.

"No. She stood buff, the old dragon. 'Twas Isabella who smoked you out."

"How . . . ? Oh, never mind." Eden began walking away from him, back along the little path that led through a small wood toward the manor. "You shouldn't have come; you must go away."

"Not very friendly, I must say. And after I've come half the length of Britain to visit you."

"What gall! I don't want you to visit me! I should think the notes I left you would have convinced you of that!"

"You didn't leave me a note, Eden." Brentwood caught her elbow, summarily ending her flight and turning her toward him. "You left the Langleys two notes, rather nasty notes, too. But not a word for me."

"I meant for you to read them and . . . and leave me alone!"

"Ah! But, Eden, if my attentions were so unwanted, all you had to do was say so. You didn't have to lie, or run away." His lifted eyebrows challenged her. "And if you really didn't want to marry, you didn't have to ask some other man to carry you off! I would gladly have done it!"

Eden retorted hotly, "That's not true! You are ready to marry, just hanging out for a wife, whether you know it or not!"

"So you ran away with a lover."

She hung her head and nodded.

"I see. And does Lady Humphrey allow him to visit you there? Perhaps she tucks the two of you in at night?"

"Don't be asinine."

"Oh, then he creeps up the back stairs at night after the household is asleep?"

"Stop it!" Eden put her hands to her ears. "That's disgusting!

"Not half so disgusting as those lying letters you left the Langleys. 'Irksome children' indeed. That hurt and offended them, quite above and beyond the pain of thinking they had misjudged your character."

Tears shimmered in Eden's eyes. "I . . . I didn't want them to search for me."

"I understand that, but I confess it surprises me that you could even think up such a cruel, crude method of achieving that aim."

"Well, now you know what a bad person I am. Why come so far just to tax me with it?" She tried to walk away again. Again he stopped her.

"Will you confide in me? Tell me the truth?"

"No."

"Well, at least you're being that truthful!" He smiled wryly. "I'll save you some trouble and the pain of additional prevarication. I know about your marriage."

Eden's normally golden complexion paled. "You do? How?"

"An informant, I don't know who, perhaps Sir Alfred Morley, told Langley. The duchess confirmed it when confronted. She also told me enough of Colville's character to make your fear understandable."

Eden searched his face in obvious puzzlement. "Then why are you here?"

"To be sure you are safe and well. Cold-hearted creature that you are, apparently it doesn't occur to you that Gwynneth, Stuart, Isabella, and I all have been worried sick about you. Those letters seemed clearly to have been written under some sort of compulsion."

She shook her head. "The duchess suggested the wording. I was so terrified, so eager to get away, I did as she suggested. The only compulsion I was under was to get safely from London before Sir Alfred informed Colville of my whereabouts and exposed the Langleys to public embarrassment or worse."

"Eden, did it not occur to you that they might have helped you? That I might have helped you?"

"What could they do that the duchess couldn't? And better, quicker? Besides, helping me would put them in danger. As for you . . ."

"Yes?"

"The only help you could offer me would have damned us both."

The green eyes darkened as he reached for her. "Ah, Eden, are you really so puritanical?"

She struggled against him, but feebly, for in his arms was just where she wanted to be. "I am a married woman. Yes, I honor that bond, though I cannot honor my husband."

"Did you marry him willingly?"

Eden hesitated, then shook her head vehemently.

"I thought not. So your bond with him is of a purely legalistic nature, not sanctified at all, is it?"

"What . . . what are you getting at, Brent?" She lifted her head, knowing she shouldn't, knowing it exposed her to his mesmerizing eyes, his tempting lips.

"I am saying that it is not a valid marriage. You could get an annulment. And when you do, I am saying that I will make you my wife, the wife of my heart, and keep you safe from that monster."

She searched his face for a long moment before relaxing the tension that held her body a fraction from his. He closed the distance instantly and pressed her lips in a searingly tender kiss.

She had never known such comfort, such a sense of well-being as that which raced through her body as she stood pressed in his embrace. A little moan escaped her lips as he pulled away for a moment to whisper, "My wife, my love," before beginning a deeper, more intimate kiss.

It was Brentwood who came to his senses first. Slowly, regretfully he ended their passionate embrace. "My darling," he whispered. "I must stop now, or I cannot be responsible . . ." He looked about him at their surroundings, then started to draw her to a cluster of trees.

Eden resisted the tug of his hands. Like one coming out of a trance she raised shaking hands to her face. "What am I about? This cannot be!"

"Yes, it can. Come, let us sit here and argue a bit." He smiled tenderly at her; she had no doubt how he meant to win the argument.

"You don't understand what kind of monster we are dealing with."

"I have some idea. The duchess suspects him of murdering two previous wives. But you are not alone anymore. I will protect you from him."

"And how will you protect your friend Langley? Think of the harm the scandal will do his political plans when it is learned that I was his governess, however briefly. And it will be learned, you know. Colville will ferret it out and make it public."

"Be damned to politics. My concern is you."

He had taken her in his arms again. This time she struggled furiously. "How selfish you are! You will risk my life, yours, endanger the cause of desperately needed reforms—all to achieve your selfish desires."

"And yours!" But Brentwood released her, frowning. These were not trivial objections. "Very well, let me ponder how to go about matters. But do not think you will get away with refusing me. I love you and I believe you love me. I don't intend to abandon you."

Baffled as to how to deal with him, Eden began walking again, almost running up the little path to the house. "I don't need or want your help! I just want to be left alone. Go back to London, Brent." She had gained the grounds; two gardeners worked within shouting distance, clearing away the over-growth of weeds from the long-neglected park.

"I won't do it! Stay here or I'll come to the house with you."

"No, you'll cost me my employment."

"Good, then you'll have to go with me."

"I won't! Go away."

The gardeners had taken note of them. They straightened up, and Brentwood could see them watching curiously.

"Do you walk every afternoon?"

"No," Eden lied. "I rarely can get away."

"Then I shall call on Lady Humphrey tomorrow. By then I shall have decided what to do."

"No! I . . . I'll meet you. Where I met you today."

Brentwood looked at her haunted face and felt a sudden un-ease. "You won't do anything drastic?"

The brown eyes didn't quite meet his. "What do you mean?"

"No throwing yourself over the cliff?"

She gasped. " 'Tis a mortal sin."

"No running away from me again?"

"I've no one to help me run this time." She looked away.

It wasn't exactly a promise to stay. He lifted her chin, forc-ing her to look at him. "Eden, will you meet me tomorrow to talk once more? As God is your witness?"

She sighed. He could feel her give in. "Yes, Brent, I will meet you once more, to explain things more fully. But you must promise me to listen and to heed what I have to say."

"That sounds ominous." But he smiled. He obviously was confident that he could carry the day in any argument with her. And Eden wasn't sure but what he was right.

Chapter Fifteen

Eden parted from Brent with her thoughts in a turmoil. She had to convince him to go back to Varnham and forget her. But how? If she met him as she had promised, she feared her attraction to him would win out over her good sense. She struggled through the usual evening activities with Lady Humphrey, then went to her chamber to ponder her predicament. She really couldn't run from him. She had very little money and nowhere at all to go.

She knew that her words had failed to convey to him the terror she felt. She wondered if she could speak to him of her past, so painful was it to her. Yet surely if he knew all that had happened to her, if he truly understood the kind of man they had to deal with in Colville, he would understand her fears and respect her wishes.

Could she bring herself to describe what had happened to her to another human being? She feared she would break down. He would comfort her, of course. Even here in her room she felt herself yearning for that comfort, so she knew if she allowed it, she would be lost.

There was one possible solution; Eden was not an eloquent writer, but if she explained herself in writing, she would not see the looks of pity, distress, anger, that must appear on Brentwood's expressive face as her story was revealed. She would then be less vulnerable to his well-intentioned but dangerous determination to meddle in her affairs.

Lighting a branch of candles, she made her way downstairs to Lady Humphrey's library, where she took out a generous supply of paper, prepared several pens, and began to write. *I will make my escape while he is reading,* she thought. *By the time he is finished, he'll know it is pointless to pursue me further.*

The next day at 2:00, she strode onto the bluff to find Brentwood there before her. "A magnificent view, is it not?" he asked as she came to stand beside him. He gestured widely over the valley, where the slate rooftops of the village shone in the hot August sun.

Eden nodded. "At first I essayed painting it. Again and again I tried my hand, but God is the supreme artist, and He kept changing his masterpiece here, by the hour, with every fluctuation of wind, every variation of sun and cloud. There is no way a mere human artist could do justice to His creation. Now I just come to enjoy the ever-changing play of light and shadow over the ranks of hills, the trees, the village rooftops below."

Brentwood pointed to the west. "I have property not far from here. There is a view from the terrace of the manor house that is almost this beautiful. I am thinking of enclosing the entire wall of the drawing room that faces onto it in glass, so that I can sit there in comfort and watch the storms chase across the countryside."

Eden's eyes widened. "It sounds lovely."

"Come there with me."

She turned away slightly and drew in a deep composing breath before facing him and thrusting into his hands the thick packet she had composed last night. "Here. Read this. Read it carefully, and then you will know my answer."

He took the sheaf of papers from her. "I already know that you mean to refuse. At least while Colville lives. I will read this, of course, but as I read I want you to consider something also. I spent several years traveling. I know where we can go and disappear into utter obscurity. We can live together as husband and wife, which before God we will be, until we can marry legally."

"And our children?"

"Children!" Brentwood thrust a hand through his straight brown hair, sifting it with agitated fingers. "I hadn't thought . . . but I would provide for them, of course. If you doubt me, we can draw up a contract—"

"Yet they would be bastards. If we have a son, he wouldn't be legitimate; therefore, he couldn't inherit your title. How might he feel, to see it go, perhaps, to a younger brother born to us after we are finally able to wed?"

"Since I hope titles will be recognized as the anachronisms they are and be obsolete by the time my children are grown, that issue may not arise."

"Langley says it may take two or three more generations before that can come to pass." She put her hands on her hips, indignation shading her voice. "You really haven't changed, have you? Marriage is nothing to you—you will marry if it is expedient, or brush it aside as of no matter. You have no concept of morality, of commitment."

"You're wrong. Entirely wrong. I have come to see the importance of commitment and monogamy. But we would be married in the eyes of God."

"Would we?" She wanted to be convinced, but she wasn't. Nor did he entirely convince himself, she guessed from his expression.

He blew out his breath on a long, despairing sigh. "I suppose not, but—"

Eden interrupted him, remembering that she had meant to avoid discussion with him. "If you will read what I have written, you will see how little good this argument can do us."

Perplexed, Brentwood opened the folded packet and began reading. Soon absorbed in its grim contents, he did not notice as Eden gradually faded back away from him before turning and silently hurrying toward the manor house.

Dear Brentwood:
    Part of what I have to tell you could be fatal to my Aunt Alicia, my mother's sister, if it is ever revealed. Please be sure to destroy this after you have read it.

You had already guessed that my father was just such a domestic tyrant as you depicted so feelingly in your famous essay. My earliest memories are of him bullying and beating my mother and myself. When I was six she took me with her to Broadhurst, my grandfather's estate in Glouster. Here we found sanctuary while she tried to obtain a legal separation, but my father successfully fought it in the courts. Grandfather protected us in the only way he could, which was by buying my father off. He was a vastly wealthy man, and my father's pockets were chronically to let.

When I was twelve, Grandfather died. Mother once again tried to obtain a legal separation from Father, but again the decision was against her. She was ordered to return to her husband's bed and board. It took two years before she had exhausted all legal efforts. Father gave her permission to live with her sister, as long as he continued to draw a generous allowance. But he insisted that I must live with him, as was his legal right.

Mother wouldn't abandon me to him, so he moved in with us at Broadhurst, having long since lost all of his own property in deep play. I cringe inwardly as I think of the reign of terror she then endured. Two long years of conflict, turmoil, and increasing violence made severe inroads on her health.

Father particularly disliked the comfort which my mother drew from her music, and had given orders for her to cease playing. He returned from a weeklong gambling and drinking binge one day to find us in the music room. She was playing her last musical composition for me, the one you heard me playing in the Langley's music room.

Brentwood looked up, hearing again in his mind the magnificent piece her mother had written. He was stunned to think that such talent had gone unrecognized. With an angry oath he returned to Eden's narrative.

Father was drunk and furious at being defied. He took a music stand and began beating her with it. When I tried to intervene he threw me out of the room and locked the door. I shall never forget her screams. When at last he left the room, there were no more screams. The servants and I carried her unconscious upstairs to her room. He refused to allow us to send for the doctor.

She did not die of the beating. She made a recovery of sorts, though she never walked but a few feet again, and was always in pain. She was so weakened that when winter came on she took an inflammation of the lungs, which led to a pneumonia.

The day before she died, the issue of *The Legacy* arrived with your essay in it. As soon as I saw it, I rushed in and read it aloud to her. Mother was so thrilled by your words. She felt that the very fact that women's plight was being discussed was a hopeful sign. Your "Manifesto" was a comfort to her on the last day of her life, which is one reason I have saved it for all of these years.

Just prior to her death Mother had formed a plan to spirit me away, for she had learned my father was about to contract a marriage for me. I was sixteen. In essence, he sold me to Colville, for the two men had agreed to share the fortune which I had inherited from my grandfather.

I was terrified of this vicious old man, who, when visiting my father, had never lost a chance to catch me in a corner and pinch me or force a brutal kiss on me. When I complained of it, Father would only laugh.

Mother swore that I would never be Colville's bride. Her sister and a faithful servant were to assist her in secretly transporting me to a school in Northumberland run by a dear friend of Aunt Alicia's, a woman who had herself suffered at the hands of a cruel and greedy husband.

But I refused to leave her while she was so ill. My father was from home when she died. He returned while she was being laid out. He came accompanied by my proposed bridegroom. I was nearly overcome with grief, yet I was informed that I would wed Colville, and instantly.

I refused to marry him.

Colville was not like my father, whose violence was triggered by anger, usually when drunk. Rather, he was soberly, calmly vicious. When I informed them that I was not going to marry him, he slapped me several times. Anger at my father, or grief, made me brave. I still defied him.

Colville then sent my father from the room. He proceeded to describe, in graphic detail, the unspeakable ways in which he had, as he put it, "persuaded" his previous two young wives to obey him. He shook his head in mock sorrow as he informed me how they were so pathetically fragile that they nearly died. He gave me to understand that their health was so compromised that they could not bear the heir he wanted; hence he had poisoned them both.

He allowed that I was of stronger stock, though I looked a bit more stubborn, too. I shall never forget the look on his face as he told me, "Still, a wife can usually be brought to do her husband's bidding." Then he crossed the room to where I sat terrified, grabbed my hand, and calmly began sticking pins into the quicks of my fingers.

No amount of struggling, no amount of screaming would stop him; he seemed to be enjoying himself thoroughly.

As he read these words Brentwood groaned out loud. He looked around for Eden, wanting to take her in his arms, but she was nowhere around. He paced up and down the cliff edge for several moments before he could bear to continue reading.

I did not last long under this torture; I am not very brave in the face of physical pain. He wanted more from me than just my assent to the marriage. My grandfather's will gave me the right to appoint one of the trustees for the substantial fortune which he had left me. At that time my appointee was my Aunt Alicia's husband. Once I married, my husband could appoint one trustee, and these two would agree upon the third. Until I married, Grandfather's solicitors in London joined with my uncle in administering the estate.

Part of Colville's purpose in torturing me was to get me to agree to replace my uncle with his choice of trustees. Then he could control all three, and thus my fortune. He wanted that little detail firmly resolved before he "consented" to marry me. I told him my uncle would never permit him to get away with his scheme. He coolly said, "Then he will have to be killed, won't he?"

Of course, I signed what he asked me to; I would have signed anything at that point.

Brentwood shook his head in amazement at her cool, dispassionate prose as she described her horrifying ordeal. She made no attempt to dramatize the events, but her account was all the more powerful for the bare but forceful retelling of the facts.

They had come with a priest, a drunken bosom beau of theirs, but a legally ordained priest—Colville would never neglect a legality like that—and a special license. We were married while my mother still lay unburied, my fingers still bloody from his pins.

They sent me upstairs with a servant, with orders to prepare myself for my wedding night. The three of them set about celebrating with brandy.

The servant was my mother's faithful Peggy, the one who had been involved in planning my escape. She immediately disguised me as a servant, in accordance with my mother's plan, and fled with me down the back stairs.

Incidentally, I left in such terror-filled haste that there was no thought of such an act of defiance as pinning your essay to the pillow. Colville made that up after the fact, to extract money from Lord Langley.

I had to leave my dear mother unburied, but I knew she would not want me to stay in that monster's power. We made our way to my aunt, who provided money and transportation to take us to a tiny village in Dorset. She did not tell my uncle, who, though he despised my father, still upheld a father's right to control his wife and children.

From sixteen until nineteen I first studied with, and then worked for, Kathryn Robinson, my aunt's friend, at her school near Alnwick. In addition to the various stratagems, which I won't bore you with, by which we covered my trail, I added five years to my age, and took the name by which you know me. When Kitty died and the school was closed, I felt myself very fortunate to find a position with Isabella's family.

So she is younger than twenty-six! Brentwood hastily calculated Eden's age. *She must be only twenty-one or twenty-two now.* She seemed so much more mature than that.

My aunt and I rarely communicated, and then in code, for Colville naturally suspected I had gone to my relatives. My uncle could quite honestly deny knowing my whereabouts. He refused to surrender his post as trustee to Colville's appointee. He was fighting Father and Colville in the courts when he was killed in a mysterious accident. Colville had made good on his threats. My uncle was a decent, upright man, though stern. He was sorely missed by his wife and children.

I have not the words to tell you how painful it is to realize that I was the cause of his demise.

How she has suffered, Brentwood thought. *Not just fear, but
guilt, too. Such a burden for so young a girl to bear!*

My uncle's death weighs heavily on my conscience.
My poor aunt lives in continual terror that Colville may
exact vengeance on herself or one of her children. When
she did not, after my uncle's death, reveal my whereabouts, he threatened to kill them one by one until she
did. Where she found the courage to persist, I don't
know, but somehow she managed to convince him that
she did not know where I was. She pretended to believe
I was dead. If I reappear, she is very likely to know his
cruel revenge. Colville is not the sort to let such defiance
go unpunished.

As for my inheritance, I assume that Colville has long
since spent it; with the death of my dear uncle there
were none to oppose him and my father, who expected
to share my inheritance with Colville once it was secured. I have often wondered about my father's sudden
death of a heart attack. Did Colville decide he wanted it
all, and have Father killed? If so, it would only be what
he deserved.

I have experienced firsthand the power of the English
husband over his wife, the English father over his children. I spoke true when I told you that nothing in your
essay had formed my opinions on the subject of marriage. It did have a powerful affirming effect on me, as
well as my mother, as I have told you.

You spoke of our being married. But, Brent, I am
afraid of marriage. I do not want to be any man's slave,
or see my children held hostage. It is true that you do not
seem to be like my father, or Colville. Nor does Lord
Langley. I admit that my brief association with you and
your friend had given me a new awareness of the possi-

bilities between man and woman. Perhaps in time I might change my views. But I am not yet able to garner the courage to trust myself to any man, and cannot swear I ever will be able to do so.

But that is a moot point right now, and as for a liaison other than marriage, that is out of the question. Odd though it may seem, given my view of marriage, I have strong moral qualms about an illicit union. Moreover, I would find social disgrace most uncomfortable.

There are also considerations of the effect on the children of such a relationship. No matter how well you might provide for them, you could not change the fact that they were illegitimate. Bastardy is a heavy burden for a child to bear; I would never willingly be a party to imposing it on a child of my own.

Could I be tempted? Yes, my dear Brent, you know that you tempt me. Would I regret it? I would. And my children would. And I suspect that you would, too. So I will not expose myself, us, to such temptation.

Finally, but perhaps most importantly, I respect the political aims of yourself and your friends. The only hope for an end to the abasement of women is a change in the laws of England. I understand better the process by which that might happen after my brief sojourn with the Langleys. I know it will take time. I could never forgive myself if I did anything to damage the cause of reform.

Once he knew I had worked in Langley's household, Colville would make it appear that we have had an illicit relationship for years. My despicable husband would enjoy pillorying Langley in the public press just as much as he enjoyed thrusting pins under my fingernails, and the results would be much more serious for many more people.

And so, dearest Brent, please go back to London and assure my friends there that I am well, reasonably content, and safe. Please find yourself a wife, take your place in the House of Lords, vote your conscience, and raise your son and heir to be of like mind. I will proudly trace the progress of reform in the newspapers, and you will always be in my prayers. More than this I cannot offer you.

By the time he had come to the end of this epistle, Brentwood had seated himself at the edge of the cliff. After he finished, he wiped away a suspicious bit of moisture from his eyes and stared off into the distance for a long, long while. Then he reread the pages again, carefully, and as he finished each one, he shredded it into hundreds of tiny pieces and let them blow off the cliff face and across the valley below.

The image of Eden as a girl, struggling futilely with that torturing, murderous brute, clutched at his heart. No wonder she wanted nothing more passionately than safety. And he, by God, was going to see that she had it, once and for all.

Chapter Sixteen

Is he lucid?"

"Aye, as lucid as his sire, the devil." Scranton, Viscount Colville's valet, walked past Norton Chriswell holding his ear, which was bright red as if it had just been violently boxed. "Watch yerself, sir. He's in a foul mood, a foul mood indeed."

"When is he ever not? Chriswell entered the room softly, diffidently. He despised his uncle Colville, but as his heir, Chriswell's interests lay in dealing well with the old monster, including helping him in his search for his long-vanished wife, so he had appeared as soon as he was summoned.

Lost in a vast bed, the skin-and-bones remnant of a once tall, powerful man watched balefully as Chriswell approached. "You mince like a streetwalker, you son of a Haymarket whore. And what in Satan's name are you wearing?" The voice originating in the bag of bones was surprisingly strong, the old blue eyes piercing as the viscount eyed the slender young man.

Moving carefully to avoid impaling himself on his high shirtpoints, Chriswell looked down defensively at his elaborately tied neckcloth, his mustard-yellow waistcoat and blue morning coat. "Assure you this attire is all the crack, Uncle." He gave his buff inexpressibles a tug as if to remove an imaginary crease.

"In my time . . ." the old man suddenly began to cough. So deep, so wracking, and so protracted was the cough that it seemed he must cough up his very soul, Chriswell thought.

That is, if he has one. He felt inexplicably like crossing himself as he reached for the cough syrup on the bedside table.

When at last his uncle was dosed and propped up on the pillows, Chriswell interrupted his tirade on the uselessness of doctors and medicine in general. "What did you call me here for, Uncle? You said it was urgent."

"That bitch! She's alive."

Chriswell did not have to ask what bitch. Since his uncle's sixteen-year-old bride had fled him, he had been obsessed with recovering her. After several years of determined effort, he had reluctantly come to believe that her relatives told the truth when they maintained she had somehow died in her attempt to escape him.

A stipulation in her grandfather's will of which Colville had been unaware had deprived him of the right to dispose of her property as he wished. He could occupy it and receive the income from it, but he could not sell it, not even if all three of her trustees agreed.

Chriswell shuddered when he remembered how soon after informing Colville of that fact the girl's father had died. A stroke, the doctor had said.

"You've found her? So much for starting legal proceedings to have her declared dead." If his uncle could establish that Lady Joanna Colville had preceded her husband in death, then he could exercise full rights to her property, as she had left no will. As Colville's heir, Chriswell did not have to pretend his interest in the fate of Lady Colville.

"Can't do it for another two years in any case. But I got this letter three weeks ago." Thin, blue veined hands searched under the throng of pillows before emerging with a single sheet of paper.

Chriswell took the proferred letter. It was quickly read. "Your wife, Joanna, Lady Colville, has been living in London with Stuart Hamilton, Lord Langley, until very recently. She pretended to be governess to the Langley children. She is now the mistress of Roger Brentwood, Earl of Dudley. She has been using the name Eden Henderson." There was no signature.

"So! Langley did have her, after all." Chriswell's eyes gleamed with amusement as he looked at his uncle. "So much for that gentleman's word of honor."

"Or knew where she was. He'll pay for this, damn him. He'll pay!" Another paroxysm of coughing wracked the old man. "He won't feel quite so clever when one of his children sickens and dies."

Chriswell closed his mind to this threat. Sometimes it was best not to think about his uncle's activities. "Wonder why he's let her surface now?"

"Doubtless has heard I'm at death's door, believes her safe from me. Hah! I'll pay him out, see if I don't."

"What are your plans, Uncle? Or do I want to know?"

"Have to know. You are part of them. Find the bitch and kill her."

Chriswell blinked. "Kill her? Me? Not in my line, uncle, I . . ." He began fiddling with an oversized button.

"You'll do it! Else I'll leave you nothing but a small entailed property and an empty title. Leave all my unentailed goods to a foundation for the betterment of wronged women. You'd like that, heh? Good choice for me, *n'est-ce pas?* A little atonement for my sins. Won't get me into heaven, but perhaps a slightly more comfortable vestibule in hell?"

The old man cackled gleefully. He didn't really believe in an afterlife, Chriswell knew, so he feared neither man nor the devil.

"I thought you said she'd been found," he whined, remembering the first part of his uncle's command.

"She was there, but has flitted again. My people learned she left there about the time this letter was sent. Not with Dudley, either, as far as can be determined. Sent my man to Varnham, where he has his seat. She'd worked nearby as a governess, but hasn't been seen lately. Must have realized she'd been recognized. I've had men searching without success. I turn to you as a last resort."

"But, Uncle, how can I help, when your people haven't been able to, who are so devilish efficient?" Chriswell shuddered at the thought of some of the rough types he knew were in his uncle's employ.

"You can move about in society, listen, ask questions of people they couldn't get near. Whoever wrote that note may be able to say where she has got to now. That bitch mustn't win! 'Tis the only thing would make me sleep uneasily in my grave, d'ye hear. I must have her, must keep her from winning."

Colville grew progressively more agitated as he spoke. Chriswell put out his hands and caught the bony shoulders as his uncle rose in his bed. "Now, Uncle, you'll bring on one of those fits of yours, getting so worked up. Calm yourself."

But the warning was too late. Suddenly a violent tremor shook the thin, wasted body. Colville's head dropped back and a howl like a wounded animal escaped his lips, then he began convulsing.

Chriswell raced from the room. "Send for the surgeon, Scranton, and see to my uncle. He's having one of his fits."

"Doctor said next one could carry him off." Scranton sounded hopeful, but dutifully hurried to carry out his commission.

Brentwood looked disdainfully at the large, unkempt structure he was approaching. Neglect and decay were everywhere. Whatever Colville had spent his three wives' fortunes on, it obviously *wasn't* maintenance of his property.

Correction, he thought, anger welling up in him. *Eden's property.* For he had learned when he began his search for her husband that Colville had made Broadhurst, Eden's grandfather's once handsome Palladian mansion, his principal home since her disappearance.

He dismounted and, seeing no sign of a footman, secured his horse to an overgrown shrub before mounting the broken stone steps of the run-down mansion. *Looks as if he's been riding horses up and down these steps,* Brentwood thought, surveying the damage. Several forceful blows on the knocker produced no response, so he opened the door for himself and entered.

No servants were in evidence on the ground floor, but above him he could hear the murmur of voices, so he mounted, following the sounds until they led him into a dirty but once magnificent bedroom. There a young dandy looked on while a surgeon bled an emaciated old man who lay across the huge bed in seeming unconsciousness.

As Brentwood took in this tableau, a servant approached him, a strongly built, battered man with a look at once servile and evil. "What business have you here, sir? Can you not see that my master is ill."

"Is that Colville?" Brentwood abruptly nodded toward the bed.

"Yes, it is." The dandy left the bedside to approach him. "And who might you be, sir?"

"I am Brentwood."

Chriswell looked at him uncomprehendingly, but on the bed, the old man's eyes suddenly opened. He thrust the surgeon from him, clamping his own hand over the wound.

"So! You have come to us, saving me a great deal of trouble, my lord. Did you bring your paramour with you?"

"I don't understand. Who is this man with murder in his eye?" Chriswell stood back uneasily at the sight of Brentwood's scowl.

"This is the Earl of Dudley, whom we so recently learned is my dear wife's lover. The earl disdains his title. He prefers to be known by his family name, isn't that so, my lord?"

"You are remarkably well-informed." Brentwood's slow but menacing steps had carried him to the bedside, where he stood gazing in disgust at the wreck of a man lying there, his thin skin covered with a scrofulous rash, spittle at the corners of his mouth.

"Well-enough informed to launch a very interesting and profitable crim.con.case!" The old man cackled as he attempted to straighten himself in bed.

"Yes, that is how I've heard you fight with men. Women, particularly young girls, you are brave enough to use more physical tactics on, aren't you, Colville." Brentwood bent and grabbed the old man by his nightshirt, lifting him with ease into midair. "But no more, do you hear? No more. Nor shall Eden suffer one more second from her very natural fear of a very unnatural husband." He began to shake the man like a rag, so that his head lolled back and forth.

"See here!" The dandy pummeled ineffectually at his shoulder. The surgeon and Scranton entered the fray. Between the two of them they managed to make him drop his prey.

"Let me go, or you two shall be next," he snarled as he struggled with them. "This vile beast deserves to swing, but since it will never happen, I've come to see that justice is served."

"It is you that will swing," the alarmed surgeon screamed. "Murdering an old man in his bed!"

"A dying old man, at that." Colville gasped the words just before swooning.

Brentwood stood there, one man hanging onto each arm, looking into the decayed face of the viscount. "*Is* he dying?" he asked the surgeon.

"Indeed, sir, he had a fit today that I made sure would carry him off. He cannot last much longer."

Studying the frail, emaciated figure, Brentwood nodded, and gradually relaxed his posture, so that the two men released their grip on him.

"Yes," he said. "I believe he is. To kill him now would almost be an act of mercy. God may show him mercy, but I will not!" He moved away from his captors and rounded on the dandy.

"At a guess, you are this beast's heir."

Chriswell drew back yet a little further from the fierce expression in the tall man's green eyes. "I am Norton Chriswell, his nephew and heir, but you and I have no quarrel, my lord. My uncle's wish to be reunited with his wife—"

"She was never really his wife and never will be!"

" . . . is, as I understand it, part of a desire for atonement on his part. I only hope he will live to ask her forgiveness." Chriswell adopted a pious look to match his soothing tone.

Brentwood gave the dandy a hard, shrewd look. "He won't. She will stay quite hidden until I have watched him lowered into the grave. And if you've any thought of continuing any vendetta against her or hers—"

"I assure you I have none!"

"Then abandon it. Eden—that is, Joanna—is not without friends now. She has many friends, and powerful ones. We mean to bring your uncle's past misdeeds under scrutiny, and your role in them, if there is any. I mean to make her my wife, and unless she dies of old age in my arms, with all her family and friends unharmed, *you* will pay."

He stepped yet closer to the trembling dandy. "And Colville is not the only one who knows how to get revenge outside of a court of law, so do not think to get away with some indirect attack."

Chriswell once more stammered out his urgent denial of any intention to harm Colville's wife or her family.

"Don't forget, for I won't. And I will make a dangerous enemy." Brentwood's eyes flashed green fire. With one last glance at the recumbent figure on the bed, he strode from the room.

A long, low whistle filled the silence that Brentwood left in his wake. "That'un means it, young sir!" Colville's valet sidled up to his master's nephew. "A right dangerous man, no mistake."

"Never mind him. Pup is afflicted with a conscience." What had moments before seemed little more than a pile of clothes began to stir, and Colville clawed his way into an upright position. "Conscience is a good man's weakness." Colville's voice took on an exuberant tone. "We're going to win, m'boy. Get this idiot out of here, Scranton, and you with him!" Thus he motioned away the surgeon and the servant who moments before had saved his life.

When they were alone, Colville motioned Chriswell to sit

on the side of his bed. "Don't have long, nephew. Know you won't grieve for me, nor would I exert myself to leave you an extra penny, except to deprive my Lady Colville of it. Still, right now we want the same thing. We want that bitch dead!"

Chriswell shook his head. "But how do we find her, Uncle? As you say, we don't have very much time."

"Young Dudley gave me the idea himself. Says she won't come out till I'm in my grave. Should have thought of it before. We'll send the announcement tomorrow. No—too soon. Mustn't be obvious."

The old man slumped back on his pillows. "But can't wait long," he gasped. "Then, once I'm buried, she'll come out of hiding, and . . . fetch me that box, m'boy. The inlaid mother-of-pearl."

Chriswell thought his uncle's clever mind had at last given way, but he complied with the request. He watched as the trembling fingers lovingly explored the array of small bottles within the chest.

"Poison, m'boy. They say it's a woman's weapon, but I've found it most useful from time to time. This in the yellow bottle, mark it well. It is perfect for my beloved wife. A tablespoon of this will paralyze almost instantly. It appears as if the victim has had a stroke. A quicker death than the bitch deserves, but I haven't time to waste on refinements now."

"But, Uncle, this revenge will come too late for you to enjoy, and just in time to make me a deadly enemy in Brentwood."

His uncle chuckled evilly. "But I won't be dead, you see. We're going to send in a false announcement of my demise to the papers, perhaps even stage a funeral, and then when that high-and-mighty young lord brings his paramour into the light of day, you'll find her, dose her, and then I'll appear, the grieving widower. Confess I faked my death to draw her out, but only, as you so delightfully put it, to make atonement. A nice touch, that. I was proud of you for once."

"I do not think that I could kill—"

"Codswallop, of course you could." Colville studied his

nephew with piercing blue eyes. "Pah, namby-pamby fellow. Perhaps not. Well, Scranton will just have to do it. One last push to earn the substantial legacy he hopes for from me, eh? In fact, I'll draw up a list, bequeath him a thousand pounds for each one he gets." Eyes gazing off into the distance, Colville began lovingly to designate his victims.

"Langley, of course, and Brentwood, that goes without saying. And my dear wife's aunt, who surely knew she was still alive all along. Then there is the judge who decided against setting aside the prohibition to sell her property, and the solicitor who refused to surrender his role as trustee."

"Uncle, you can't kill all of those people without its being noticed.

"Why do I care if it's noticed? I'll be dead. It'll be Scranton's problem, not mine, nor yours, so don't fly up in the boughs.

"Now, pay attention, Norton. See this little purple vial? Once the deed is done, and the bitch's inheritance is secured to you, I will have had enough of life. Brentwood was right about that. It would be a mercy to die, at this point.

"After I've claimed Joanna's fortune once and for all, we'll drink a last toast together, and then I'll shuffle off and leave you to enjoy my money and title in peace. The contents of this purple vial in my brandy and I'll go peacefully, painlessly to sleep. Promise me you'll se to it, m'boy, when the time comes."

Chriswell looked solemnly at his uncle. "I promise."

Chapter Seventeen

Eden stood on the windswept bluff overlooking the valley, tears streaming down her cheeks. The loss was not unexpected, but it still pained her.

She had been right to fear that Lady Humphrey's health would be irrevocably damaged by her demanding daughters' behavior. Their chief concern had been that Eden might replace them in their mother's affection. They had showed this concern by bullying the elderly lady into showing them her most recent will.

She had summoned her solicitor, who assured them that the bequest which Lady Humphrey had added for Eden Henderson was a reasonable one, but they insisted on reading it for themselves.

They were only slightly mollified upon learning that her inheritance was merely a thousand pounds plus the right to continue her employment as housekeeper at Humphrey Manor for her lifetime if she so wished. The daughters were united in viewing this legacy as excessively generous, and threatened Eden with dire consequences if she exerted any influence to get their mother to change the will.

Eden angrily denied any intention to do so. "I not only won't try to influence her, but if she left me more than she already has planned, I would feel honor bound to refuse." This assertion was received with arrogant skepticism.

Their complaining and criticism had exhausted Lady Humphrey's irritable nerves to the extent that she had a very serious attack, which she barely survived.

After they finally left, Lady Humphrey mournfully observed, "They spent their entire time and energy bullying me about their inheritance. Not once did they note how well I had been feeling before they arrived, or compliment you on how much better the house and grounds are, though I know from the delighted compliments of callers that it is so."

Eden patted Lady Humphrey's hand, "No child would want their parent to be intimidated or taken advantage of by an adventuress."

"Don't try to wrap it up in clean linen, my dear." Looking almost as gaunt as she had when Eden arrived, Lady Humphrey sank against the pillows. "They care nothing for me. They'll be glad when I'm gone, so they can have my money and property."

Gazing across the valley, Eden dashed a tear from her eye, remembering the old woman's forlorn voice. Lady Humphrey had never really recovered from the attack she had suffered during her daughters' visit. Each day she seemed progressively weaker and less connected to life. Two weeks later, she had been discovered dead in her bed.

Eden had fled to the cliff after the funeral to avoid exchanging hot words with the daughters, who made a great show of grief after their mother was gone. She must gather her courage to return to the house, for she had been summoned to meet them in the library at 4:00 to "discuss her situation," which she took to mean that they were going to try to circumvent the will somehow.

She wouldn't be able to fight them in court, so it looked as if once more she would have to find a place of refuge. Where could she go now? The dowager Duchess of Carminster had written her condolences, but knowing of Lady Humphrey's bequest, thought Eden still safely settled.

"As I plan to take up residence here, your services would be redundant," Mrs. Aimsley, the eldest of the two daughters, observed as soon as Eden had seated herself in the library with the sisters. "I am quite a good manager, and do not require a housekeeper."

Eden said nothing, waiting for the two women to make whatever offer they intended. Though she could not fight them in court if they decided to cheat her, it occurred to her that they could not know that.

Mrs. Aimsley cleared her throat. "You were promised by the terms of my mother's will that you would have employment for life here if you wished it, but I am sure this is far too isolated a situation for a handsome young woman like yourself to wish to retire to permanently. With a thousand pounds for a dowry, you surely can find a suitable husband."

Eden remained silent, which unnerved Mrs. Aimsley slightly. "Of course, we will compensate you—"

"What my sister intends is to offer you an additional two hundred pounds for quitting Humphrey manor now, without any legal action, surrendering your claim to further compensation. That is the equivalent of four years' salary, and you surely would not wish to stay here longer than that." Mrs. Lloyd smiled insinuatingly.

Eden thought of the magnificent view from the bluff. She had learned to love this Welsh countryside, and was beginning to master the language of its people. In truth she would not mind spending a lifetime here. But even if she dared to fight the sisters for strict adherence to the provision of the will, she did not like to stay where she would be unwanted and unneeded.

"Very well. I agree to that, provided that I receive a bank draft for the entire 1,200 pounds prior to my removal."

The two women looked somewhat stunned by the quick capitulation. "It . . . it will take us a week or two to raise that sum."

"I shall pack and be ready to leave on the instant that I receive it. Will that be satisfactory?"

"Eminently satisfactory." Now that she had achieved her end, Mrs. Aimsley decided she could be magnanimous. "I shall provide you with a reference. You *have* done a good job of keeping the place up."

"I thank you," Eden said dismissively, "but Lady Humphrey

has already given me a reference, dictated to the vicar on one of his many kind visits. Ladies." She curtsied politely and left the room to keep from saying all that was in her heart regarding their treatment of their mother.

"The morning post, Miss Henderson." The butler who once had resented her assumption of the reins of power in the household now let his regret at her leaving show in his voice on this last day. He and the other servants had expressed their sorrow at losing her. Eden wryly thought it was intensified by the realization that they would now be working for the unpleasant Mrs. Aimsley.

"Thank you, Archer." *The Times* was on top of the pile. Sighing as she remembered how much Lady Humphrey had loved to have the gossip columns read to her, Eden set it aside and sorted through the mail. To her intense surprise, there were four letters for her.

Astonished, she opened the first. As she expected from the ornate handwriting, it was from Gwynneth Langley:

Dearest ———
    I am not at all sure what to call you. You aren't Eden Henderson, yet I can't think of you as Joanna. And I'm sure you don't want to be called Lady Colville.
    Brentwood says to call you Rosie, for now, and that I needn't explain why. Silly man. He has gone off to attend the funeral.
    He says to tell you to stay put until he comes for you, which will be as soon as he has seen the old wretch put into the ground.
    Then we hope you will come to us here, but perhaps you have someone nearer and dearer to you to visit first. At any rate, we are eager to see you and congratulate you on your release.

Eden's heart began pounding. Could this letter possibly mean what she thought it meant?

Eagerly she took the newspaper she had put aside and opened it. She skimmed past the shocking accounts of "Peterloo," the massacre at Manchester. Before long she found the story she sought, an obituary of her husband which included a brief retelling of her disappearance.

When Archer came in a few minutes later to remove her breakfast dishes, he found her staring out the window, tears streaming down her face.

"Eh, miss, what is it? Something in the post o'erset you?"

"No, Archer, it's just that . . . I've only just found out . . . Oh, Archer, I'm free!" She turned a glorious smile on him. Astonished and offended, the old butler retreated, to tell the staff below stairs that he had misjudged Miss Henderson.

"Thought she'd loved our mistress, and regretted leaving Humphrey manor, yet here she is crying for joy that she's leaving."

Eden opened the other letters, one at a time. The one from Isabella gushed with pleasure at Eden's newfound freedom. The dowager duchess was more restrained, but Eden was touched by the invitation to come and stay with them in London.

"I can help establish you in society," the duchess wrote. "Any ninny who thinks he can snub you for refusing to live with that odious man shall have to deal with me."

She saved what she guessed was Brentwood's missive for the last.

Dear Rose by any other name,

I didn't kill him, I swear. I went there to do so, but found him at death's door, and decided not to grant him the mercy of a swift death.

I am going to attend the burial, and make very sure the monster is in the ground and his nephew suitably impressed with the danger of molesting you, then I will come for you. DO NOT LEAVE LADY HUMPHREY until then. For aught we know, Colville is a vampire. If I find that he is, I will require a little extra time to drive a stake through his black heart.

Eden smiled at the letter. It was so much in Brentwood's style. What a ridiculous notion. Did he think to frighten her into waiting until he came to tempt her to do that which she was determined not to do?

Yet even while she mentally scolded him, she realized that her happiness was increased by the knowledge she had not succeeded in driving Brentwood to abandon all interest in her.

Something strange had been happening to Eden ever since she had written that long letter to him. She had found him constantly in her thoughts, in ways she had previously denied herself. She had begun to deeply regret sending Brentwood away without any hope.

Ever since she had escaped to Wales to live with Lady Humphrey, she had experienced moments of deep longing for his presence, usually when she saw something that amused her, and imagined the way his green eyes would light up as he shared the joke with her.

But since she sent him away, her feelings had intensified. She yearned to have him there to help her deal with Lady Humphrey's illness. She wished she could turn the two unpleasant sisters over to him, feeling sure he would know how to deal with them. Most of all, she found herself wanting the comfort of his arms in her grief when her employer had died.

When these emotions came over her, she found herself deeply regretting telling him to find himself a wife. Agonies of jealousy possessed her at the thought of his courting another woman.

This letter from him proved that he still cared for her, that he had in no way given up on her, but in fact was actively involved with her life. His joke about Colville being a vampire was doubtless a cover for his serious wish to be the one to escort her back into society. If she had not been virtually kicked out the door of Humphrey manor, she would have waited for him, too, glad to lean on his strength and take courage from his humor as she faced people once again as her real self.

But it could not be. The bank draft had been presented. She was packed. Indeed, the hackney had already been summoned. Lady Aimsley had not wavered in her fervent desire to see Eden gone, so Eden must go.

At least now she knew where to go!

Joyfully she penned a note to her Aunt Alicia, informing her of her intention of visiting her first. *I can't wait to meet my dear cousins, to see again my childhood friends,* she thought.

She then wrote notes informing Gwynneth and the dowager duchess of her intentions. Lastly she wrote to tell Brentwood her plans, promising to see him in London after she had visited with her family for a few weeks. She wasn't sure where to send it, so dispatched one copy to the Langleys in London, and one to Varnham, where she was sure the redoubtable Briggs would see that he received it.

The 1,200 pounds which she would receive from Lady Humphrey's estate would permit her to make a new beginning. She placed no reliance on any of her inheritance having survived Colville's possession, but a judicious use of the Humphrey legacy, carefully invested, might gain her an independence.

As Eden happily ascended the carriage that was to take her to her aunt, she began to plan for a dream she had cherished since Kitty Robinson's death: she would open a school of her own, a school for especially bright and talented young women, which would encourage them to develop all of their talents, and not merely their social skills.

As for Brentwood? As for marriage? That was a possibility both frightening and alluring. She would make no hasty decisions. But she realized she no longer firmly rejected all possibility of entering parson's mousetrap.

Of all the welcomes she could have imagined from her Aunt Alicia, Eden never would have expected this one. The servants, some of whom she remembered, looked at her as if she had the plague as she was escorted into the house, and now as she approached the woman who had once saved her from a terrible fate, she saw fear, rather than joy, etching the lines on a face astoundingly like her mother's.

"Oh, Eden, you shouldn't have come. Didn't Mr. Brentwood warn you?" Alicia drew her to a couch and hugged her, tears streaming down her cheeks. "I hate to start you traveling again when you surely are exhausted, but you must leave, we both must."

"Why, whatever are you talking about?" A feeling of deep dread almost overwhelmed Eden.

"Brentwood doesn't think Colville is dead."

"What? But the papers . . ."

"He thinks it is a trick. He rode over here to see me after he went to Broadhurst. He had intended to view the body, but he learned that Colville left there alive.

"Mr. Brentwood thinks the death announcement is a ploy to get you to show yourself, and that Colville is not dead at all. And would it not be just like that wicked man?"

Eden was not one to faint, but suddenly it seemed she had no blood in her veins, no air in her lungs. Dimly and from far off she heard her aunt calling to her. The pungent vapors of a vinaigrette forced her to a consciousness she almost felt she couldn't bear.

When at last she could speak, her mind had already begun to grapple with the implications of Aunt Alicia's words. "Not dead? Then it is a trick, and I've walked right into his trap."

"That is what we fear. Here is a note Mr. Brentwood wrote you, in case you came here."

Dearest Rosie:

As I was unable to drive the stake in the vampire's heart at Broadhurst, I shall pursue him to Wiltshire. Never fear—I shall see that he keeps his appointment in hell.

Remain with your aunt and follow her instructions. I

shall come for you when I know one way or the other
whether your husband is still above ground.

Eden looked up at her aunt. "He says I am to follow your
instructions. What is his plan?"

"Mr. Brentwood has informed all of my servants, and we've
hired some villagers to stand guard. He said to stay here, keeping indoors, but I feel we should flee. He does not know
Colville as we do."

"Where would we go?"

Aunt Alicia looked at a loss. "I can't think. I don't want to
bring this plague on any of my children's houses."

"No more do I." Eden straightened suddenly. "Nor do I
want you to take any more risks for me. You must go, but I
will stay. That way, if Colville is alive, he'll concentrate on
trying to get to me, and you can be safe."

"But I—"

"I won't take no for an answer, Aunt Alicia. You've suffered enough for my sake."

Her aunt bent her head. "I feel such a coward, but that
dreadful man—I'm so terrified of him."

"Then you must leave, and take some armed men to guard
you."

Eden finally managed to convince her aunt to leave. "Don't
tell me where you are going. I don't want to know. Until Mr.
Brentwood comes for me, I'll stay here. I'll use our code to
put a notice in the papers when I feel it is safe."

After her aunt's departure, Eden enlisted one of the hired
guards, a village lad, to show her how to fire a gun. She appro-
priated her dead uncle's dueling pistols, thinking grimly it
would be a type of poetic justice if she should succeed in
killing Colville with one of them.

When dark fell and what seemed to her to be a pitifully
small army of armed servants and villagers had been de-
ployed, Eden retired to a bedroom. She locked the windows
and the door, and shoved a table in front of the door, not so
much because it would stop a determined intruder, but because

she hoped the scraping it would make when it was shoved aside would wake her. She was exhausted, and knew that no amount of determination or nerves could keep her awake this night.

The night passed without event, and Eden arose the next morning to exchange greetings with a relieved staff. She went down to the kitchen to warn the cook of what he already knew, that Colville had been accused of using poison.

"Yes, my lady," the cook nodded sagely. "My mistress told me. I'm to cook everything with my own hands and keep a careful watch on the supplies. Plain food, no sauces."

"I see you've been well instructed." Eden thanked him and then went in search of a footman to accompany her for a walk through the shrubberies. She was tense, geared for action, and there was nothing to do. The day passed so slowly, it seemed like ten years.

Often through the day she found herself yearning for Brentwood. She realized with a shock that she would only feel safe once he was with her. When had he so firmly embedded himself in her life?

Brentwood should have been back from Colville's estate near Chippenham by early evening, she calculated. Her apprehension for his safety grew with each long hour. Somehow that monster Colville must have killed him. Fear, guilt, and grief almost threatened to overwhelm her.

When night fell, she once again looked to the priming on the pistols, before locking herself in her room. She read until late in the night, too keyed up to sleep this time.

But sleep at last she did. The scraping noise of the table being pushed aside by the opening door penetrated a ghastly, phantasmagoric dream in which she was being chased by someone with Colville's features, but the strong body of a much younger man. In her dream she was running toward Brentwood, but she could never seem to reach him.

Eden sat up abruptly in bed, scrabbling to get the pistols she had placed on the bedstand. The scraping came again. She was surprised to see a line of light under the door, and hear a soft murmur of masculine voices. Colville or his hired assassins must be very sure of themselves, not to use all the stealth at their command. How had they gotten past the guards? She wondered grimly how many of them had been killed.

Terror suggested strategy. Eden slipped away from the bed, which sat in a pool of moonlight, into the deepest darkness of the room, beside the massive wardrobe. A heavy pistol in each trembling hand, she waited for the door to open completely so she wouldn't miss her target.

Chapter Eighteen

E den, Eden. Wake up!"

"The door's blocked, sir."

"Damn it, why doesn't she answer?" The table scraped and bounced in response to a vigorous shove, and two men stood silhouetted in the door.

"She's not in her bed! Eden?"

A loud clunk drew the men's attention to the darkness beside the wardrobe. The taller of the two strode over and peered into the darkness. "Eden?"

A second loud clunk sounded as the other dueling pistol fell from her hand, and suddenly Eden launched herself out of the darkness into Brentwood's arms. "Oh, Brent, Brent. I was so terrified. I thought you'd never come. Is it safe? What did you find out? Is he really dead?"

Brentwood held her close and rocked her, taking as much comfort from the embrace as she did. "Yes, my darling, quite, quite dead. I was very suspicious, for all his servants had been dismissed but that one. However, in the village I found the carpenter who built his coffin. He swore Colville was the one he measured for it."

Eden gave a long sigh of relief, then suddenly covered her mouth, her eyes wide. "Oh, Brent, I almost shot you."

He bent and picked up the pistols. "Never knew you were such a high stickler. Just because two men come barging into your bedroom at night."

Eden gave a watery laugh as she watched him disarm the pistols.

"That would have been fine thanks after all I've been through for you," Brentwood grumbled, but a fond half-smile softened his words. He handed the pistols to the young man who still stood in the door. "Thank you for your assistance, Carl. That will be all."

Eden didn't even demur when Carl left them alone. She was still shaking, and willingly curled up on the small sofa beside Brentwood, with his arms around her. She demanded, "Tell me all!"

Brentwood related his initial encounter with Colville. "He looked on death's door, physically, and yet in those eyes was so much evil vitality! When I learned he had died so soon after I left, I was suspicious. I took a notion that he might try to trick you by staging his death. So I went to Broadhurst, as I wrote you, to make sure he was dead.

"When I learned he had left there alive, I followed him home. There I was told he'd been buried that morning. I'd a mind to dig him up to be sure, but the nephew objected strongly."

She could feel Brentwood's muscular arms flexing a little as he relived that confrontation with the nephew. "He is a weakling compared to Colville, yet there was something so uneasy in his manner, it only served to enhance my suspicions. I am glad I was able to locate the carpenter, and that he had known Colville previously."

Eden snuggled closer, her head on his shoulder. "I'm so grateful to you. I know I am terrible to be so glad of another person's death, but—"

"Where Colville is concerned, I think you are only one of many. The nephew was considerably less than grief-stricken. His principal objection to opening the coffin seems to have been the fear of contagion." Brentwood chuckled. "Rightly so. The old man had already begun to rot while he was yet alive.

"When I warned him any thoughts of carrying out a vendetta for his uncle would result in his own untimely trip to meet his Maker, Chriswell assured me he had no hard feelings against you for being so inconsiderate as to outlive Colville, though it cost him a substantial inheritance."

"Why should that be?" Eden had so long ago resigned herself to the loss of her grandfather's estate that she couldn't immediately take in the implications of Brentwood's story.

"It seems that Colville was unable to acquire more than a life interest in the property you inherited, according to the terms of your grandfather's will."

Eden twisted so she could look Brentwood in the face. "Are you saying what I think you are saying, Brent?" Rising hope warred with incredulity in her voice.

"I am saying that you are an heiress, my dear."

"Oh!" Eden raised a trembling hand to her mouth. "Can it be true?"

"I'll doubtless never stand a chance with you now." He shook his head consideringly. "I have it! I shall encourage young Carl to gossip and force you to marry me to avoid being compromised. Does this give you a feeling of déjà vu?"

Eden smiled up at him. "It should give you one, my lord Dudley. For I'll still not be taken by such a strategem."

"Oh, well, I'll try something else, then." He abruptly kissed her. Startled at first, she found she liked the sensation excessively. She offered no resistance when he twisted with her in his arms so that they were all but lying down side by side on the sofa, their bodies pressed together. His hands roamed hungrily along her back as his lips melted against her own. They were both breathing heavily when he broke off the encounter.

"Is it working?" he asked, eyebrows lifted hopefully.

"Do you know," Eden replied in wonder, "I think it is." She raised her face eagerly. "Try it again."

Brentwood was only too happy to comply. Eden had never guessed the magic that a woman could find in a man's arms. She made a little moan of protest in her throat when Brentwood broke off the kiss and sat up, putting some distance between them on the sofa.

"Wh-what?" Disoriented by passion, she reached for him. He took her hands and held them between his own.

"If I am not to act the utter cad, we must cease this at once. I've no intention of sneaking into your bed when terror has made you vulnerable . . ."

Eden pulled her hands free, closed the distance between them, and threw her arms about his neck. "It's not like that, not at all. Ever since I wrote that letter for you, I've regretted telling you to marry someone else. I was sure I'd driven you away forever, and too late I realized that I"—shyness made her lower her eyelashes—"I think I love you."

"Oh, Eden." Hungrily he hugged her to him. "I never believed in love at all, much less love at first sight, yet that first day—"

"I know. It was not like being attracted to a stranger, was it? It was as if we recognized one another."

"That is the very word! Instant recognition!" Of one accord they came together for another kiss, a long, sweet, intimate kiss that left both of them panting.

"I hope we can be married right away," he murmured into her hair as he worked his fingers through her braid to comb the long silky tresses down over her shoulders. "I don't want to wait too long."

Eden caught her breath. "Marry? I . . . perhaps we could . . ." She wiggled a little distance away from him. "I've been thinking about what you said about America. Perhaps we could go there and just live together."

"No, Eden, you aren't thinking at all, right now." He gave her a tender smile. "Have you forgotten about the children? Because I certainly haven't. You were right about that."

She slumped back down against his chest. "I was?"

He stroked her hair soothingly. "Yes, you were. You've heard several references to my experiences in America, I know."

She stiffened. "Ah, yes, your harem." She lifted questioning eyes, surprising a look of dread and shame on Brent's usually pleasant features.

"I categorically deny that there was a harem, but . . ." Brentwood struggled with himself. He wanted to tell her the whole story, yet he feared to put her newfound love for him to such a severe test.

"I saw what happened to some women who let themselves believe in promises that fell short of marriage. They and their children were abandoned and had no legal recourse. American society is no less unforgiving than our own toward women caught in such a situation. For all its shortcomings, marriage does provide women and children some protection."

"Yes, I know. Yet it's so hard to think of putting myself back into a man's power, any man, even one as dear as you, after what I've been through."

"I understand. I had meant to say I'd wait as long as it took for you to trust me, but after this evening . . ." He didn't really need to explain; another kiss spoke for him.

Wrapped in this sweet cocoon, Eden capitulated completely. "Let's not wait. In my rational moments I know you could never treat me as my father did my mother. You've too calm and pleasant a temperament. As for Colville—"

"Colville was evil," Brentwood broke in. "Until I met him, I'd never been in the presence of an actively evil person. I've always believed that people who do bad things do so out of misguided motives or a lack of understanding of the consequences, but there seemed to be an almost palpable emanation of evil from that man."

Eden shuddered. "I'm so glad it's over." A sudden thought brought a beatific smile to her face. "There's one excellent reason for marrying right away."

"You mean in addition to the danger that we'll both go up in flames if we don't? What's that, love?" Brentwood's hands were on a leisurely, delicious journey of exploration of Eden's contours as he listened.

"I don't want to be known as Lady Colville. I can't bear the thought of carrying his name!"

Grinning, he queried, "Speaking of names, what about your first name? How do you like Rosie?"

Eden giggled. "I thought it very sweet, but in truth, I believe I shall remain Eden. And I don't want my despicable father's name, either. I believe I shall stay Eden Henderson until we are wed."

"Ah, I am glad you said that." He left off his exploration in the interest of self-control, instead cradling her head in his hands. "I know I will always think of you as Eden, my lovely Eden. And will you be content to be Mrs. Brentwood? If you prefer Lady Dudley, I will certainly . . ."

She shushed him with a gentle finger across his firm lips. "Eden Brentwood is a lovely name. I shall be proud to be known by it."

"Eden Brentwood. It can't happen too soon, my love." After one last, tender kiss, he stood and led her to her bed.

"Get some sleep," he commanded. "Tomorrow your life begins again!"

"We did it! We fooled him." Viscount Colville was wheezing, but his tone was gleeful as his henchman lifted him from the priest's hole in which he had hidden while Brentwood, returned from his successful queries in the village, threatened Chriswell if any vendetta should be continued against Eden or her friends and family. The earl had just ridden off, satisfied that Colville was dead.

"Brilliant notion of yours, Norton, bribing the carpenter to say he placed me in the coffin. You show signs of being a true Colville, worthy of my title."

Norton Chriswell bit his lower lip as he watched Scranton set his uncle down gently. "Yes, but if you go through with murdering Lady Colville—"

"Bah! 'Fraid of your own shadow. Hasn't Scranton got Dudley on his list too?"

" 'Deed I do, my lord. And I'll see to it with pleasure. Thinks he's a nonesuch, that one!" Scranton spoke with the bravery of a man who plans to hire several thugs to do his dangerous work.

"Have to add that carpenter to the list. Can't leave any loose ends like that." Colville gave both men an admonitory shake of the finger.

"Right you are, gov'ner." Scranton lifted the old man up when he proved too weak to climb the stairs.

Chriswell followed gloomily behind, glancing around at the handsome furnishings. Colville had kept his family seat in good repair, unlike the various properties of his wife, which he had taken pleasure in destroying.

I could have a fine life here, on the income from these lands, Chriswell thought. *Not rich, but certainly independent. No need to fear Brentwood's revenge or Scranton's blackmail, if the old man would just die now, before Scranton has a chance to kill Lady Colville and the others.*

Thoughts like these, which had been tumbling around in Chriswell's head for days now, had come to a head with Brentwood's convincing threat of retribution. In fact, he had taken the yellow and purple vials from the inlaid chest while the servant had been seeing Brentwood out the door. They were in his pocket right now. But doubtless Scranton would only find more of the poison to do his uncle's dirty work.

"I'll run ahead and open the doors," Chriswell offered. They had dismissed all servants but Scranton, to prevent word of the viscount's "resurrection" from being bruited about prematurely.

Now, thought Chriswell. *The tide in men's lives. To be or not to be. If t'were done, t'wer best done quickly.* Fortifying himself with famous quotations, he hastened up the stairs.

Head pounding with exertion and sheer terror, he dashed ahead of Scranton into his uncle's room and picked up the bottle of laudanum-laced cough syrup that always sat by his bedside. It was the work of an instant to tip the contents of the purple bottle into it.

"Join me downstairs after you make him comfortable, Scranton." Chriswell edged toward the door. "We'll discuss strategy."

Half an hour later Scranton strolled into the library. His steps were confident, even cocky, and Colville's nephew shivered at the look in the valet's eyes as he surveyed the room. *He sees himself as the true master here.* Chriswell thought.

The valet's manner toward Chriswell had become far from servile since this plot had been hatched.

"Sleeping like a baby," Scranton murmured as he sank without permission into the chair across from Chriswell, who had stationed himself behind the massive desk. "Gave him some of his medicine to quiet him down.

"Good, good." Chriswell patted a sudden burst of perspiration from his forehead. Then he tented his fingers and regarded the burly servant hopefully over them. "I say, Scranton, when my uncle shoves off, there'll be plenty here to share. No real need to do in Lady Colville and her friends. What say we just—"

"Ah, no, gov'ner. Couldn't do that. Old devil'd come back and haunt me. He swore he would, and if anyone could do it, he could." Scranton shivered visibly. "Asides, we might as well have her blunt. Share it between us, like."

"Ah, well, then. Just thought I'd ask. Commend you for your faithfulness. Tell you what. Let's have a drink to seal our partnership—Uncle's best French brandy. Unless you are averse to drinking his private stock before his demise?"

Scranton's mouth all but watered. "Aye, a drink. He'll never miss it, will he, young sir?"

"That he won't." Chriswell stood a little unsteadily and walked to a cabinet. His key gained him entry to the colorful display of decanters, from which he selected a fine crystal one and two matching glasses. "Drink up, then. To our partnership."

"Aye, may it be a long and profitable one." While Chriswell watched, Scranton tossed back the brandy, looking extremely pleased with himself.

"In a way I blame myself."

"Now, my lord, no need to do so. Obviously a stroke, nothing that you could have done to prevent it." The coroner stood, shaking his head.

"But I let Scranton carry that heavy coffin all by himself. He never really recovered from it. Uncle had dismissed all the other servants in a fit of pique. Scranton swore it was no burden for him. So loyal as he was to my uncle, I think he didn't want to share this last office with anyone. I should have remembered he wasn't a young man anymore."

"And doubtless he would have resented you for reminding him. Still, you can't blame yourself for what was, after all, an act of God."

Chriswell shuddered, fingering the little yellow vial in his pocket. "That's true. Because Scranton was so devoted to my uncle, I think I'll lay him to rest beside him. I don't believe he has any kin."

"Very generous, my lord. And may I say that I cannot help feeling sanguine about your stepping into your uncle's shoes. I mean to say, he—"

Chriswell held up his hand. "Please. I know my uncle wasn't perfect, but still, he was my relative, and now is not the time to speak ill of the dead. You'll send the carpenter to prepare the coffin?"

The coroner assented, accepted his fee, and bowed his way from the new Lord Colville's presence, thinking that even though the young lord might be misguided in his loyalty to his evil uncle, his sentiments did him credit, and showed clearly that he was a very different sort of man.

Chapter Nineteen

I'm so very glad you are going to marry him."
Eden half-turned her head from the window through which she was watching Brentwood's departing form. "Are you, Aunt Alicia?"

"Yes, I was afraid after what you'd been through, you might never marry again. And I think he is a fine young man, not at all what one might have expected from his reputation."

"He wasn't what I'd expected, either." Eden turned pensively away from the window. "It is so strange—all those years of hiding from Colville, of being on my own, yet I never felt lonely. Now, when I am away from him, I feel lonely. Already, I miss him, and he's just ridden out of sight."

"Well, he'll be back soon. He was a bit vague about this errand in Liverpool, I thought."

"Yes." Eden frowned and joined her aunt on the couch. "He said it was a package coming from America, and that he wanted it to be a surprise." She tried to shake off the feeling of unease she had about his half-amused, half-excited demeanor as he told her he must leave her for a short while before the wedding.

"Well, my dear. I have a bit of a surprise for you, too."

Eden looked fondly at her aunt. It had been more than a week now since they had been reunited following the confirmation of Colville's death. In that time her cousins had come to call, all healthy and happily married young people. She had looked with delight and envy on the baby of her oldest female cousin, and watched in deep satisfaction as Brentwood played with the three-year-old son of another. This week's visit had done much to heal her spirit and whet her appetite for married life.

"What is it, Aunt Alicia?" she prompted as she saw the older woman hesitate.

"I . . . I've decided to marry, also."

"What?" Eden stared at her. "Who is it?"

"Mr. Haveril. You met him."

"Oh, yes," Eden was surprised. She had seen no sign of partiality on either her aunt or Mr. Haveril's part during his brief call.

"He asked me two years ago, but I feared to say yes. I feared Colville might harm him."

Tears standing in her eyes, Eden embraced her aunt. "How that evil man marked us all!"

"I couldn't tell him then why I had to refuse, for fear he'd try to challenge the man directly. So now I will have to court him a bit, I fear." Alicia bit her lower lip. "Flirt with him, let him know my feelings have altered. Though they haven't, really. I yearned to accept him then."

"Is there any way I can help?" Eden wished with all her heart she could do something for her aunt to make up for the suffering and sacrifice the dear woman had made on her behalf.

"No, my dear, but I did want to ask you never to let him know why I refused him. I'm afraid it might hurt his pride to know I felt it necessary to protect him."

Eden quickly agreed. "I have an idea. When Brent returns with our license, we can invite Mr. Haveril to be one of the wedding party."

"That would be lovely, dear."

Of all the people to have been in the crowd awaiting the disembarkation of passengers from the children's ship, almost the last one Brentwood would have expected to appear was Alana Morley. What would bring her to Liverpool? He was not at all happy to see her, or anyone else who might gossip and spread the news of his visitors before he had a chance to prepare Eden.

He tried to ignore her, hoping she wouldn't see him as he lifted up the largest of the three toddlers, a red-haired boy, and swung him around. Lady Morley, however, would not be ignored. He let none of his consternation show on his face as he returned her determined greetings.

"Why, Mr. Brentwood. It seems you have acquired a family."

"In a manner of speaking, yes." He swung the boy down and stroked the dark curly heads of the two shy little girls. Lady Morley's eyes darted from the children to Brentwood and back again in avid speculation.

"And where is their mother? Or is it mothers?" She swung her gaze from the boy's bright red hair to that of the young woman hastening to catch up with the children. "Ah, here she is, I think."

"No, this is Miss Thomason, the children's governess. Miss Thomason, Lady Morley."

Miss Thomason, looking somewhat frazzled, curtsied briefly before rounding up her charges. "We'd better get them in the carriage, sir, before they manage to fall into the water."

"My thoughts exactly. Alana." He tipped his hat to her and started to turn away.

"The remnants of your American experience, I take it?" Alana's expression was sly, insinuating.

"That's one way of putting it." He realized the need to turn Alana up sweet, in hopes of stopping her tongue, but he felt distaste for the task. Compared to his Eden, she seemed somehow tainted. Still, he must try to win her over for a little while at least, so he gave her one of his most charming smiles.

Alana responded with warmth. "You needn't worry that I'll judge you, Mr. Brentwood." She put one hand on his sleeve in a gesture that was meant to be reassuring. "I think you know that my views on the relationship between the sexes are quite liberal."

"Yes, I haven't forgotten. Our little American experiment

was not so different from an English country house party, after all."

Alana giggled. "Naughty boy," she said approvingly.

"Perhaps you would do me the favor of not speaking of this meeting to our London acquaintances until I have had time to introduce the children in my own way?"

Alana's smile was sweetly reassuring. "I quite understand. I never was the one for brewing scandal broth. You may rely upon me, my lord."

Feeling a bit more warmth toward her at this response, Brentwood once again tipped his hat to her and climbed into the carriage after Miss Thomason and the children.

Alana's eyes narrowed thoughtfully as she watched the merry party drive off. *I wonder if his* chére amie, *the recently widowed Viscountess Colville, knows of that brood?* Alana had followed the Colville's affairs more closely than most members of the *ton,* to whom the viscount's death and his wife's immediate reappearance was a mere nine-day wonder. She wondered if Brentwood planned to marry the creature now she was free.

She was not pleased with the thought. She had a sense of having been cheated and cast aside, and would have liked nothing better than to stop the match. Did his request for her silence mean that Lady Colville did not know of the children's existence? Would she cut up stiff if she learned of them? Alana's eyes narrowed in speculation.

"Alana, where is your mind? I've called you three times." She turned to find her young, recently widowed cousin Esmerelda standing next to her, a scowl marring her pretty face. "What good is it to meet me if you are going to leave me standing here on the dock while you stare into space?"

"Esmerelda, see that group in that carriage? The three children with the red-haired governess. They were on the ship with you. Miss Thomason, I think her name is?"

"That is what *she* calls herself. But she is a *bit* more than a governess. My dear, such a scandal. But you know something of it from my letters."

Gleefully Alana hustled her cousin into the waiting carriage. "Tell me all," she demanded eagerly.

Eden opened the letter from her solicitor. She was looking forward to taking control of her fortune. She eagerly embraced the knowledge that she could now afford the fine gowns, horses, and carriages that she had only been able to admire from a distance. But even more so did she look forward to being able to restore Broadhurst, to remove every trace of Colville from it and return it to its former splendor.

Along with this project went the need to restore the land and repair the cottages of her tenants, and to upgrade livestock and farming techniques. Though as Brentwood's wife she would be largely an absentee landlord, she would certainly not be a negligent one.

Her face fell as she read that the solicitor insisted she must come to London right away to unscramble her tangled legal affairs.

"Bother. How am I to go to London now, when Brent may well be on his way back here?" Eden exclaimed impatiently as her aunt lent a sympathetic ear.

"If you send a messenger on horseback, he probably should be able to catch him at Varnham. Wasn't he going to stop by there before returning to us for the wedding? Though shouldn't you just wait until after you are married, and then your husband could handle your business for you?"

"No, Aunt Alicia. The solicitor says it is urgent. Besides, Brent and I have agreed to keep our finances separate insofar as possible. He respects my need for independence. He is planning to have a settlement drawn up along the lines of the one Lord Langley had made for his wife. It goes a long way toward correcting the inequities toward wives in the common law."

Her aunt shook her head. "So much independence. Is it good for either of you, I wonder? Doesn't it speak of a want of trust?"

Eden gazed at her aunt fondly. She had been a loved, trea-

sured, even cosseted wife until the untimely death of her husband. Though she had learned to manage her own affairs, she
had never liked doing so, and looked forward to the day when
she could turn them over to Mr. Haveril. No wonder she
couldn't understand Eden's need for control of her own life.

"The messenger is a good idea. Briggs will certainly see
that he receives the message. I don't want to wait until Brent
arrives here to leave for London, for it will only delay our
marriage, which I am sure would displease him as much as it
would me."

"I don't wish you to travel to London alone, especially with
so much unrest in the countryside. If I can convince Mr.
Haveril to escort us, would you like me to accompany you?"

"I should like that of all things. We can both shop for our
trousseaus!" There was to be no pretense of wearing mourning
for such a husband. Eden was looking forward to a complete,
fashionable new wardrobe. Smiling, she hurried from the
room to give the necessary instructions to the servants.

"I don't understand what you are saying, Mr. Alpert." Eden
frowned at the slight, balding man who sat across the desk
from her. "Viscount Colville left everything that wasn't entailed to establish a home for ruined women? Odd, ironic, but
admirable. Why should I contest his will?"

Elbows on his desk, Mr. Alpert tented his fingers. "We
think the will is invalid, since it ignores your dower rights entirely. And we can find no evidence that your father made a
marriage settlement that would have replaced them."

"No," Eden murmured. "My father was not concerned with
my interests. What did you mean by the new viscount's having
gone mad?"

"When he heard the provision in your husband's will that
left everything to him if you predeceased your husband, but to
the foundation for ruined women otherwise, he began raving
and fell down in a fit. He hasn't recovered yet, and may never
do so. Incidentally, if any of his insane ravings are founded on
fact, he did you a great favor."

Eden lifted her eyebrows. "What? And why? I don't even know the man."

"As for the what, he raves of 'resurrecting the dead,' and then of having poisoned your husband, his valet, and a carpenter, apparently to foil a plot to kill you and your intended, among others."

Eden felt tremors of shock run through her. "So Brentwood's suspicions were justified!"

"Colville's will castigated the nephew as a spineless jellyfish for letting you live. Apparently the jellyfish found enough backbone to do in the uncle and two others, however. What a family!"

"I still don't understand why. If he is such a villain, why kill Colville to save me?"

"Who can understand madness? It must be in their blood. At any rate, the nephew is in no condition to put up a strong defense if you contest the will. You could claim a goodly portion of Colville's estate. In fact, you might claim guardianship of the nephew and control the whole thing."

"I don't want anything of Colville's. All I want is the return of my inheritance from my grandfather."

"Now, that is a very short-sighted and emotional view of matters. A woman's emotions often rule her head. You must allow your trustees to decide." Mr. Alpert's manner was at once agitated and patronizing.

"I am two-and-twenty, sir. I've no need of trustees."

"Mr. Biscane and I have faithfully served you for five years, at some personal risk, I might add. Shouldn't you trust us to look out for your best interests now?"

Eden looked at him sadly. "I trust you to look after my financial interests, yes. But I won't take anything from Colville's estate, for I never regarded him as my husband; the marriage was a travesty."

"Perhaps you should wait until you have married Lord Dudley, ah, . . . Mr. Brentwood. Then your husband can decide for you?"

Eden lowered her eyes. Something told her Mr. Alpert

would not approve of the marriage settlement she and Brent were planning. Still, she would let her fiancé deal with the man, thereby saving herself a good deal of bother. She had a sudden insight into her aunt's willingness to turn all unpleasant duties over to Mr. Haveril.

"Very well, Mr. Alpert, I will consult with my fiancé. And I do want to thank you for your efforts on my behalf."

"Very glad to do it. Admired your grandfather tremendously. It was an honor to preserve his legacy for his granddaughter."

Eden turned back at the door. "Mr. Alpert, has the current Viscount Colville enough to keep him in comfort?"

"In comfort, though not in style. But a madman has little need of style, does he?" Alpert smiled at his little joke. "Don't worry about him, my dear. He intervened to your benefit, but you may be sure it was for motives of his own. He poisoned his elderly uncle and two others without a qualm, which indicates he was no less evil than the uncle, only perhaps a trifle less bold. If he ever recovers, it will only be for hanging."

Eden shuddered. "The Colville line will die out, then?"

"I believe the title will become extinct if the current viscount dies without an heir."

"I am sure you will understand when I say I cannot regret it."

"Perfectly understandable." Mr. Alpert bowed her out the door before mopping his brow. For a moment there, he'd feared the chit would stand firm. Getting the Colville money for his client would mean a substantial increase in his fee, and he was loathe to lose it to a feminine whim.

"A home for ruined females?" Brentwood threw his head back and roared with laughter. He was seated by Eden in the sitting room of her suite at the Pulteney Hotel. "But that is perfect, since I am sure he contributed more than his share of such unfortunate creatures to our nation."

"It strikes me as the only good that will have come from his life—if it can be made to stand." Eden briefly detailed the suggested challenge to the will.

Brentwood shook his head. "No, you are quite right. You don't want any of his property. It would be pointless to contest his will. Besides, I rather like the delicious irony of it."

"Yes, so do I." She tilted her head up for a kiss, which he very obligingly bestowed. With a sigh she snuggled against his side, delighting in the feel of his strong arm around her.

"Did you get your business in Liverpool taken care of?"

Brentwood nodded. "All right and tight."

"And did you bring me my surprise?"

Suddenly his cravat seemed a little too tight. "No, I, er . . . you have to marry me and come to Varnham to see it."

She lifted trusting eyes to his. "I can't wait!"

I must tell her, he thought. *This is the perfect opportunity.* He cleared his throat, preparatory to his confession, when her voice interrupted him, sounding suddenly rather tense.

"Brent, I have been wanting to ask you something."

"Yes, love?"

"Do you want a large family?"

He moved away enough to get a better view of her large brown eyes, tilted up to study the expression on his face. *Now why had she asked that? And at this moment, of all times?* "I've never given it a great deal of thought. I am fond of children, though. Aren't you?"

"Yes, I am, but . . . well, there are other things I want to do with my life, too. I will want to be a good mother, and I think that takes a large investment of time, so I would prefer not to always be breeding. I know it's very bold of me to mention this, but—"

"We are to be married in a fortnight. I hope we can speak frankly to one another." His calm voice and accepting expression relieved her embarrassment.

"You see, I want to found a school. A special school, for gifted young women, along the lines of Eton and Harrow, where they can study the classics, mathematics, all the things that men learn. I also envision an academy attached to the school, for advanced students to study art, music, even natural history."

Brentwood did not immediately reply, and his frown surprised her. "I thought you'd be pleased, as much as you and Lord Langley have harped on women's need for more and better educational opportunities."

"It is a wonderful idea, Eden. It's just that . . . " Brentwood felt renewed anxiety about whether his "American surprise" would be a welcome one to Eden, or a burden she would resent. And to think, he had been about to tell her the whole.

"I'm not saying we won't have any children. But surely a couple would be sufficient? Or perhaps three? I know there are ways . . ." She lowered her head, once again embarrassed.

"Yes. There are. Spare your blushes, Eden. I would not wish to wear you out with breeding, and I think your school sounds wonderful." Troubled, Brentwood gathered his courage to tell Eden his secret.

She looked up at him curiously. His voice did not sound quite as accepting as his words. He took his arm from around her and leaned forward, elbows on his knees. For a long moment he stared into space. Rarely had she known him to look so solemn for so long a space of time.

"Brent? What's wrong?"

"Eden, have you ever done anything you are really ashamed of?"

His question surprised her, but she gave it careful consideration. "Yes, when I ran off, leaving the Langleys and you with a false impression about me that upset people I cared about, people who had been very good to me."

He dropped his head into his hands. Speaking in a low, muffled tone, he admitted, "I've done something much worse. I think the time has come to tell you about it. You have heard occasional reference to my participation in a social experiment in America?"

"Oh, was that what it was?"

He glanced around to see a teasing smile on her face. "Yes. Why are you laughing?"

"Your harem?"

"There never was a harem!"

"I believe you, sweetheart. You could never do anything so despicable. Please tell me, though, what you did do. I confess I have been horribly curious about it."

Brent studied her face with trepidation. What would be her reaction? Must she know the whole of it? She looked so merry, so trusting as she waited.

"Before I left England, I had written up a Utopian scheme based upon some ideas from Robert Owen, some from the *Philosophes,* some from Godwin, and some from his disciple and now son-in-law, Shelley. It was to include a form of group marriage. You see, I was painfully aware of the fact that many men and women have a great deal of difficulty confining themselves to monogamy." Brentwood grimaced as he thought of his parents, both so busy pursuing other lovers that they had little time for their children.

"I was aware that just doing away with marriage altogether could result in total chaos, with no basis for the support of children—or their mothers, for that matter."

A sudden thought made Eden interrupt his narrative. "Oh, Brent, you didn't abandon some poor woman, did you? Or worse, woman and child? It seems so unlike you."

"No, I didn't abandon anyone, that much I can proudly deny, but . . . oh! I expect I'm overdramatizing the whole episode." He essayed a disarming grin. "What we did was no worse, and in fact not much different than your typical English country house party."

Eden stiffened and pulled away from him, frowning. This did not seem at all an appropriate time or subject for his levity. "How can you joke—"

"You are right. I shouldn't, for the results were far from funny." He abandoned the attempt to make light of his confession.

"My idea was that we would pledge ourselves in marriage to the group, agreeing to give one another freedom to associate with members of the opposite sex in the group without guilt or repercussions. We would agree that all of the children born in the group would be regarded as the children of all of the adults, regardless of whether they were actually of our body or not.

"I wrote of this scheme to my cousin, Dominique, who eagerly adopted it as the social basis for his trading company. By the time I reached America, he had already started a small colony deep in the Northwest Territories of the United States. I joined him fully expecting to take my vows and enter the family."

More than a little shocked, Eden asked, "How many were involved in this?"

"There were six couples." He shook his head. "How idealistic I was, to think such a thing could work. I was startled and alarmed by the reality. For one thing, half the women were more suited to a bordello than a hardworking frontier community. Then there was the unhappiness of three very decent young women who, for one reason or another, had let themselves be drawn into the scheme. They were not free, as I had expected, but enmeshed in constant jealousy and turmoil. They received little respect from the men in the group, who seemed to have trouble distinguishing between the decent females and the . . . uh . . . other kind.

"The worst problem was the children. Rather than all of the men accepting responsibility for all of them, as I had planned, it became clear that where paternity was unsure, none of them would accept responsibility for any of them."

Eden was quite horrified by now. "And you participated in this . . . this . . ."

"No. As I told you, I arrived to find it already launched. After observing for a few days, I was appalled. I convinced my cousin to end the experiment. He was more than ready to do so, as the group was not functioning well at all, either as a social or economic entity."

"And what became of these unfortunate women and children?"

Brentwood looked into the serious, somber depths of his

sweetheart's brown eyes. "Some of the women found husbands within the group. Some headed back to the bordellos from whence they came. As for the rest—women and children alike—I felt responsible for their plight. I made provisions for them."

He struggled to find the words to continue his revelation, but Eden pitied his misery and rushed to soothe him. "It is a shocking episode, Brent, but I am proud that you recognized your responsibilities. And after all, it is all in the past, isn't it? And half a world away." She slid her arms around him in a comforting gesture.

When he stiffened as if resisting her embrace, she frowned anxiously. "Isn't it?"

What was he to do? It certainly wasn't over, and was less than half a day's ride away. But he had heard the disgust in her voice, read the alarm in her face. If he told her the rest of his secret right now, she might back out of the marriage. He couldn't bear the thought of losing her. Better to keep quiet and hope she'd accept the situation once they were married.

Taking a deep breath, feeling his conscience prick him like knives, Brentwood drew her back against him and crooned reassuringly. "Yes, my love. All in the past."

Chapter Twenty

This is such fun!" Eden held up a shining bolt of gold satin for Brentwood's admiration. "Now that the tedious job of taking measurements is behind me, I am in alt over getting to select a new wardrobe."

"It needn't have been a tedious job, if you'd only have let *me* measure you instead of that *soi-disant* French modiste." Brentwood lifted one expressive eyebrow suggestively as he draped the material over her shoulder. "Yes, perfect. Gold is your color."

Eden cut her eyes at him and tossed her head. "Behave yourself, or I'll send you away, and ask Aunt Alicia to shop with me."

"Cruel creature. First you refuse to let me measure you—I daresay I would have been much more thorough—and now you threaten to deprive me of the pleasures of dressing you."

Eden chuckled. He had been having as much fun as she on this, her first real shopping spree. Indeed, he wanted her to have every fashionable design the modistes suggested, made up in every color available, so that she, giggling, had to countermand most of his suggestions.

He was indefatigable, too. When she was ready to quit for the day, he insisted she go to the bootmaker, and from there he found himself irresistibly drawn to a cheerful display of bonnets and pulled her into a hat shop.

It felt so wonderful to be free, to know that she was loved, and to have money! Still, she resisted the hats. "Mercy," she gasped. "Let us quit now. I am exhausted."

"Very well, but first we must order a parasol to go with each of your walking dresses."

"No, not now." She pulled on his arm. "Ices! Gunthers for ices, I beg of you. I am not only exhausted, but thirsty as well." The late September day was almost as warm as a high summer's day, and the thought of such a treat made Eden's mouth water.

"Ices! Well, why didn't you say so!" He dropped the dainty parasol he had been handling and offered her his arm, eager to escort her to Gunthers.

In contrast to the last time they had eaten ices there, Eden could sit calmly in Brentwood's curricle, unafraid of being recognized. Oh, she knew there was some gossip, but for the most part she had attracted little attention. At any rate, without Colville to fear, gossip seemed but a minor annoyance.

She was pleased that her brief connection with the Langleys had not been remarked in the press. As she reemerged into society in her aunt's company, it was accepted that her family had somehow helped her avoid her odious husband. Few blamed her for wishing to do so, partially because Chriswell's ravings had been widely reported. Society felt that her actions had been justified by the old viscount's bloodthirsty vendetta against her.

She sighed with contentment as she tipped a delicious spoonful of raspberry ice into her mouth. "It is all things wonderful to sit here with you, unafraid!"

The green eyes caressed her face tenderly. "But you should be afraid—afraid I may carry you off at any moment and ravish you."

"Do your worst, sir. Just keep in mind that this time if you compromise me you must marry me!"

"About to be shackled at last, and I'm not even struggling." His eyes grew serious. "You are even more beautiful now than before, now you are relaxed and happy. Dare I think our approaching nuptials form part of your happiness?"

"A very great part. It cannot be too soon for me!" She used a minute adjustment to his impeccably tied cravat as an excuse to touch him, letting her fingers graze his chin lightly, delighting in the slight rasp of beard on his cleanly shaven face. They shared an intimate look, and the five days that remained until they would be married quietly at the Duchess of Carminster's home seemed a very long time indeed.

That touch, that intimate look was observed from another carriage by a pair of bright blue eyes that glittered with jealous annoyance. "Look at them," Lady Alana Morley snapped to her American cousin, Mrs. Esmerelda Penworthy. "They positively reek of April and May."

"She'll regret marrying that rakehell, mind my words!" Alana's cousin sniffed disdainfully. "Doubtless find herself forced to share a bed with the whore he brought from America, and even, perhaps, with her so-called husband!"

"You must speak to her, Esmerelda! It is your duty as a Christian."

"Why do you not?" Esmerelda gave Alana a sly look, for she understood her cousin very well, and thus more than suspected jealousy was the wellspring of Alana's interest in Miss Henderson's welfare.

"She wouldn't listen to me, I think. But you have firsthand knowledge—"

Esmerelda nodded judiciously. "The things that hussy Mrs. Thomason told me!" Her righteous indignation was fueled by a wounded *amour-propre,* because in New York Brentwood had failed to respond to the lures she had cast out to him. *I wouldn't mind putting a spoke in Brentwood's wheels now,* was her vindictive thought.

"You have the right of it, Alana. 'Tis my Christian duty to alert that poor young woman to his true villainy. But how am I to approach her?"

"A properly worded note should gain you a hearing. I do not think she is high in the instep. Not yet, anyway."

"I will do it! After all, Lady Colville, or Miss Henderson, or whatever she calls herself, should know what kind of man she's marrying."

"I have some ideas about how to present the matter to her."

Alana signaled her driver to move on and put her head near her cousin's, spelling out her plans.

"What is it, dear?" Eden's aunt crossed the room to look at the letter her niece was holding as if it might burn her.

"This! Some woman from America asking for an audience. It is very vaguely worded, but the gist of it is, she claims to have information that is vital to my 'continued well-being.' "

"Oh, pooh. Doubtless another drummer or beggar." Since Eden's fortune had become common knowledge, she had been deluged with letters and callers seeking to sell her something or borrow money.

"Doubtless you are right. Still, she writes well and has a respectable address. Perhaps I had best see her."

"If you think so, dear." Aunt Alicia was distracted by her own approaching nuptials, and was content to let her niece make her own decisions.

Eden consulted her appointment book and then wrote a short note informing Mrs. Penworthy that she could call on the morrow at 10 A.M. "And heaven help her if she is selling another nostrum for preventing freckles or spots or wrinkles!" Eden shook her head over the weird collection of cosmetics she had been offered. "The last such a one looked as if she had been pickled in brine."

Eden and Alicia shared a chuckle over this bit of irony.

"I think you would be adorable with a few freckles," a deep, amused voice rumbled from the doorway. Brentwood crossed to give her a kiss on the cheek.

"Varlet! You gave me a start. How long have you been standing there?"

"Long enough to guess your soft heart is overriding your common sense again."

"Who knows? Perhaps I'll find just the right potion to make me irresistible." She quirked a challenging eyebrow at him.

"You already have," he growled into her ear.

"If you do find such, be sure to share it with me," Aunt Alicia exclaimed as Brentwood shepherded Eden out the door. "Give my regards to Lord and Lady Langley."

"I will." Eden was a little nervous over the coming reunion, although Brentwood insisted that the Langleys understood the terror that had caused her to flee and had forgiven her for the notes. "I can't wait to see the children again. I expect they've grown a great deal."

Eden studied her morning visitor with interest as she settled down to the requested tête-à-tête. Mrs. Penworthy, dressed in half-mourning, was short and plump, with silver-blond hair. The pretty widow was somewhat past the prime of youth, having perhaps thirty years in her dish. She had a loud, aggressive voice, and charged straight into her subject with no attempt at subtlety.

"Miss Henderson, you are about to make a terrible mistake. You are about to marry a man who in his own way is as much of a depraved beast as Viscount Colville."

Eden gave a little gasp of indignation. "Explain yourself, madam."

"I am lately come from New York City. Your finacé gained considerable notoriety there when he and several other young men formed an association—"

"My fiancé has told me of his unorthodox social experiment in America."

"Did he tell you that they lured young women to it by pretending they would marry them, and then shared them like common whores?"

"No, because that is not what happened." Eden's heart began racing. She stood, anxious to end this interview.

"Did he tell you that one of the women was legally married to one of the men, not knowing his intentions, and that he forced her to participate."

"Forced!" Her voice choked. "I do not believe—"

"Indeed, yes. The poor child innocently married a Mr. Rosewood, and once they were wed, she had no choice but to play the whore to the others."

"If you have not made this up out of whole cloth, then it is just vile rumor, and in any case has nothing to do with my fiancé. In actuality, Brentwood did not really participate in this association. It broke up shortly after he arrived."

"I am sorry to destroy your illusions, Miss Henderson, but on the ship from America with me was one of their women, a very pretty red-haired woman named Margaret Thomason. We became fast friends, and she told me the whole of it, a shameful and alarming tale."

Eden felt sick that the story was spreading. She must attempt to stem the gossip. "Mr. Brentwood himself put an end to the scheme because he saw clearly how harmful it was."

Esmerelda gave her a pitying look. "I can understand your wish to defend him. He is a plausible rascal, to be sure. Unfortunately, his scheme is far from ended, and the latest incarnation of it includes you."

Eden's instincts told her this woman was not credible. The malicious glee with which she delivered this shocking news argued against it. But she felt compelled to hear her out. "Me, ma'am? How?"

"The young woman I told you of was supervising three children of almost identical ages. One was the image of herself, but the others little resembled either her or the man she had embraced before leaving, and whom she had claimed was her husband. She called herself the children's governess, in spite of the fact that one of them was obviously her child.

"I became curious about her. I gained her confidence and learned that she was on her way to England to rejoin Roger Brentwood, Earl of Dudley. The children were the products of these illicit unions of which we just spoke.

"Mrs. Thomason told me that Brentwood had gone ahead to England to prepare the way, and had sent for them to join him there. From what she said, and what she left unsaid, it was perfectly clear that their plan is to quietly and unobtrusively re-create on Brentwood's estate this disgusting 'family' they started in America. To avoid the kinds of problems they had in America, the group is to be composed of legally married couples. Since you are to be married soon, obviously Brentwood intends for you to participate in this new version of their group marriage."

Eden drew in her breath sharply. *Surely he wouldn't do such a thing to her.*

Encouraged by Eden's obvious distress, Mrs. Penworthy continued. "I pitied Mrs. Thomason greatly, for she really wished to be free of the whole disgusting situation, but she had no way to support her child or the other two, whom she was unwilling to abandon, though their own parents had done so. Thus she was forced to accept whatever provision Mr. Brentwood made for her."

"I made provisions for them." Brentwood's words suddenly slammed into Eden's consciousness. She clutched at her throat. *This woman has to be lying,* she told herself. But the doubts that assailed her made her almost physically ill.

Relentlessly Mrs. Penworthy pursued her story. "When I told her no Englishwoman would willingly be party to such a scheme, Mrs. Thomason said he would not tell an English bride ahead of time, and reminded me that once a woman is married in England, she must do as her husband bids her. An English wife has fewer rights than an indentured servant in America, I am told."

Eden nodded her head in acknowledgment. "Unfortunately, that is very nearly the truth. But Mr. Brentwood would never expect such a thing of me! You are mistaken. I think this young woman is engaged in air-dreaming."

"No, Miss Henderson." Mrs. Penworthy shook her head sadly. "I saw Mr. Brentwood at the docks in Liverpool when I disembarked recently. We had a slight acquaintance in New York. I presumed upon it to chasten him for his unrepentant ways. He just made a great joke of it. Said it would be very little different from an English country house party, after all."

Eden gasped. Brentwood's very words! He had attempted to tease her out of her disgust of his American scheme with that very comment. "I just cannot credit this!" But her protests were really attempts to convince herself, to stave off the horrible doubts that began to assail her.

"I have no motive for saying this other than to save a young woman from an intolerable situation. Of course, perhaps it has some appeal for you? Mrs. Thomason's husband was quite handsome. There *are* women who enjoy variety quite as much as men do, I am told." She cocked her head to one side, considering her horrified hostess in an insulting manner.

Eden stood up abruptly. "Thank you for your concern, Mrs. Penworthy. I will question Mr. Brentwood closely about this matter, but what you may not know is that he is quite a jokester. When he made that remark, very likely he was funning, and—"

With great dignity Esmerelda Penworthy stalked to the door. "It is the sort of funning which no lady could tolerate, Miss Henderson. It bespeaks a very degenerate sense of humor. I begin to think I have come in vain, but I hope that you can free yourself from his influence, before he drags you into the same moral morass he is in."

As she shut the door on her caller, Eden's mind raced. Surely it couldn't be true. And yet . . . and yet . . . When Brentwood had revealed his secret, she had felt that there was more to it than he told her. She realized now as she thought back on the conversation that she had rather glossed it over than encouraged a full revelation.

No! It couldn't be! He knew she wouldn't go along with such a scheme.

Yet that remark about the English house party! Eden felt her cheeks flush at the implications. And the details of Mrs. Penworthy's story matched what he had told her so well that it was clear she had considerable knowledge of what had happened.

And Brent had hinted at a surprise, somehow connected to America, awaiting her at Varnham. He had refused to tell her about it until they were married. Was the surprise a ready-made family, with extra husbands and co-wives?

"You aren't dressed!" Looking extremely handsome in his fashionable black evening clothes and snowy cravat accented with an emerald as green as his eyes, Brentwood strode into the drawing room anxiously. "Are you ill? You look pulled."

"I am not ill, but I have had rather a shock. Please have a seat." Her formal tone barely disguised the quaver in her voice.

"You alarm me. Have you learned that I secretly ordered you ten parasols?" He reached for her, but she stepped away and gestured to a chair. Shrugging, he took it.

"I have had a caller."

"Always a fatiguing business." His dry tone masked the tremor of alarm that ran through him at his fiancée's grim expression.

Eden shook her head. "I really am not in the mood for your nonsense tonight. My caller was a Mrs. Penworthy, lately of New York, recently arrived on the Liverpool packet."

"Ah! Definitely not the parasols, then. Let me see—she told you about the children? And their pretty red-haired governess?"

"Then you don't deny it?" Eden felt her last hope sinking.

"I did tell you I had made provisions for them."

"You didn't tell me you expected me to live with them."

Brentwood scowled. "I meant to, but at the last moment I couldn't. I feared to lose you."

A low moan escaped Eden's lips. "Then it's true? Oh, my God."

Alarmed and yet disappointed by her reaction, Brentwood hopefully insisted, "You have a loving heart. You will soon come to love them all as I do."

"I do not think our definitions of love are at all the same." Eden removed the ring he had given her. "Our engagement is at an end."

"No, Eden, you can't mean that! I won't believe it of you. Once you meet them, you will grow to love them. You can't help but. The children are well-behaved, sweet—"

"And the governess?"

"As for that, I think you will like her, though it little signifies. She is not really their governess, but the mother of one of the children, as you have guessed. She is now the lawful wife of an American friend of mine. We called her their governess to try to avoid scandal. Rotten luck for Esmerelda Penworthy to be on board!"

It little signifies. Suddenly Eden felt the same horror she had known when Colville had told her that a husband can eventually get his wife to obey him. She shuddered at her narrow escape.

"Rotten luck for you, and for her *other* husband! A piece of great good fortune for me." Eden shakily placed the ring on the small table near where he sat.

Brentwood stood. "You don't understand."

Eden stared at him as if she had never seen him before. "I'm afraid I do. You said someday we'd each know all of the other's secrets. But there was one you were saving until I was firmly, irrevocably wed to you, wasn't there!

"That's rot! You know I would never insist—"

"Do I? Mrs. Rosewood's husband insisted."

Her last hope deserted her as Brentwood visibly blanched at the name. He drew in his breath sharply. "Damn. So she found out about that, too. But, Eden, I'm not Rosewood. Surely you don't think I would be so lost to all sensibility as to . . ." Brentwood's dawning comprehension of her suspicions rendered him suddenly speechless.

Eden half turned away from him. "I don't think I know you at all. I've spent too much time hiding out from the world to have much knowledge of all the varieties of vice in it. I think I was blinded by how different you were from Colville. I ran to you to get away from such as he, forgetting that scoundrels come in all sorts of different guises."

A choked sound made her turn her head. What she saw almost turned her to stone. Brentwood's face was a mask of fury. She had often seen that expression in her father's eyes. It froze her blood to see such an angry man standing inches from her, towering over her.

Eden wanted to run. It cost her a great deal to stand her ground. She couldn't control the trembling that began in her limbs and threatened to completely overset her. "I think you had best leave." Even her voice shook.

Brentwood worked his clenched fists. A muscle jumped in his jaw. "Perhaps you are right," he growled.

Eden could not restrain herself from flinging her final condemnation as he stalked from the room. "I am almost more disgusted at your plans for their potential consequences for Lord Langley's political struggle than for myself.

"How horrified he will be when he finds out. Your actions are putting the entire reform movement in jeopardy. Here he is trying to stop the government from passing those infamous Six Acts repressing British freedoms, yet once your little scheme becomes known, he will lose influence with those whose support he needs. He will be blamed and pilloried right along with you. And it *will* come out! Mrs. Penworthy does not seem a discreet woman to me. Why did you not stay in America, if you could not conform to civilized modes of behavior?"

"Ah, a beast like me thinks of nothing but his own carnal pleasure. Surely you realize that by now. I am a monster of selfishness, hiding my own depravity in a cloak of specious philosophical rantings." A twisted grin contorted his features. The green eyes blazed. "You have indeed had a narrow escape. I bid you adieu, Miss Henderson."

Chapter Twenty-one

Y ou can't just let her go!"

"Can't I?" Brentwood smoothly parried Langley's advancing sword. "And am I to force her to stay? *That* would certainly set her mind at ease!"

"But it's perfectly obvious that she has misunderstood." Langley nimbly sidestepped Brentwood's retaliating thrust.

"A misunderstanding that is hardly flattering to me, would you say?" His face was hidden by the fencing mask, but Brentwood's disgust was clear in his tone of voice.

"The minute you realized she thought you intended to share her with other men, you should have explained."

Brentwood gave his head an angry shake. "I couldn't. I was so furious that she could believe such a thing, I could hardly speak. And to make matters worse, she cringed from me, trembling all over as if I might do her an injury. Now I find myself wondering if she has any genuine feelings for me at all. How could she, and think so ill of me?" He attempted to get under his opponent's guard, but was neatly parried.

Scorn edged Langley's voice. "You'd let her go out of wounded pride? Your love is easily killed. As well she cried off."

"What do you think I should do, then?" Brentwood dropped his guard.

"Touché!" Langley's foil penetrated easily to the padding over Brentwood's heart. "Perhaps we should decide whether to fence or talk. You are not a very challenging opponent right now."

Brentwood lifted his mask to reveal a solemn face. "That's true. And my enemy cannot be conquered by the sword."

"So now she's your enemy." Langley wiped the sweat from his face and stalked to the side of the fencing studio, disgust with his companion marring his expression.

"Not Eden. Mrs. Esmerelda Penworthy, cousin to Lady Alana Morley. And she's very much your enemy, too."

Langley turned slowly to regard his protégé with surprise. "What do you mean?"

"She obviously told Eden a highly colored account of my American experience, embellished suitably with my dastardly plans for Eden once I had her to wife. Doubtless Esmerelda'll dine out on such lurid tales for weeks in scandal-hungry London. Eden was almost as upset for you, for the damage such tales would do the cause of reform, as for herself."

"My God!"

"So you see, much as my first wish is to pursue Eden, persuade her of her error, and convince her to forgive me for mine, before I can do so, I must draw that female viper's fangs."

Langley nodded. "Regrettably, I agree. Though how you are to do it I can't quite imagine. Threatening her in any way would only make matters worse."

"Give me credit for some sense, Stu!" Brentwood's voice was muffled by the towel he was applying to his face, but his irritation was obvious.

"Shall Gwynneth or I write Eden? Or perhaps I could go see her on your behalf?"

"I appreciate that, but no. I think only I can deal with Eden. I also think that some delay, though I chafe at it, will do her good. Yesterday she alluded to her small experience of the world. I started to think last night, how true that was. And I've selfishly rushed her into a commitment before she's had a chance to try her wings a while. The truth will speak for itself, but perhaps it will be more readily believed after a little time."

Langley shook his head as the two men drew on their vests

and morning coats. "I admire such patience, though I confess I lack the virtue myself."

"If it be a virtue. Perhaps I am just being a coward, avoiding putting our love to the final test." Brentwood smiled ruefully. "Come, old friend. We are going to go on a snake hunt."

Shivering a bit in the chill October air, Eden signaled her horse to stop at the crest of a small hill overlooking Broadhurst. Below her was a scene of frenzied activity that should have given Eden a deep sense of satisfaction. Workmen swarmed over her grandfather's home, repairing the depredations of the late Viscount Colville's occupation. Soon it would be restored to its original magnificence, and the last traces of its recent odious occupant erased.

Then and only then would she consent to occupy it. She had been staying with her aunt, supervising the repairs and renovations by driving or riding over two or three times a week.

After three weeks, she had thought herself on the road to healing from the painful blow of discovering Brentwood's true nature, but several recent items of gossip about him she had read in the *Times* had upset her so much that she realized she had only concealed the wound from herself and others. The latest bit of gossip, shared with her by her aunt over breakfast this morning, had put her spirits in a turmoil.

What was she to make of the scandal broth served up in the *Times?* Referring to Brentwood by his title, it had chronicled his frequent appearances as the escort of Mrs. Penworthy. This morning the *Times* had reported that Dudley had all but publicly declared his intention to wed the American widow. Eden had also been surprised and disquieted to read that Mrs. Penworthy was Lady Alana Morley's cousin.

I should be sufficiently weaned of any affection for Brentwood not to care who he courts, she thought. Instead, she felt betrayed. She realized that some part of her had expected, had wanted, Brentwood to follow her, to explain his actions, or at least to repent of them, to beg her forgiveness and attempt to win her back.

She had pictured to herself various scenarios when he did so. In one, she haughtily refused to see him at all. In another, she graciously listened to his pleas, but sternly refused him. The most cherished version was the one she tried to keep herself from envisioning—but it just *would* come, invading her dreams or her unguarded waking moments. In this one, he explained all his actions to her satisfaction, and she went into his arms to feel again that delicious sense of safety and warmth which once she had known there.

Instead of obligingly playing his part in any of these scenes, he had taken up with the American widow, a woman, moreover, who had professed to despise him, who supposedly regarded him as morally depraved.

It was this latter aspect of the situation that was primarily responsible for Eden's turmoil. If Mrs. Penworthy had told the truth, why would she have anything to do with the man? Most particularly, why would she be contemplating marriage to him?

And if she hadn't told the truth, then why had she told Eden such lies? And why had Brentwood then admitted to her lies, and in fact embellished his confession with that scathing self-denunciation?

And if they were lies, then what *was* the truth?

She found herself going over and over her last conversation with Brentwood, seeking some explanation, some clue. Had she misunderstood him? Had he misunderstood her?

Knowing his frequent use of irony for humorous purposes, should she see his admission of depravity as angry irony?

Ever since seeing the gossip in the *Times,* all her doubts about the widow's story had begun to surface. Surely the man she had come to love would not have contemplated betraying her trust so horribly? His anger, so alarming at the time, could be understood if she had vilely misjudged him.

As her horse stamped restlessly beneath her, Eden relived her terror at seeing Brentwood so thoroughly enraged. Yes, he had been furious. *And yet, he did not hurt me.* Eden lingered over this soothing realization.

However angry he had been, he had not made even the slightest threatening move toward her. *Nor would he,* a little voice whispered in her ear. *He is a man in control of himself; your father was a giant spoiled child.*

And yet . . . and yet . . . He was such a large man. She could still see his hands, clenching and unclenching, his working jaw. What if he lost control?

Thus Eden's thoughts spun around and around. *I shall go mad,* she thought. *I must think of something else—anything else. I must put Brentwood out of my mind.*

Relaxing the reins, she urged her horse down the path toward Broadhurst. She hoped that inspecting the work which had been completed, and discussing next week's plans, might distract her from her spinning, confused thoughts.

That evening when Eden returned to her aunt's, she found a letter awaiting her from Isabella. It was a thick missive, full of London gossip and the excitement of a pretty young girl enjoying her first outings in society. Her grandmother had begun to take her about during the little season, the better to keep an eye on her. Eden read the letter with a rueful smile, slightly envious of her former pupil's opportunity to enjoy such an experience.

She frowned as she reread the last few paragraphs, her perplexity and turmoil of the morning returning full force:

And, Eden, all of London is wondering about the mystery of Lord Dudley's keeping company with Mrs. Penworthy, or rather, I should say, of her keeping company with him.

Just at the time you left us so abruptly she was putting about a scurrilous story about him that, if true, would explain the sudden termination of your engagement. Indeed, many supposed that to be the reason.

But now she says she was mistaken in the matter, that she had confused Lord Dudley with someone else and done him a disservice. You should see how she preens herself as she says "Lord Dudley." Lady Alana Morley casts quite killing looks her way. I wonder why?

And, Eden, why did he take up his title again? It seems to be in order to court that nonentity of an American widow who is so impressed with it.

I taxed him with it at a rout and he only smiled and said something in his usual enigmatic style to the effect that it was a touchy business drawing poison from vipers without being bitten yourself.

I am not sure what to make of it, but I am more than a little disappointed in him, and so I told him. I liked him better as a misguided but sincere polygamist!

Eden threw back her head and laughed. She could just imagine the young, innocent-looking Isabella delivering this sophisticated, rather naughty set-down with wide eyes shining and dimples peeping.

Folding the letter thoughtfully, she turned her mind once again to the puzzle of Brentwood's behavior. She was glad for the Langleys' sake that Mrs. Penworthy had been stopped from spreading malicious gossip. Relief flooded her as she drew some conclusions about the purpose of Brentwood's recent amorous activities.

"And when I had finished outlining my plans for our future, she told me to go to the devil!"

Langley could not recall when he had laughed harder. Mopping his eyes, he observed, "I wish I could have seen her face when you told her you expected her to act as mother and governess to the three children and give you at least six more besides."

"Actually, it was when I informed her of the puritanical mode of dress and behavior I would expect her to follow that she turned puce."

"Thus ended your very short engagement!" Langley managed to choke out this obituary over his chuckles.

"Firmly and definitively. When she said all it wanted was

for me to tell her I was abdicating the title, and I asked her how she had guessed, that cinched it!"

Langley wondered at how far Brentwood had been willing to go to alienate Mrs. Penworthy. "You ran quite a risk. She might not have cried off in spite of all, just to discomfit Alana."

Green eyes twinkling, Brentwood waved a dismissive hand. "I had half a dozen other repellent ideas to suggest to her if need be. Now, because she was so obviously willing to marry me, she can no longer spread her tales of my immoral behavior, without tarring herself with the same brush. Remember how she gleefully agreed when I said how happy I was to find a dear friend from my sojourn in America, one who could give the lie to the ridiculous gossip that had pursued me hither?"

Langley lifted his brandy snifter in silent toast to the other man. "Well done, my friend. You've managed better than I dreamed possible. I cannot wait to see how you now plan to undo the damage she did with Eden."

"B-Brentwood! You gave me a start!" Eden had been standing in the middle of the newly refurbished ballroom at Broadhurst, daydreaming of balls she had never had the opportunity to attend, when she heard the door softly close and whirled to see her former fiancé, tall, elegantly clad, and somber of mien.

"I shan't begin by apologizing, as I shall have enough of that to do later. Get your cloak, Eden."

She eyed him nervously, not understanding his mood. This was certainly not like any of the reconciliation scenes she had imagined. "Why? I am not going anywhere."

"Yes, you are. I am abducting you." He advanced on her, the green eyes dark as a stormy sea.

"Don't be ridiculous!"

"I am taking you by force to Gretna Green to be married."

Eden lifted her eyebrows and raised troubled, puzzled brown eyes to his. "You are?"

"Didn't I just say so, woman? You know what a villain I am."

His features were stony, his stance menacing. Eden realized she should have been frightened, but wasn't. She allowed that interesting detail to sink in before replying to him. "Ah, yes. I do recall . . . but why now? Why not a week ago? Why not a month ago?"

"I had some matters to attend to."

Warily she regarded him as he loomed over her. "Something to do with drawing the fangs of American vipers?"

Only the tiniest quirk of his mouth, a fractional lift of an eyebrow, accompanied his dry response. "Ah, I see Isabella is a faithful reporter."

"May I take it that your intention of abducting me indicates that your romance with Mrs. Penworthy is at an end?"

"Of course not. You know my true nature now; why should I hide it? She will make an admirable mistress, just one of many, of course, while you, my pretty heiress, will learn to be a biddable wife." He reached for her, catching her elbow and drawing her to him.

"Hmmmm. A biddable wife. That is to be my role?"

"And a rich one." He lowered his head to kiss her. She did not refuse him.

Eden sighed as the kiss ended. "Very well, then. Let me get my cloak."

"What?" Passion warred with perplexity in Brentwood's features. He had come prepared for a great deal more resistance.

"My cloak. You said to get my cloak. As a biddable wife, I must do as you say." She lowered her eyes demurely.

Somewhat bemused, he followed her out of the ballroom. She proceeded down the stairs and plucked her cloak off the stair railing. Silently she let Brentwood arrange it around her shoulders, then, giving him an arch look, marched bravely through the open door.

She hesitated a little when she saw that the vehicle standing in her drive was in fact a traveling carriage, encumbered with considerable luggage. "You don't believe in traveling light for elopements, I see."

He smiled for the first time. "Get in the carriage and you'll understand."

For just a few seconds more she hesitated, searching his face for something. Then she returned the smile with a blinding one of her own, and began walking down the steps.

Suddenly three small heads popped into view in the carriage window.

"Is this the pretty lady you said we were going to visit?"

"Can we get out now?"

"I'm hungry."

Eden's smile changed into a grin. "Eloping with three children. What a unique approach."

"I thought it might set a new fashion."

She peered over the children's heads, trying to see into the depths of the carriage. "No pretty red-haired governesses?"

"Alas, no. Mrs. Thomason had to return to her husband in America. We can get another one, though, if you like."

Eden frowned. "She gave up her child?"

Bowing his head so he could whisper in her ear, Brentwood explained, "It cost her many bitter tears, but her new husband, while willing to forgive and forget her past, was unwilling to take in the child who would forever remind him of it."

He waited for some sign of reluctance from her. Instead, she lifted large brown eyes with a suspicious sheen to them. "Poor thing."

He cleared his throat. "So you see, Eden, my only secret was the children. I wasn't sure you'd want them." He searched her features for a clue to her feelings, but it was her turn to look inscrutable.

"If you don't, I will do as I always intended, and make other provisions for them."

Almost sadly, Eden whispered, "Oh, Brent."

He took her elbow and urged her toward the carriage. "First, yes, this is the pretty lady; second, no you can't get out now because third, your hunger is to be appeased at Miss Henderson's aunt's house."

"Is Aunt Alicia in on this?" Eden peered at him, eyes dancing mirthfully as she ruffled the small boy's red hair.

"Only to the extent of agreeing that you should meet my children before I throw myself at your feet and beg for your forgiveness, your heart, and your hand."

"Now *that* is more like." Eden settled herself on the squabs and pulled the smallest of the three children onto her lap. "Introduce me to my family, sir."

Epilogue

November, 1824

Roger Brentwood entered the door of his town house wearily and handed his dripping many-caped coat to Briggs. "My wife?"

"The library, sir."

"Thank you, Briggs."

"Sir? It will pass next time."

A slight flash of amusement lit the green eyes. "Ever the mind reader, Briggs. I hope you are prescient, too."

It was quiet and warm in the library. Surprised not to see her immediately, Brentwood stole around the high-backed sofa to find Eden dozing, her head pillowed on the arm, a robe across her legs. Smiling tenderly he sat beside her and leaned forward to give her a kiss on the cheek.

"Ummm?" She slid her arms up around his neck and turned for a real kiss. Afterward he drew back and she exclaimed at the look on his face. "Not again!"

"Afraid so. Refused even to bring it up for a reading, in fact. Everyone is preoccupied with whether to recognize the independence of Spain's South American colonies. Stuart is mightily discouraged, I can tell you."

"As am I. Will England never outlaw climbing boys? It is unconscionable!"

He stood and drew her to her feet. "Sometimes I think perhaps we should give up. America beckons at times like these."

"Where they enslave Negroes and confiscate the lands of the natives? No, there is evil enough on both sides of the ocean. But oh! I did think something would be done this time."

"I am afraid Stuart has the right of it. Nothing can be done until the suffrage is extended. Let's visit the schoolroom, I could use some cheering up."

Slowly, arm in arm, they climbed the stairs together. They spent a pleasant hour romping with the three children, giving their exhausted governess a much-needed respite.

Brentwood's spirits had revived by the time they left the schoolroom. "We're invited to the Langleys' for a postmortem this evening. I guess I'll have to go."

"What about me?"

He frowned a little. "You were sleeping in the library in the middle of the day. I think you must have been overdoing a bit with all your work for the academy. And it won't be a happy occasion. Perhaps you'd like to stay at home."

"Oh, definitely not. I'd like to go and tell Stuart that reinforcements are on the way."

The dancing light in her eyes alerted him. "What is that supposed to mean?"

"You know how he's always lecturing poor Martin about how he must study the issues, as doubtless reform will still be required when *he* takes his seat in Lords?"

A long pause ensued while Brent stared in disbelief at his wife. Finally he managed to speak. "Are you trying to hint to me that there is to be another Brentwood unleashed upon the world?"

"You must promise me you'll let him out of his cradle before beginning to indoctrinate him."

"When?" Brentwood's delight lit up his face.

"In about five months."

Shocked, he drew her down onto the sofa. He put an experimental hand to her stomach, which seemed to him no more rounded than normal. "Are you sure? Why haven't you told me before? Why all the secrecy when you knew how delighted I'd be?"

"I wanted to be sure first, after so many years of hoping and being disappointed."

"Always keeping secrets! You might have at least given me a hint!" Brentwood put his hands on her shoulders and gave her a gentle, exasperated shake.

"Oh, but I know how much you like surprises, Mr. Brentwood."